Sword of the Golden City

By Jane Harris and Ruston Jones

For Gavin, who always loved all the weapons, and for Olivia, who could decipher every clue – Ruston

For my indispensable writing team: Jacob, Aidan, Brea, Goldie, and Craig, who suffered through innumerable drafts with patience and wisdom, and whose support never diminished. It really does take a village. And to Ruston, who trusted me with his story in the first place - Jane

Contents

PROLOGUE

The eagle soared through the Czech sky in a wide circle. Her feathers of red, orange, and black bristled in the jet stream. Below her sat the mountain, cloaked in a forest of dark trees running from its summit down its slopes. The eagle did as her ancestors had done for generation upon generation: she soared and she watched.

As with every day, a wandering procession of men, women, and children hiked in and out of the mountain. They explored the crumbling stone chapel, the ruins of ancient battles, and the entrance to the cave of slumbering knights, who were said to be waiting for the call to awaken and save Prague in the time of the city's greatest need. The eagle had watched over Mount Blaník since she had learned to fly.

But on this day, something caught her eye. Far from the well-worn tourist footpath that carved a zig-zag pattern into the mountain, a pair of men trekked through the thickest part of the forest. Although the eagle hadn't seen humans travel this way in her living memory, she knew where the men were going. Somewhere beneath the dense cover of green was an entrance to a cave that hadn't been seen by human eyes since the eagle's ancestors began their watch over the mountain dozens of generations ago.

The men pushed their way behind a large bush and...disappeared.

"Keeh!" the eagle fretted, tilting her head.

Something was happening. Foreboding menace itched inside the eagle's hollow bones. She circled higher and did as she always had.

She soared and she watched.

* * *

Hundreds of feet below the surface of Mount Blaník, two men stood in a winding tunnel. The fraying rope they'd been following led directly over the edge of a cliff, where it passed through a rusting piton and descended into total darkness. The older of the two men, Damek Maracek, leaned forward to peer past the precipice. His headlight's meager glow petered out after fifty feet. With the jagged edge of a small dagger, he struck a flare from his utility belt. A brilliant light hissed awake in his palm, washing the cavern in red. He held it out over the ledge and let go.

A ring of illuminated stone closed around the red-orange flame as it fell, as if the flare were being swallowed in a giant's throat. Eventually, the hissing light reduced to a pinpoint of red below them. A moment later, it was gone. In a blink, only green-blue afterimages remained in the men's eyes, along with the faint scent of sulfur hanging in the air.

A muted *ping* echoed up the chasm. It had taken the flare almost six seconds to reach the bottom.

"About 150 meters," Damek noted. "Give or take."

"Are you sure this is the only way down?" Kyril Zeman, the younger of the two, questioned. His usually strong, cheerful voice wavered ever so slightly in the dark.

The corners of Damek's nearly-white mustache arched up as his mouth twisted into a wry grin. It wasn't often he heard his sturdy, barrel-chested friend so unnerved. At age 50, Kyril Zeman was nearly thirty years Damek

Maracek's junior. He'd been Damek's attorney for the past 25 years, his squire for the past 11, and his friend since the day they met.

"Afraid so." Damek clapped Kyril on the back with his calloused hand just hard enough to make Kyril flinch and step back from the edge. "Suddenly afraid of heights?"

"Not heights," Kyril's voice rumbled. "Ancient ropes, rusting pitons, and cursed crypts on the other hand..."

Damek's smile evaporated. Descending the rope would be treacherous and slow, but doable. The time it would take to climb back up, however, meant a speedy retreat would be impossible.

"This goes beyond anything either of us could have imagined when you agreed to become my squire," Damek said. "You have served me faithfully, Kyril. But when we reach the bottom of this rope, there will be no turning back."

"You're not getting rid of me just when things get interesting," Kyril huffed. "Besides, you need me, old knight. You can hardly fasten your own harness these days without help. Do you really think you can destroy Prague's ancient enemy alone? Without your *lawyer?*"

Damek chuckled. Kyril had a way of lifting his spirits. "Thank you, my friend," Damek said. "I'm grateful for your company."

"Well," Kyril grumbled, "don't think I won't remember this the next time you ask if I'd like to do a little sightseeing. Sightseeing in a tunnel under Mount Blaník! I can't see a single thing, even with the headlamps!"

"Can you see that?" Damek indicated a spot on the rock wall just above Kyril's head.

Kyril turned and gazed up. In the glow of both headlamps loomed a faded, carved figure with massive wings and foot-long talons. "The Red Eagle!" His gasp echoed off the rock walls soaring overhead. "You were right,

Damek. The legends are linked! The evil wizard, the Knights of Blaník, the Sword of the Golden City..."

A sudden, howling gust of wind rushed up at them from the abyss below, blowing dust from the earthen path and flapping their sweat-damp clothes. Damek clutched his headlamp before it could fly off. Then, just as soon as it came, the wind vanished, leaving the two standing in silence once again.

Kyril looked at Damek. Neither man needed to say it out loud: there had been nothing natural about that wind. The squire started forward with a carabiner ready to attach to the rope.

"No," Damek stopped him. "I'll go first. Give me a few seconds of lead, then follow."

Sharp spindles from the hemp rope dug into Damek's calloused hands as he lowered himself over the edge. In his vest pocket, a small, time-faded wooden box pressed firmly against his chest. It seemed to grow heavier as he descended. Almost as if it was *pulling* him in the direction it wanted to go. A terrible thought. Maybe this expedition hadn't been such a brilliant idea after all.

Focus! Damek scolded himself. The time for second guessing has long since passed

Damek Maracek had spent his entire adult life researching legends, tracking down myths, excavating ruins, and uncovering artifacts rumored to hold curses or magical properties. But in all those years, he'd never once believed ghost stories or curses held any genuine power.

Until recently.

Now he wasn't sure he would ever feel safe again. Because he knew. He knew that something...*evil*...had awakened. Something others would probably discount as a bedtime story used to frighten children.

Damek wanted to dismiss his fear as feeble thinking brought on by old age, but events of recent weeks had been too alarming to ignore. Not to mention the dreams...

But it didn't matter. He'd read the clues. He'd followed where they led. And now there was nothing to do but descend further and further into the darkness that awaited them, all to try and rid the world of the darkness that awaited everyone.

CHAPTER ONE - Night Terrors

A scream pierced the night.

Nick bolted upright in his bed, heart pounding a mile a minute. A moment later, a second muffled shriek rang out. This time he sighed heavily. No matter how many times it happened, he'd never get used to being yanked from sleep by his little sister's screams.

Throwing off his covers, he swung his bare feet to the floor and rushed to Kat's room, ignoring the ache in his right leg as he limped through her door.

Kat's bed was empty. Nick found her curled in a tight, terrified ball in the far corner next to the dollhouse their uncle had built for her.

Her huge, brown eyes stared in wide-open horror at her closet door. Her feet scrabbled against the thick wool rug on the floor as she tried to push her small body further away from the closet, even though her back was already flat against the wall. She clutched her head in her skinny arms, pressing her palms against her ears. Her lips stretched wide around the black hole of her screams.

Nick dropped down next to her on the rug.

"Kat," he whispered, trying to pry her hands away from her ears. "Kat, shhh, it's okay. It isn't real. It's just a dream."

But Kat kept screaming as if Nick wasn't there at all. So he wrapped his arms around her and hummed a lullaby, slowly rocking back and forth on his knees.

Gradually, Kat's screams faded; her arms relaxed and dropped to her sides. Knees aching, Nick kept rocking until she quieted completely.

After several seconds of silence, Kat inhaled sharply. "Oh!" she cried as she realized Nick was holding her. Throwing her arms around her big brother, she buried her head in his shoulder and began to sob.

"Hey," Nick said softly. "It's okay, Kat. I've got you. I won't ever let anything hurt you, remember?"

She nodded and squeezed him tight. "I remember," she said, her voice small and hoarse. And then, "I'm sorry, Nicky. I woke you up, didn't I?"

"Sorry? Nah. I was already awake," Nick lied. "Come on, let's get you back in bed. Your fingers are like icicles!"

Nick tucked Kat into bed and handed her the cup of water sitting on her nightstand. "Do you want to talk about it?"

Sometimes she didn't. Sometimes she couldn't even remember what had frightened her so badly. But lately she'd needed him to reassure her that whatever she'd seen wasn't real, that she was safe.

Kat gripped the glass in her hand, glancing at her open closet. Nick stood, walked over, and shut the closet doors.

"There was a crooked old man." Kat shivered and looked up at her big brother.

Nick sat down next to her on the bed. Kat leaned her head against his shoulder before she continued. "I thought he was nice, even though I couldn't see his face, only his arms and hands and the top of his bald head. He was doing a puppet show for us...for all the girls and boys...and our parents, too."

Nick watched Kat's face, listening. She stared into the middle distance, eyes bright with remembered colors and magic.

"It was so pretty, Nicky," she sighed. "The crooked man could make the puppets dance and twirl like Uncle Damek can, but even faster. He must have been magic, because I couldn't see any strings!" As she spoke, Kat sat up, moving her arms and hands as if she were pulling the strings of an invisible marionette in front of her on the bed. "He was telling the same story Uncle Damek told last time he was here, about King Winnie Sauce taking food to poor people when they were hungry in the winter."

Nick smiled. "King Wenceslaus," he corrected. "Go on."

But her smile faltered, and the light in her eyes faded like a snuffed-out candle. "When the puppet show was over, we all clapped and cheered and dropped coins in the man's hat," she whispered, as if she was afraid someone besides Nick might hear. "I think he didn't have lots of money, because his clothes were dirty and he had rags tied around his feet, even though there was snow on the ground and everyone else had capes and boots. The crooked little man kept his head down and never looked at anyone, only the ground. I didn't look in his eyes, Nicky," Kat said, "I promise."

"Hey." Nick put his arm around her shoulders. "It's okay. You didn't do anything wrong."

"Yes, I did." Kat pulled away from Nick and stared at him, her lips trembling.

A tickle of dread crawled up Nick's spine. He'd never heard his little sister speak in such a serious voice before.

"I watched the crooked man put his puppets in a big sack," Kat said. "He lifted it on his back like this." She moved to her knees, hunching over the bed so her arms touched the quilt and her neck drew down to her chest. "Then I... I followed him, Nicky. But I was really quiet, and he didn't know I was there. He walked and walked for a long time, and then he stopped and dropped his sack on the ground and made a fire."

Unease grew in the pit of Nick's stomach as he watched Kat's small body mimic the actions of the crooked old man from her nightmare. Listening to her dreams usually didn't bother him, but this time he could almost see the flames of the crooked man's fire casting shadows on Kat's bedroom wall.

Knock it off, he scolded himself. She had a bad dream, end of story. *You're going to make this worse if she thinks you're spooked.*

"What happened next?" he asked, keeping his voice steady.

"He dumped out his hat on the snow and counted his coins," she said.

Her body bent lower as she counted invisible coins, her face so close to the quilt that Nick could barely hear her. He leaned in closer.

"Then he picked a long stick from the fire and scratched something in the snow," she continued.

Nick watched, mesmerized, as her small finger traced shapes on her quilt.

"But I couldn't see, so I sneaked closer." Kat's voice wavered, and she started to cry. "I saw what he wrote..."

"What did you see, Kat?" Nick urged before silently cursing himself. *It doesn't matter what she saw! Just tell her it wasn't real and that she's safe!* But he just couldn't help himself. "What did the man scratch in the snow?"

"It was your name, Nicky!" she sobbed. "He scratched 'Nicholas' in the snow. And he...he saw me..."

Her voice grew hushed and her eyes unfocused, as if she were seeing the dream play out in front of her again. "He looked right in my eyes and he laughed and laughed like a mean old witch!" She moaned. "I'm sorry, Nicky! Now he knows where we live."

A chill swept through Nick's bones. It was all he could do to keep from shivering. He gathered his little sister in his arms again and patted her long, brown hair.

"No one knows where we live, Kat," Nick soothed. "It wasn't real. We're okay. It was just a bad bad dream."

Kat sniffed. "*Really* really?"

"*Really* really," Nick said. "First of all, it's the middle of summer, right? It's definitely not snowing here any time soon. And second, when's the last time you saw anyone in Chicago wearing a cape?"

"Oh, yeah," Kat said. "That would be silly."

"Ready to go back to bed?" Nick asked.

To his surprise, Kat shook her head. "I'm scared to go to sleep. What if the crooked man comes back?"

Nick sighed, on the verge of promising her the crooked man wouldn't come back. But something stopped him. What would happen if she had another bad dream and the crooked man *did* come back? Would she trust him the next time he made a promise?

"Want me to tell you a story?" he asked instead.

Kat's eyes lit up. "Yes! The one about how Bruncvik saved the lion and gave him two tails!"

So, Nick leaned back and cleared his throat. "Beyond seven mountain ranges, beyond seven rivers, there was a brave knight named Bruncvik..."

CHAPTER TWO - A Friendly Voice

An hour later, Nick trudged wearily out of Kat's room, his bad leg aching. With one last look to make sure she was sleeping soundly, he pulled the door almost shut, leaving it open just a crack. He looked down the hall in the direction of Mom's room, the soft spinning of her fan only faintly audible.

The skin on the back of his neck tingled, as if he were being watched. Mom said the dreams were probably just a phase Kat would grow out of, but she was having them almost every night now, and they seemed to be getting worse. Two nights ago, she'd dreamed about being chased by a statue. The night before that, it was a giant spider under her bed. But this dream with the crooked old puppet master scratching Nick's name in the snow...

Nick shuddered, shaking the thought from his head. Why was comforting Kat his job anyway? He was only 13. But like always, Mom had slept through the entire thing.

He knew it wasn't fair of him to be upset with Mom. She worked hard to pay the bills. She'd started cleaning houses on her days off from the daycare center, which meant she didn't even get to sleep in on the weekends.

Not that Nick did, either. Kat liked to get up early on weekends to watch cartoons.

What a crap summer break, he thought to himself. Then he sighed. It wasn't Mom's fault life was so expensive. It wasn't Mom's fault Dad was gone. None of this was anyone's fault.

It sucked not having anyone to blame.

Nick stopped in the bathroom and opened a drawer beside the sink. Inside sat a box of heavy-duty earplugs Mom gave him last time he'd complained about Kat waking him up. He'd tried them once; they blocked out everything except the sound of his own breath and heartbeat.

Kat had never had two episodes in the same night, but her nightmares *were* becoming more frequent. Nick would never forgive himself if she needed him and he slept through it. He shut the drawer.

Nick had been seven when Kat was born. On the day he first met her, he'd taken one look at her through the nursery window, one look at how tiny and fragile she was – all swaddled up like a little burrito in her hospital crib – and swore right then and there he would always protect her. Mom and Dad had joked that Kat had Nick wrapped around her little finger.

It was true.

From the time she was old enough to walk, she called for Nick first when she needed anything: when she fell down and scraped her knee, when the neighbor's dog chewed the head off her favorite doll, when Mom scolded her for tracking mud into the house.

So, yeah, the night terrors were a pain, but it gave Nick a sense of pride to know how much faith Kat had in him.

Nick returned to his room and laid back down in bed. He was just contemplating getting back up and opening his door – just in case – when his heavy eyelids drooped shut and he drifted off to sleep.

* * *

Nick woke to pounding at his door. The impulse to run flooded through him, but his bed sheets tangled around his legs.

It took a second for him to realize he was in his bed, in his room, in his house in Chicago, not...

...not on the lip of a chasm shrouded in fog. On his right, a bottomless drop over the side of a cliff, on his left, an enormous door set in the rocky face of a mountainside.

A dream, he told himself. *It was just a dream.*

The pounding continued. "All right! I'm awake, I'll be out in a second!"

Except the pounding wasn't coming from his bedroom door.

He whipped around, staring at his closet, expecting to see the wooden door splinter apart at the force of the repeated blows. Easing from the sheets, he limped toward the closet, reached to grasp the knob, and...

...the pounding stopped.

See? It's just a regular closet.

He pulled open the door.

An enormous, blood-red eagle stood emblazoned above the massive door embedded deep in the side of a rocky cliff face. On either side of the door, a huge mural that stretched from the ground to the top of the mountainside depicted a two-tailed lion rearing up on its powerful hind legs.

The pounding from the other side of the door shivered through the timber, rattling the door's frame.

Whatever lay trapped behind the door wanted out. Bad. And Nick didn't want to find out what it was. His eyes fell on an enormous metal padlock securing the latch.

Nick sighed in relief. Surely nothing could break through a padlock that big.

A gale-force wind surrounded Nick, lifting him off his feet and hurtling him toward the edge of the cliff.

Nick jolted awake. Sweat soaked his pajamas and his pulse hammered in his ears. No pounding, no cliff, no wind.

He wiped at the perspiration beading on his forehead with the back of his arm. He was safe in his room. In his bed. His chest ached with anxiety. Why wouldn't his heartbeat slow down?

He grabbed for the framed photo sitting on his nightstand. In it, a young Damek Maracek – Nick's uncle – held a huge, fish-shaped figurine in his gloved hands. Dust caked his uncle's face and neatly trimmed beard, but the teeth in his ear-to-ear smile gleamed white. According to Damek, he'd dug the tarnished object out from under the crumbling ruins of a Romanesque chapel. It was made of pure silver: Myslík's famed Silver Fish.

Nick loved this story. In it, a man melted down all his wealth and had it cast into a single, silver fish. He'd had to leave it behind when fleeing Prague during a battle. Years later, a poor city clerk found the fish in the rubble after being ordered to tear down the old house. Selling it allowed the clerk to rebuild his own house, serving as a reminder that one man's misfortune could always become another's good luck.

Of course, that didn't stop Nick's mom from joking that the photo looked more like a souvenir from a fishing trip than documentation of a news-worthy archeological find.

As Nick held the photo, the fear and panic melted away. He had never met anyone as cool as Uncle Damek. He was actually Mom's uncle – Nick and Kat's great uncle – but Mom said she was happy to share since neither she nor Dad had any siblings. Nick's bond with his uncle was created the day he was born, when his parents named him Nicholas *Damek* Gordon.

Before they'd ever met in person, Nick had spent hours flipping through albums filled with photos of the tall, sophisticated man while Mom told stories of his travels and discoveries. Mom described Uncle Damek as a gentleman scholar: an expert in ancient languages and mythology who dabbled in archeology. But to Nick, he was bigger than that. He was a real, live Indiana Jones, who'd lived a life full of dangerous adventures, narrowly escaping death on numerous occasions.

Maybe that explained why thoughts of his uncle's adventures always calmed Nick down? Damek had survived so many perilous quests. Maybe being his namesake meant that his uncle's bravery and luck would somehow rub off on him.

Nick missed Damek. It had been months since they'd last talked to him. All at once, he decided: if Damek's photo helped calm him down, talking to him would dispel the unsettled feeling entirely. And who knew? Maybe Damek knew of an ancient remedy to stop Kat's night terrors! Nick climbed out of bed, put on his cushioned slippers, and headed downstairs to call his uncle.

Mmmm...what was that smell? Was that bacon?

Mom usually woke him before she left for work so he could baby-sit Kat, who got up at the butt-crack of dawn. But Mom never had time to cook actual breakfast before she left for work. What was going on?

"Morning, sleepy head," Mom said from the stove where she was frying eggs.

"Morning, Nicky!" Kat beamed at him from where she sat on a barstool next to the stove. Her voice was ever-so-slightly hoarse but happy. She wore a little apron around her waist over her night shirt, and had a giant oven mitt on each hand.

The microwave clock read 9:30 A.M.

"I didn't realize it was so late," Nick said. "Sorry I overslept. You should have woken me up. Aren't you working today?"

"Kat told me she had another nightmare last night." Mom set her spatula down and ruffled Nick's hair after wiping her hands on a towel. "Thank you for helping her again, son. I'm not sure how I keep sleeping through them."

She smiled in apology, but Nick noticed how tired her eyes looked. And when she picked up the spatula, he noticed her hands were dry and cracked.

He swallowed around a lump in his throat. Nick remembered when Mom used to take Kat on 'girl dates' to the nail salon for manis and pedis. Her hands had been smooth back then, and her nails polished. But that had stopped more than a year ago. Now the only somewhat smooth spot on her hands was the small band of skin on her right pointer finger which was usually covered by the only ring she still wore.

Right now, the ring rested on the windowsill. She always took it off when she cooked or cleaned. It was a family heirloom, given to her by her own mother, who had passed away before Nick was born. Apparently, Mom hadn't even been able to look at the ring for the first couple of years after the funeral. The memory of her loss had been too painful. Now she was never more than a few feet away from it.

"It's okay, Mom," he said. "I don't mind waking up with her. It's not a big deal.

"Yuh-huh," Kat said. "I love you, Nicky. I'm sorry I keep having scary dreams."

"It's not your fault, Kitty Kat." Mom kissed Kat's forehead the way she did when checking for a fever. "Goodness, young lady, you're as cold as a popsicle! Are you sure you're feeling alright? No sore throat? No earache?"

"Maybe I'm not a kitty cat." Kat slid off her stool and held out her hands for the plate of bacon, which Mom handed her. "Maybe I'm a penguin. Penguins like to be cold!" She waddled to the table, wiggling her arms like flippers.

"Well," Mom said, "luckily, I've been talking to a doctor who has some experience with penguins. I think I've finally found someone who can help us get these night terrors sorted out."

"But I thought you lost your health insurance..."

Mom whipped around before Nick could finish his question, her eyes wide with embarrassment.

"Sorry," Nick said awkwardly. Obviously, he wasn't supposed to know about that. "I heard you talking on the phone about it."

"Neither of you have anything to be sorry about," Mom said. "It's not your job to worry about those kinds of things. I've got everything under control. Don't you know how tough your Mama is?" She flexed her biceps.

Kat snorted and Nick grinned. She *was* actually kind of buff – for a mom, anyway – and it always made Kat giggle when she acted tough like that.

"Hey, Mom," Nick asked, remembering why he'd come downstairs in the first place, "would it be okay if I call Uncle Damek? I haven't talked to him in a while."

"Funny you should ask." Mom took her phone from her pocket and handed it to him. "Your uncle called this morning before either of you were up. You know what they say about great minds!"

Nick grinned and clicked on Damek's number, doing the math in his head to figure out what time it was in Prague while the line rang. Prague was seven hours ahead of Chicago time, so it would be just after 4:30 P.M.

"Hello?" he asked when he heard the line pick up.

"Aha!" An elegant voice came from the speaker. "The young knight!"

"Uncle Damek!" Nick practically shouted.

"Hello, Nicholas," Damek said. "How are you and your sister this morning?"

"I'm great! Kat's okay, too, I guess. How are you? I've missed you! Are you working on any new projects?"

"I miss you, too." Damek's tone was warm, if a little tired. "But what on Earth made you say your little sister is only okay? Has something happened? Is she in good health?"

"Yeah, she's fine. It's just..." Nick paused, looking over his shoulder to see if Kat was listening. She wasn't. She was busy covering her French toast with way too much whipped cream. Still, Nick lowered his voice before he continued. "She's been having these nightmares for a few months. Mom calls them night terrors. They've gotten worse lately. She wakes up screaming almost every night. Last night she told me she's afraid to go to sleep."

"I'm sorry to hear that," Damek's tone was grave. "What about you, Nicholas? Have your dreams been troubled lately?"

"Up until last night they've been fine."

"Our family has a long history with dreaming, as I've mentioned before," Damek remarked. "Will you tell me about the dream you had last night?"

"It was just really weird. I even thought I woke up once and sat up in bed, but it turns out I was still dreaming."

"A dream within a dream," Damek mused. "What else do you remember?"

Nick stepped around the corner from the kitchen into the family room and sat down on the couch. "Well, there was this huge door carved into a mountain. It had a giant red eagle painted above it and a two-tailed lion on both sides. Someone – or some*thing* – was pounding on the door from the other side. I don't even know what was back there, but I was really creeped out and I wanted to run. But then I noticed a huge lock on the door, so I felt better, until a *really* strong wind slammed into me and..." He trailed off. Now, in the light of day with a plate of bacon and eggs waiting for him on the table and his uncle on the other end of the line, telling Damek about his fear of hurtling over the cliff's edge and plummeting to his death felt silly.

"Nicholas? Are you there? What were you about to say? How did the dream end?"

"I... I guess I forgot," Nick said. "It's no big deal, just some weird dream. Are you working on a new project? Any cool translations or digs?"

"Ah, you know me so well! I've actually been working on some new research I think you'll be fascinated with. It's one of the reasons I called. It regards not one but *two* cursed family heirlooms. It has required intensive studying, but you know what I always say."

Nick grinned. "The real adventure always begins with learning." It was one of Damek's favorite phrases. Nick had spent hours with Damek in his study looking through musty old books and brittle parchments well before Nick could understand what he was seeing. Uncle Damek had such a gift for storytelling, making old myths and legends come alive in Nick's mind. He could spin something as boring as an archeological dig's inventory of equipment into an adventure. And short of going on mythical adventures himself – hardly likely to ever happen – Nick loved living them in his imagination with Damek's guidance.

"Indeed! So glad you remember." Damek laughed goodnaturedly. "And what an adventure it's led to this time. In fact, I even did a bit of spelunking recently, if you can believe it."

"Really?" Nick's eyebrows shot up. "You went cave-diving? How deep did you go? Were you looking for buried treasure? Can you take me some time?" Nick stopped all of a sudden. "I mean, I don't know when we'll be able to visit you in Prague..." He didn't want to say that he wasn't sure they could afford the trip – not while Mom could hear.

"If I recall correctly, young knight, Illinois has some cave structures worth exploring. Perhaps we'll visit one while I'm in town."

"Maybe, but I don't know how Mom would feel about me cave diving with my messed-up leg... Wait. While you're in town!?" Nick gripped the phone tight. "You're coming to visit us in Chicago?"

He looked up to see Mom leaning against the door frame between the kitchen and the family room, watching him with a smile on her face. The next second, Kat barreled past Mom, planting herself in front of Nick. He didn't realize he'd spoken so loud.

"Uncle Damek is coming to visit?" Kat clapped her hands. "Really?" She danced from foot to foot.

Mom gently pulled Kat back to the kitchen. "Shhh," she whispered, "It'll be your turn in a few minutes."

"Sounds like I've stirred up quite the ruckus," Damek chuckled. "I still have some affairs to put in order, so my visit won't be for another three weeks, but I'm hoping to stay at least that long, if you put up with me."

Nick's smile grew bigger and bigger. Almost a whole month with his uncle in town? It was almost too good to be true. "You should stay longer. For the whole summer!"

"I make no promises, young knight. Besides, if I stay in Chicago forever, how will you be able to visit me here in Prague? It's been far too long since you've come to see our fine city."

"Yeah, it has been." Nick had only been five or maybe six. Kat's age. But the city had made a huge impression on him. It had been like visiting a real-life magical kingdom, straight out of a fantasy movie.

"Now, young knight," Damek interrupted Nick's memory, "if my suspicions are correct, your sister has been waiting very patiently for her turn at the phone."

Nick grinned. His great uncle had a sixth sense. Kat was, at that very moment, hopping up and down just past the door to the kitchen, kept in place by Mom's firm grip on her apron strings.

"Patiently's an interesting word," Nick joked.

"She is lucky to have you as her older brother," Damek replied, voice warm. "I thank you for taking your responsibility seriously. It may not always be easy, but I take great comfort in knowing you will watch after and protect her, no matter what dangerous circumstances may arise."

"I...erm...thanks."

Damek had such a sincere way of praising him, Nick could almost believe he was as cool as his uncle thought he was.

"Nick!" Kat had either escaped Mom's clutches or been let go. She poked him in the ribs. "It's *my* turn!"

"Well, I gotta go before Kat skewers me to death. Oh, I forgot to say: Mom did say she found a doctor who might be able to help Kat with her dreams. I should have mentioned that. I don't want you to worry."

"I am not at all worried, young knight," Damek answered, "and neither should you be. In fact, I have every reason to believe neither of you will be plagued with sinister dreams again."

"Really?" The confidence in Damek's voice rolled over Nick like a wave of relief, washing away the anxiety that had nagged him since Kat's screams had startled him awake.

"Really," Damek answered. "Of course, everyone dreams. I, myself, have more experience than I'd care to remember with bothersome dreams. But, that is a conversation for another day. Now, I'm afraid you will face very real peril quite soon if you don't hand over the phone to your younger sister."

"I can't wait 'til you get here," Nick said. "Good-bye Uncle Damek!"

"One more thing, Nicholas," Damek said. "Don't hesitate to call anytime day or night if you need me for any reason. Promise me you'll let me know if anything unusual happens."

"I promise!" Nick barely got out before Kat made a grab for the phone with her syrup-sticky hands.

"I knew you'd be happy to hear from your uncle." Mom had her purse slung over her shoulder and her car keys in her hand. "And you thought I couldn't keep surprises!"

"He's coming to visit!" Kat chirped, hugging the phone against her chest like it was her favorite stuffed animal. "I can't wait! I can show him all of my new puppet tricks!"

Mom laughed and reclaimed her phone, a cleaning wipe in her hand. "Well, if you're going to practice more today, please tidy up after yourself when you're done. You'll make sure she does, Nick?"

"Yep!"

"I'll see you both this evening. Call if you need anything. You'll be good for your big brother, won't you, Kat?

Kat's little face grew serious. "I will, Mommy. Uncle Damek said I have to always listen to Nicky because he's my knight in shining armor." She launched herself at Nick, squeezing him tight around his waist.

Nick groaned and rolled his eyes. "I'm not a knight, Kat, that's just Damek's nickname for me.

"Yuh-huh," Kat said. "Uncle said *you're* a knight, *he's* a knight and *his dad* was a knight, and *his dad's dad* was a knight..." her voice trailed off as she skipped up the stairs to her room. At the top of the staircase she paused and yelled down, "Hey! Why don't girls get to be knights?" But she skipped off again before Nick could think of an answer.

Damek had told Nick the same story about their ancestors being knights when he'd been young. He'd spend hours daydreaming about wielding a sword and fighting enemies.

"Bye Nick," Mom said. "Thanks again for your help with Kat. Your sister adores you. You know that, don't you?"

"I know."

Nick ascended the stairs as fast as his bad leg allowed, already calling to Kat. "Hey, Kat! Wanna put on a puppet show? About Bruncvik and his two-tailed lion? You can be the knight this time and I'll be the lion, and we'll defeat the crooked old man from your dream. Want to?"

Kat's head popped out of her bedroom door. "You can't be the lion, silly! Uncle Damek says I'm the lion, because my name is Kat and lions are cats. And look," she picked up her long hair in two sections. "I have two tails!"

CHAPTER THREE - The Acolyte

Damek whistled to himself as he returned home from the hospital, a strong wind blowing his rainjacket back and forth behind him. Despite his worries about his squire, Damek knew Kyril was in good care. And, while doctors insisted on keeping Kyril for the rest of the week to monitor his oxygen levels, they'd assured Damek his friend's lungs and hip would eventually heal...provided Kyril didn't attempt any further underground explorations.

They had accomplished their mission. Their journey beneath Mount Blaník had gone according to plan.

Why, then, did something feel so...off?

Damek wracked his brain as he pulled the keys to his front door from his pocket. Work had been work: tiring, but not worrying, mostly consisting of planning for the one lecture he was scheduled to teach during the coming semester. Kyril Zeman – his loyal friend and squire – lay wounded in Hospital Na Františku, but was recovering quite nicely. So why could Damek not shake the sense of impending doom?

His thoughts wandered as he turned the key in the lock, eventually settling on young Nicholas and Katarina. He smiled. It had been too long since he'd seen his dear niece Anna and her children. He couldn't think of a better way to relax and celebrate after such a harrowing few months. And being able to assure both his great niece and nephew that they needn't worry about troubling dreams any longer was worth celebrating.

Even now, when he knew the threat had passed, Damek couldn't stop his hand from trembling on the doorknob as the memory of his own recent troubled dreams rose in his mind. A hunched man dressed in rags. A chill, disembodied voice riding the wind. Those very dreams had been the catalyst that sent him and Kyril under Mount Blaník in the first place...

Damek shuddered and straightened his shoulders, reminding himself he was safe. Nicholas' mention of the red eagle and the door set in the mountain was strange, though. *Remember, you raised him on the legends of Czechoslovakia,* he reasoned with himself. *Calm yourself, old man. The battle has been won.*

He pushed open the door.

It slammed shut in his face.

Damek leapt back. He glanced up and down the street, but it was empty, save for a man – who seemed completely unaware of any commotion – passing by with a bag of groceries.

Damek frowned. There had been wind and scattered showers all day, but not wind strong enough to snatch the door from his fingers like that. What if he'd miscalculated somehow? What if something had gone wrong?

Now, now, he chided himself as he smoothed his rumpled jacket. *Everything is fine. You are jumping at shadows! You just need a good night's rest.*

This time, he heard the gust before it manifested. It whistled in his ears, a high-pitched whine harmonizing with a low, mournful howl.

The wind smashed into him, shoving against his chest like an icy, open-handed slap. Not hard enough to lift him off his feet, but certainly hard enough to upset his balance. He tumbled backward to the ground.

"Dr. Maracek, are you all right?"

The man with the bag of groceries raced toward him, scarf and wool coat trailing behind him as he ran. *Wool coat? In the summer?* He looked to be in his early twenties – *one of my lecture students, perhaps?* – and had a mop of dark hair pushed greasily to one side across his forehead. He hastily set his bag of groceries on Damek's porch before reaching out a gloved hand to help Damek up.

"I'm alright," Damek said, accepting the man's help. "Nothing broken out of place, at least."

"Lost your footing, did you?" the stranger asked.

"Lost my footing? Not at all! Surely you saw that?" Damek sputtered. "The wind knocked me flat!"

"Wind?" The man cocked one thin eyebrow. "What wind?"

Damek nodded at the red and gold stripes of the Prague flag jutting from the corner. They rustled slightly.

"Nothing but a breeze," the man shrugged. "Surely you are not suggesting the wind holds a personal vendetta against you?"

Was he joking? Damek peered more closely at the stranger. He was not as young as he'd first appeared. Fine lines creased his forehead and gray streaked his unkempt hair. Definitely not a student. Damek would have remembered a face so pinched and narrow, so pale. Yet something about the nervous, twitching way he moved seemed familiar.

"Excuse me," Damek asked, "have we met? You know my name, yet I am at a loss..."

One side of the man's mouth jerked up in a half-smile as if at a poorly told joke, then he bent stiffly to retrieve his paper bag.

"We have never met," the man replied after straightening, "though I hear much of you in the world. The Maracek name has become quite celebrated due to your endeavors."

"Celebrated in a very limited, academic circle, perhaps." Something was off. The stranger stared at him through his one visible eye – the other being concealed behind a shock of unwashed hair – with such a humorless expression that it caught Damek off guard. "Look here, you must forgive my poor manners, but are you quite sure we've never met?"

"Quite positive. Though it is strange, perhaps, given my passion and your profession," the man said, taking one step closer.

"Oh?" Damek could now see inside the bag. Not groceries after all. Rather an assortment of what looked and smelled like dried roots and rotting herbs.

"I own a small antiques shop in the Jewish Quarter," the man said, "and I've been told you have quite the collection of antiquities that I am *very* interested in."

From the corner of his eye, Damek watched the Prague flag begin to flap briskly in a sudden breeze. He took a step back from the stranger, his senses uncomfortably heightened.

"Perhaps you would like some assistance getting inside?" The stranger cut him off, sweeping his hand grandly toward Damek's front door. "You seem out of sorts. We could talk about possible acquisitions of your collectibles?"

"Thank you for your concern," Damek said, struggling to keep his tone light. "I assure you, I'm not as feeble as I must look."

"I only thought you might still be recovering from your recent...*mis*adventure...shall we say? If you will invite me inside, I will see to your injuries. I dabble in the apothecary," he said, indicating his foul-smelling bag.

"I want none of your healing." Damek pulled himself up to his full height and fixed the stranger with the considerable command and authority he had accrued through his life. "You will never touch any artifacts in my possession. You will leave now and never return."

With a knowing light in his eyes, the stranger obeyed, turning to leave. Though once he reached the border of the property, he turned for one last remark: "I take my leave of you for now, Damek Maracek...or do you prefer Old Knight?...but I *will* return, and I will have what I seek." With that, the strange man's long legs strode quickly around the corner, the collar of his wool coat turned up against the sudden wind that tore down the street.

Behind Damek, the window shutters rattled as if desperate to escape their fastenings, and for a moment, he swore he heard voices chanting evil spells. *Eybik ibn...*

Quickly, he opened his front door and slipped inside, wrestling against the wind that battered against it from the other side. Once it was closed, he quickly bolted the chain, then sagged against the wooden frame, panting for breath.

A deep, mournful groan welled up in Damek's chest. Had that been...

No, he thought. *I studied every passage, deciphered every clue, translated every word.*

But even as he thought the words, he knew he'd taken a huge risk in acting so quickly. Even one small error, one word or punctuation mark out of place, could change the entire meaning of the passage he'd examined

"What have I done?" he whispered.

As if in reply, a memory from beneath the mountain seized him...

..."RUN!"

This time, Kyril yanked roughly on Damek's climbing harness.

Damek turned on his heel, pushing his squire toward the mouth of the tomb. His back hunched against the searing heat, he lumbered after Kyril, crouching low to avoid the boiling tendrils of flame that raced out from the tomb and swirled across the walls and ceiling toward the entrance.

Damek's jacket caught fire. He struggled to free his arms as he forged ahead. In front of him Kyril doubled over, racked with coughing. The squire sank to his knees.

Growing dread hung on Damek like an anchor chain. They weren't going to make it.

"Du kenst mikh nit tseshten! Eybik ibn..."

The haunting voice melded with the screech of twisting metal chains behind him.

The shrill whistle of the tea kettle snapped Damek out of his trance. He couldn't remember putting the kettle on, let alone walking to his kitchen from the front door. Now was *certainly* not the time to be losing track of things. He needed to focus.

"You cannot destroy me," the bodiless voice beneath the mountain had taunted him in Yiddish. *"Eybik ibn..."* Those two words were from a different language. Old High Germanic if he wasn't mistaken. Eternal life.

The memory of that haunting voice filled every bone in his body. The shutters outside his study windows creaked, and the screens rattled in their frames as the unnatural wind tested for weaknesses, searching for entrance.

He had work to do.

CHAPTER FOUR - The Itsy Bitsy Spider

"The icky ibin spider crawled up the water spout." Kat sang and danced around the garage with her spider puppet. "Down came the rain and swooshed the spider out..."

Nick grinned. Uncle Damek had sent them both marionettes to celebrate the end of the last school year. The knight had been left unfinished so Nick could practice his woodworking skills. It needed some work, but Nick still had over a week to finish it up before Damek arrived. The spider – complete with creepy, googly eyes and pincers on the ends of each limb – was for Kat to practice puppetry with. Its eight arms made it perfect for learning how to handle more complicated set-ups. Of course, Kat made him promise they would share their marionettes with each other, but it shouldn't have surprised him that she loved the spider most. His little sister could be fearless – when she was awake, at least.

"Up came the sun and dried up all the rain..." Kat heaved the spider high up above her head. She'd painted each of the legs a different color, and they dangled like rainbow raindrops in the air before she swung the puppet back to the ground. "And the icky ibin spider crawled up the spout again!"

"Nice work." Nick clapped. She wasn't using the paddles to control the body and legs like a puppeteer was supposed to. Instead, she held all the strings in one fist. But she was six. There was plenty of time for her to practice.

Kat bowed.

"You know it's 'itsy bitsy spider,' though, right?" he asked. "Not whatever you were singing."

"I like my way better," Kat shrugged, placing her spider back in its box. "I heard it in my dream. It makes things wake up, I think." She twirled and then jumped into the air, flapping her arms like a bird.

Nick glanced up at his sister from where he sat at the old workbench. "Was it a scary dream?" he asked.

"Not tooooo scary," she said. "The crooked man found a sleeping rabbit and put it in his pot. And he said: *"Icky ibin, icky ibin,"* over and over and wiggled his fingers like this," Kat said, hunching her shoulders and wiggling her fingers. "Then the rabbit woke up and hopped out of the pot. And the crooked man laughed and clapped his hands and danced." Kat demonstrated, clapping and dancing from foot to foot.

A sense of unease crept up on Nick as he watched Kat doing her weird little jig. Her eyes seemed too bright as she stared past his head, clearly seeing the dream play out again in her mind. He glanced over his shoulder, sure he'd see the crooked man sneaking toward him. But there was nothing, only empty cardboard boxes piled in the corner.

He turned back to face Kat, who had stopped dancing and stood silently, as if waiting. "And then what?" he asked.

"Then he grabbed the rabbit..." Kat clutched her spider puppet, both hands around its neck, "and... SNAP!"

Behind Kat, a stiff wind blew her hair across her face and slammed the door from the garage to the kitchen shut, causing them both to jump.

"Kat!" In shock, Nick jumped up and rushed to his sister. He took hold of both her shoulders and shook her slightly.

Kat blinked, confused. She looked down at her hands. "Oh no, Nicky!" she cried, looking up at him with wide, sad eyes. "I think I broke him."

Nick stared at the ruined puppet, eight limp arms in Kat's left hand, and grinning, googley-eyed head in her right.

Just then, the automatic garage door went up, and Mom's van pulled into the driveway.

Kat dropped her puppet and rushed to the driver-side door. Mom unrolled the window and Kat chatted with her while she pulled into the garage, telling her all about their day.

Quickly, Nick bent over and retrieved the broken puppet and placed it on the workbench behind his dad's old tools.

"Kitty-Kat, will you help me take in the groceries?" Mom asked, opening the van door.

"I can help, too," Nick said.

"You keep working," Mom said. "I need some one-on-one time with my girl."

The summer day had been hot and muggy, but now a breeze slipped in through the open garage door and cooled Nick's face. It did nothing, however, to quiet his anxious nerves.

What had just happened?

He picked up the spider's body and head. The neck hadn't been very thick, but he still wasn't sure he'd have been able to snap it in two like that. More disturbing than that, though, was the creepy look in Kat's eyes as she'd danced around like the little old man. Almost as if *she'd* been the puppet and someone had been pulling *her* strings.

The door to the house creaked open. Nick startled, hiding the spider behind his back.

Mom poked her head into the garage. "Sweetheart, are you forgetting what day it is?"

Nick stared at her blankly. Then, with a start, he realized: Damek said he'd call today. He glanced at his watch. It was almost time.

"Thanks, Mom!" he said. "I'll just put my stuff away and be right in." Damek would make everything all right. Damek would know what to do about Kat.

"My phone's on the counter!" Mom called over her shoulder. "Please make sure the garage door is shut when you come in. I keep finding doors open, and bugs are getting in. And brush off! I don't need sawdust in the carpet!"

After putting his tools back in the tool box, Nick headed inside. As he grabbed the doorknob to pull it shut, the wind snatched it away from him.

The wind? From where? Wind from *inside* the house?

Nick's pulse picked up as the uneasiness he'd felt earlier returned.

He gripped the doorknob with both hands this time and it swung easily. He let go, allowing the momentum to do the rest. At the last second, it sped up, crashing into the frame.

"For heaven's sake, Nick," Mom's voice called from upstairs. "Are you trying to knock the house over?"

"Sorry!" he called back.

The phone rang.

"Hey Uncle Damek!" Nick said, breathless from his quick sprint to pick it up before it went to voicemail.

"Nicholas, is everything all right?" Damek asked, clearly concerned. "You sound exhausted."

"No, just fighting the wind and running in here to get to the phone. I was working on my knight puppet out in the garage and lost track of time."

"Fighting the wind?"

The sudden alarm in Damek's voice caught Nick off guard. "Oh, not for real," he said, wanting to reassure his uncle. "I just... Sorry, the doors just keep slamming for some reason. I wasn't really fighting anything. I'm okay, I promise."

"And Katarina?" Damek asked, his voice calmer. "How is she? No more troubling dreams for either of you, I hope?"

Nick thought for a second. "Hmmm, I haven't had any dreams that I remember. Kat said she had a *weird* dream, but nothing scary since I talked to you last time. But..." He hesitated, unsure whether he should mention Kat's strange behavior. His uncle sounded worried this time, his voice strained. Nick didn't want to bother him. Then again, Damek *had* asked Nick to let him know if anything unusual happened.

"What is it, young knight?"

"There *was* something strange. You know the spider marionette you sent Kat? Well, she broke it."

"Ah, yes, the creepy spider. That isn't so bad," Damek's voice sounded instantly brighter. "Accidents happen, and she's very young. The spider wasn't expensive. It was meant to be played with. Perhaps we can repair it when I visit."

"Maybe, but..." Nick glanced around to make sure no one was listening. "She broke it on purpose. It was really weird."

"Weird how?"

"She was playing with her puppet and singing a song – the Itsy Bitsy Spider," Nick explained, "but she was singing it wrong, and I teased her about it. She said she'd heard it in a dream. That a crooked old man was singing it while he made rabbit stew or something. Anyway, it didn't make any sense. She said the dream wasn't scary, but she was just being *weird* about it when she told me, like she was still in the dream or something. She was holding the spider and suddenly just snapped its head clean off."

Damek didn't answer. Nick waited for the wise, comforting words he knew would come. He realized his pulse had sped up while he'd told the story. Damek would probably say it was nothing. Everybody dreams, after all. And he was probably right...

"Nicholas, where is your sister now?" Damek asked, interrupting Nick's thoughts.

"Oh, I'm not sure. One sec." Nick hit the mute button on Mom's phone and called out. "Kat? Uncle Damek's on the phone! He wants to talk to you!"

After a moment, Mom appeared at the top of the stairs. "Nick, please tell your uncle that Kat isn't feeling well and I've put her in the bath to warm her up. Tell him she's sorry to miss him and will call back tomorrow."

Nick relayed the message.

"I see," Damek said, with no trace of his usual good humor. "I'm sorry to hear Katarina isn't feeling well. Perhaps that accounts for her odd behavior earlier."

Of course that was it. Nick breathed in relief. Damek always knew how to put his mind at ease.

"Nicholas, you mentioned there was an old man in Katarina's dream. Did she happen to tell you anything else about him?"

"Just that his back was hunched. Except, she didn't actually *say* that. She showed me. She said he was 'crooked.' He was in her other dream, the night terror I told you about." Nick considered telling Damek about the part that had scared Kat: the part about the crooked man writing Nick's name in the snow. But he felt stupid saying it out loud.

"And the words to the song? Do you remember the words to the song?"

"Kind of? It was the Itsy Bitsy Spider, but like I said, she was singing it wrong. Something like, 'The eye-bick ick-bin spider.' Sorry, I can't remember exactly."

Again, Damek remained silent.

"Uncle Damek?" Nick asked after waiting several seconds. "Is everything alright?"

"Yes, yes, of course!" Damek replied. "Nothing to worry about, I'm sure. Though, you will continue to keep a close eye on Katarina for me, won't you? Let her know I will call in the next few days to check in on her. "

"Yeah, of course," Nick replied, a little unnerved by the urgent tone in Damek's voice.

"That's a good lad," Damek said. "You know, young knight, sometimes unsettling dreams are unavoidable. For people like you and me, they can even help us to work out problems in our waking lives. Though your sister is too young to understand such things." Damek hesitated for a moment before saying: "Tell Katarina that when I visit, I'll bring something for her that will protect her dreams from crooked men."

"I'll tell her," Nick said. That should cheer Kat up if she wasn't feeling good. "Uhm, well... I'm excited you'll be here soon."

"As am I," Damek replied, and his voice sounded normal again. "As am I. Have you looked into any of the caves we've discussed? I'm eager to hear which of them you think best deserve our attention."

Nick grinned, his anxiety slipping away at the prospect of spelunking. "Well, we have a couple options..."

CHAPTER FIVE - Twelve Layers Deep

The solid thunk of a hammer hitting a chisel filled Damek's house tonight just like it had the better part of the last week. Wood shavings curled in piles all around, and sawdust topped every surface in a fine layer, hanging suspended in the air.

Then finally, all was quiet.

Damek wiped his shirtsleeve across his sweaty brow and stepped back to survey his handiwork. Intricate, looping lines and angular shapes decorated the inside archway of the front door and ran up and down both sides. Similar patterns embellished every other entrance to the house, including the windows and even the inside of the chimney.

He'd worked with only short breaks for hastily prepared food and a few hours each night of restless sleep, carving the runes meant to ward off evil spirits. Runes he'd discovered in the book written by his ancestors about an ancient legend he'd scoffed at.

Until recently.

Laying down his tools, he put the kettle on.

His disbelief had been his first mistake. His first of many.

Damek's hands trembled as he poured hot water over the bag in his tea cup. With the protective runes in place, he could no longer ignore the heavy, tattered book on the table.

The book lay next to the same small, time-worn wooden box Damek had carried in his shirt pocket below the mountain. For a moment, he stared at the box with narrowed eyes, almost as if he expected it to do something peculiar. When it remained motionless, he picked up the leather-bound book, opening it and turning to the page he'd marked. The same page he'd gone over at least a hundred times in the past few months, ever since the dreams began.

His second mistake had been ignoring the dreams.

What started as occasional glimpses of a crooked man and his puppet shows had quickly escalated to nightly terrors involving sinister plots and ghastly crimes. And from the very beginning, a voice had called out to him.

Soft and muffled at first, the voice permeated the dream like the eerie soundtrack from an old, black and white horror film. In the beginning it was a young voice...a lost voice. It begged Damek for help. But night after night, the voice grew older. Darker. Before long, another sound joined the voice: the cold rattling of prison chains.

If only I'd recognized them for what they were sooner, Damek grieved silently to himself, *I would have had more time. More time to research, more time to study!*

But that wasn't quite true. He'd had decades since his father – on his deathbed – had told him what was hidden in a secret compartment buried beneath the floor of the attic. Decades he'd spent studying and teaching myths and legends as evidence of common human hopes and fears, debunking superstition, offering logical explanations for what gullible people called magic.

Even as a young boy he doubted his father's insistence that dreaming ran in their family, as if it were some kind of superpower. He also dismissed bedtime stories about mythological monsters like the golem – a creature made of mud and brought to life by a magic spell, or the Noon Witch – who kidnaps disobedient children.

Damek's mother scolded her husband for trying to frighten the young boy, afraid her son would have nightmares. But Damek wasn't afraid of make-believe and told his mother as much. When his father gave him the lion pendant to ward against unpleasant dreams, Damek wore it to bed on a leather cord around his neck for a few weeks to put both his parents' minds at ease and then wrapped it in a bit of his mother's sewing scraps and squirreled it away in his sock drawer. He'd always been a sound sleeper, rarely remembering his dreams. He'd never had nightmares.

Until recently.

Now, he could only regret the years he'd spent believing that the last legend his father had told him before passing was just another make-believe bedtime story. All those years he could have been researching, preparing. Instead, once he'd finally realized the identity of the figure who had wriggled into his dreams, time was very close to running out.

So, he'd done what any professor would do: dived into researching the artifacts he'd found hidden beneath the attic floorboards. He devoured his family history, immersing himself in the very book that sat before him now. And yes. With his newly squired friend Kyril, he'd gone off half-cocked, completely confident in his ability to defeat the centuries old threat his knighted ancestors had sworn to protect against.

And he had failed.

But how?

If his suspicions were correct, he had not just failed to destroy the ancient evil that had awakened and wriggled into his dreams only months earlier, he had somehow...*strengthened* it. It was the only explanation.

He turned back to the passage he'd carefully marked on the yellowed page.

Death piles stones twelve layers deep,

The Crimson Eagles sacred secrets keep

He read the stanza in English rather than the ancient Bohemian it was written in, no longer needing to consult the translation he'd made in his own notebook. These two lines had been what led him under Mount Blaník in the first place, descending through *at least* 12 levels of tunnels and past the faded crimson eagle fresco guarding the entrance to the crypt.

Strike the light and fan the flame,

Without the body will the soul remain?

The inferno he'd wrought in the crypt under the mountain should have been enough to annihilate anything, body *and* soul...

...for a moment, the flames slowed, receding back along the walls, sucking cool air in from the mouth of the tomb.

Eyes stinging, lungs screaming for breath, Damek inhaled deeply. Then, with a burst of adrenaline he surged forward, lifting his squire from the ground. The only hope they had was to make it to the door and seal the chamber.

"Leave me," Kyril panted weakly.

Damek didn't waste any breath scolding him. He pushed forward, supporting his friend.

The howling blaze cast the entrance in deep relief, revealing thousands of ancient runes carved into every inch of the doorway. The same faded runes criss-crossed the small, time-worn box resting in Damek's shirt pocket. On either side of the door, the chiseled image of a two-tailed lion reared on its hind legs. Above the door, stretching to the top of the cavern, perched the likeness of a blood-red eagle.

Another violent wave of coughing wracked Kyril's muscular frame. When it passed, his full weight sagged against the old knight.

"Hold on, old friend," Damek murmured, half-dragging, half-carrying his squire as they staggered the last few steps to the entrance.

"Ih rufe thaz winda; in himil wart mir giwisan."

The shriek rose from the crypt, echoing off the walls and piercing Damek's ear drums until he was sure they would burst.

"Alle solla binnan tjenan. Prag vet zeyn mayn!"

A gale-force wind blasted the foreign words through the tunnel straight at Damek and his unconscious squire.

With his final ounce of strength, Damek slammed the stone door shut.

Damek opened his eyes, breath catching. His tea had turned cold in its cup, yet sweat beaded his brow, drawn out by the memory of the blaze beneath the mountain.

The words had been in High German. He didn't need a transcription to remember them clearly enough to translate them:

"I call the wind; it shall serve me."

"All shall bend to serve. Prague will be mine!"

He could no longer ignore obvious facts: the sorcerer had awakened.

Taking a shaky sip of cold tea, Damek turned his eyes back to the page and scanned the last three stanzas of the riddle his ancestors had written. The answer to where he'd gone wrong must be in these stanzas.

Time guards the key to hidden power,

A reflection of pride when the clock strikes the hour

Beneath the place where heroes kneel

The Knight and Squire will reforge steel

Trust the Lion or all is lost

When Evil arrives at the Foot of the Cross.

He'd been so sure of his translation of the passages he'd found scattered throughout the thick tome by his ancestors. Had that surety cost him everything? Was it too late now?

CRASH.

The window beside the fireplace flung itself open. Damek bolted out of his chair. A gust of howling wind whipped across his face, followed by a bright blue flash of light and a crackle of electricity.

In less than a second, the wind and the light had disappeared, leaving behind the faint stink of singed hair. The curtains hung limply in place. Damek took a few hesitant steps forward and drew the curtains closed again. When five seconds passed in silence, he crowded his desk with maps and notebooks.

The runes had worked.

The runes had prevented evil from entering the house.

The sorcerer lived, and Damek was marked.

He had work to do.

CHAPTER SIX - To Cross a Creek

Nick leaned forward, pressing hard as he sanded down a particularly tricky edge along his puppet's arms. He always hated this part, but after he was done, he could finally start using the paints he'd picked out to finish it up. And he had to move fast, too. He only had five more days before Damek arrived.

A nice breeze blew in through the opened garage door, ruffling through a stack of old newspapers Mom collected to use in the fireplace during the winter. Somewhere in the neighborhood, a dog barked, and the distant sound of a lawnmower signaled a peaceful summer evening.

Behind him, the door to the house opened. "Sweetie, Jeremy's at the front door asking if you can join him and your friends for some night games," Mom's cheerful voice called from the top of the steps leading down from the laundry room. "Just be home before 9:00 P.M., okay?"

Nick's shoulders drooped. Mom knew as well as he did that he didn't have any friends besides Jeremy. But Nick knew pretending he did made her happy. He just didn't know if he was up for any pretending tonight.

"Um," he said, turning in his chair, "I'd rather just stay home, actually. I haven't finished sanding yet, and then I'll still need to paint him before I can practice..."

"Oh, come on." Mom sounded like she was asking a favor. "It's important to socialize with other kids your age. Besides, you haven't seen Jeremy in weeks. He probably misses you."

"I doubt it," Nick said, turning around in his chair. The disappointment on Mom's face changed his mind. "Oh, fine," Nick groaned. "I'll go."

"Don't forget your flashlight!" Mom pushed the button to close the garage door, giving Nick just enough time to grab the flashlight and duck out, awkwardly hopping over the sensor.

Jeremy stood on the sidewalk, waiting for Nick to join him. "The puppet master himself!" he called out as Nick walked out to him

Nick didn't usually like other kids calling him that, but it was Jeremy, so he let it slide. "Hey, Jeremy. How was Alaska?"

"Dope," Jeremy said. "I'll have to show you the pics I took. Come on. Everyone's waiting for us."

* * *

Damek stood up from his hunched position in the attic. The different lengths of sleek, polished wood fit together seamlessly, and the gears turned so precisely that a master clockmaker would applaud. Pride and fear battled in his heart. Pride at what he had made, working tirelessly for the last several days. Fear because of its purpose, should he fail in his mission again.

He paused at his door. Was he doing the right thing? Was he really about to leave the safety of his own home in the earliest hours of the day, before the sun had even risen? But he had no other choice. It was a gamble, to be sure, but if he was right this time...if he found the clue he prayed would be there...the finish line would be in sight. Then he could truly rest. Then, no one else would suffer.

He stowed his notebook in his trenchcoat pocket – only Kyril could decipher the cryptic scrawlings and sketches it contained. He'd wanted to visit Kyril at the hospital one last time – the doctors planned to release him by the week's end – but the wind made leaving the house all but impossible in the last few days. Damek considered calling his squire on the phone, but he couldn't risk Kyril's keen perception. If his friend knew what he was about to attempt, he would go to great lengths to prevent Damek from going alone.

Oh, my old friend, Damek thought. *I would not fear the dark and the wind nearly so much with you by my side tonight.*

Damek rubbed his eyes. Several sleepless nights in a row made them red and bleary, but his mind still functioned clearly enough to know what must be done. Before he left the home that had been in his family for generations, possibly for the last time, he must transfer the protection of the Brotherhood. The same protection his father had bestowed on him from his deathbed. The protection he'd never needed – or let alone believed in – until very recently. If only he could protect all three of his last remaining relatives.

Damek opened the book again, this time to the very last page, and spoke the words written there: "Štít projde. Nicholas, rytíři řádu, čas nést toto břemeno je nyní na tobě."

As the words left his mouth, the wind howled around his house, pummelling the windows and doors. The lights in his study flickered, then went out.

Damek took a deep breath, closed the door to his study, and went to the kitchen to retrieve some brown packing paper. With the transfer completed, he still had one trick up his sleeve. Something that would appear innocuous should it fall into the wrong hands, but would hopefully hold meaning for Nicholas.

* * *

The sun, which had lingered late on the horizon, slipped all at once below the skyline and vanished. Nick and Jeremy chatted as they walked in the growing dark to where the neighborhood ended and the woods began.

Maybe Mom was right. Jeremy is a good friend, Nick thought. They'd grown up playing Astronauts and Aliens in the forest together, and Jeremy always had time for him when the other kids didn't. *Maybe I should be more social.*

Six flashlight beams strobed over them as they left the sidewalk and crossed the empty lot. Jeers and jokes from The Pack – as the group of neighborhood kids called themselves – floated to them from behind the fence line.

"Hurry up, laggers!" a voice called. "We've been waiting for *hours*!

"Yeah, yeah, we're coming," Jeremy called back as they reached the fence. Nick held the two middle barbed wires apart as Jeremy slipped through. Jeremy did the same for Nick.

And then, the other kids were all just...gone.

"C'mon!" Jeremy shouted over his shoulder.

Nick switched on his flashlight and he and Jeremy took off after The Pack. Six beams sliced through the undergrowth and thick-branched canopy, throwing creepy shadows across the path. The other kids dodged around tree trunks, scrambled over fallen logs, and swung from low-hanging branches, whooping and hollering deeper into the forest on their way to the creek as Nick quickly fell behind.

*Did you really expect any different?? * Nick limped after them. It stung that part of him always held out hope that one day they'd include him.

Jeremy ran a few yards in front of him, halfway between Nick and The Pack, occasionally glancing back over his shoulder to make sure Nick hadn't gotten left in the dust. Nick tried his hardest to keep up, his flashlight's beam wobbling slightly as he hobbled after them.

"Just go," Nick called, doing his best to keep from panting "I'll catch up!"

"You sure?" Jeremy asked

"I'm sure. I'm right behind you!"

Jeremy sped up, and Nick slowed to a fast walk, his hip joint throbbing with pain. Bitter thoughts chased each other through his mind: *Why does Jeremy keep inviting me to do stuff with The Pack? Why can't we just hang out together? He had to know this would happen. Did the other kids put him up to it?*

The Pack consisted of two girls and five boys, ranging in age from nine to fourteen. But even Josh – the smallest nine-year-old – easily outpaced Nick. And every single one of them except for Jeremy had taken turns tormenting Nick about his disability for as long as he could remember.

The sole of Nick's right shoe was thicker than the left. He'd been born with CFD: Congenital Femoral Deficiency, which basically meant his hips and right knee were all screwed up, and his right leg was shorter than his left.

Not that any of the kids in his neighborhood or at school had ever bothered asking why he 'walked funny'. Or why he limped when he ran. Or why it took him longer to get anywhere. It's almost like they thought he'd *chosen* to be disabled and hated him for it. Like they thought if they bullied him enough, he'd just disappear and they wouldn't have to watch him stumble along anymore.

He'd heard a million times from adults that he was lucky and should count his blessings. There were lots of people with CFD who couldn't walk at all without a brace or a prosthetic. He didn't feel lucky, though. He felt angry.

Angry at Mom for not letting him stay home and work on his puppet. Angry at Jeremy for inviting him. Angry at himself for hoping it would ever get better.

Ahead of him, the bouncing flashlights converged one by one in a small clearing. A chorus of crickets and rushing water filtered through the trees.

The creek.

Inviting him on a night they were going to the creek was borderline cruel. Maybe Jeremy wasn't such a good friend after all.

They'd had several summer rain storms the last couple weeks. By the sound of it, the rushing water reached the top of the bank.

Just turn around now and go back, he urged himself. *There's no way you'll make it. They'll forget you were even here if you turn around now!*

Too late. His forward momentum carried him awkwardly into the middle of the clearing. All six flashlights trained on him like a giant spotlight. He shielded his eyes.

"Nice of you to join us, snail," Becca jeered. She'd taken great pleasure in hiding his backpack in English last year to make him perpetually late for lunch and always had to wait at the end of a hopelessly long line.

Nick ignored her, focused on the creek. A pit of dread grew in his stomach.

Years ago, some genius had scaled the trunk of the huge oak tree whose broad branches stretched out across the creek, and tied a thick rope to it. Big knots had been worked into the rope to grip onto with arms, legs, and feet.

Sometimes, barely any water trickled along the bed of the creek and Nick could step across from stone to stone without getting his feet wet. He'd even used the rope to swing over when it was halfway full. The problem wasn't his arms. They were plenty strong. But when the creek swelled to the top of its banks, like it did now, even the biggest, most athletic kid would need to get a good running start before grabbing the rope to make it to the other side. Nick couldn't even count how many times Mom had made him promise to stay away from the creek when it was full.

In Nick's neighborhood, swinging across the full creek was a rite of passage. Everyone in The Pack had done it by age 11.

Everyone except Nick.

He aimed his flashlight on the rope hanging out over the water. The chorus of crickets seemed to be holding its breath as The Pack stared him down.

Tony, Nick's least favorite of The Pack finally broke the silence.. "You're all a bunch of grandmas," he jeered, then backed up clear to the boulder at the edge of the clearing. "Hold the lights steady, jeez! You think I wanna break my neck? If I miss the rope and land in the creek in that much water, I'll crack something for sure!"

But there wasn't even a hint of fear in Tony's voice. He just liked sounding tough. He backed up to the top of the sloped clearing, paused for dramatic effect, then whooped as he pelted past his audience. No one was at all surprised when his hands easily grabbed the top knot as he ran past, launching himself out over the water. His stocky upper-body made it easy for him to hang on. He didn't even bother clutching for the bottom or middle knots with his feet or knees. One second his feet left the ground. The next, he was crowing on the opposite bank.

Cheers drowned out the crickets, and every member of the pack rushed to catch the rope as Tony flung it back. But it was no contest. Freckle-faced Curtis, at 14 years old, was taller than anyone else by several inches, and had the wingspan of a full-grown silverback gorilla. He easily snagged the returning rope and backed up even further than Tony had, almost until he was on the other side of the slope before sailing across the creek.

One by one, the other boys and girls caught the rope and flew across the water, laughing, cheering, yelling like Tarzan. And, of course, voting on who had the best landing. Nick stood with Jeremy at the back, the churning in his stomach ramping up as the line in front of him shrank. Finally, it was just Jeremy and Nick.

Jeremy grabbed the rope in one hand, clapping Nick on the back with the other. "See you on the other side!." He grinned at Nick before backing up and launching himself into the air. His excited 'yeeeee-haaaaaaw!' hung in the night sky just a fraction of a second too long.

But Jeremy let go a split second too late. The rope had already reached its full extension and reversed trajectory, causing him to land awkwardly on the edge of the bank. His yell choked off suddenly as gravity claimed his body, and his arms windmilled as he fell backwards toward the rocks lying just under the shallow water in the creek bed.

"Jeremy!" Sara screamed. She dropped her flashlight with a thud and rushed forward. But before she reached him, Curtis – who was closer – reached out lightning-fast and snagged the front of Jeremy's sweatshirt, hauling him back to safety.

"Psych!" Jeremy said, when he regained his footing, but his voice was wobbly. "Nice reflexes, though, man!" He clapped Curtis on the back.

"You're such an idiot!" Sara swatted at Jeremy, who ducked his head just in time to avoid being knocked on his back.

In the dim light from across the creek, Nick could just make out Jeremy's sheepish grin. But Nick wasn't fooled. His friend had almost landed on the bottom of the creek bed.

Curtis flung the rope back across. "Okay, Nick!" he called. "You're up!"

Nick caught the rope. He looked hard at the deep creek bed, the muddy water, the boulders poking up here and there, and at his own stupid leg and

Frankenstein shoe. Without raising his head, he called across the water. "I better not. My mom will kill me if I end up getting wet."

"No worries, man," Curtis called back. "I'll catch you!"

Nick winced. No way was Curtis trying to be nice. *He knows I can't...won't...do it,* Nick guessed. *He just wants to make me look stupid.* The whole pack stared at him, their eyes drilling into him in the dark, waiting.

"Nah." Nick swung the rope back across. "I'm supposed to be home by nine. I'd better go."

"Don't be a baby!" Tony caught the rope. "It's barely eight-thirty. You can swing right back. We're all supposed to be home by nine."

"Knock it off, Tony," Jeremy muttered half-heartedly.

Nick's shirt stuck to his back, damp with sweat from his stumbling jog through the forest. But the sweat slicking his hand when he caught the rope was all nerves.

"Oh, because he's *disabled,*" Tony mocked, "Jeremy, everyone knows you're only nice to him because you feel sorry for him. You've been making excuses for him since kindergarten and it's getting old.

Nick's face flushed hot in the darkness. He half-considered letting go of the rope and leaving them all stranded on the other side. But they'd just pay him back the next time they saw him. Instead, he threw it as hard as he could, turned around, and stumbled back the way he'd come.

"That's right, little Nicky," Tony shouted. "Hurry home to your mommy!"

Nick hunched his shoulders against the laughter that followed him up the slope. As soon as he reached the cover of the forest, he sped his awkward steps to a hobbling jog back down the path. The last thing he wanted right now was for Jeremy to swing back across and come after him.

* * *

Tentatively, Damek peered through the kitchen window blinds. A streetlamp shone on the empty cobblestone, glistening with a misting of dew. The neighborhood slept.

Picking up the rectangular paper package, Damek examined its carefully taped edges. He'd addressed it to Nicholas Damek Gordon in Park Ridge, Illinois. Securing the bottom seam with one more piece of packing tape, he placed the package under his left arm. He stowed a flashlight in the deep front pocket of his trench coat, and in the other, he placed a large, hastily carved runestone. For a moment, he paused with his hand resting on the doorknob. *What would my colleagues think if they could see me now?* he wondered. With a shake of his head, he stepped out through the back door and into the night.

After locking the door behind him, Damek surveyed his surroundings. Nothing so much as a breeze stirred the leaves of the trees. But his tense shoulders didn't relax. It was too much to hope that the sorcerer had suddenly lost interest in him. The possibility occurred to him that the ancient evil power had somehow sensed he no longer held the Brotherhood's protection. But if it no longer considered Damek a threat, could it also sense the identity of the new heir?

Fear lurched in his gut. He must not fail again. Nicholas's life depended on it.

With a whispered prayer, he stepped into the dark streets of Prague under a midnight crescent moon. At the corner, he stopped at a mailbox and scanned his surroundings again. Once he was certain no one had followed him, he dropped the neatly-wrapped package in the box before continuing on his way down the deserted street.

The grating of his heels on the sidewalk echoed in his ears as he strolled briskly through the night, which had become suddenly cold. The cemetery was a few blocks north-west of his home. He hurried his step, his head constantly swiveling this way and that, every sense on high alert. His left hand clutched the runestone in his pocket. Of course, he saw nothing. The sort of predator that stalked him wouldn't be visible unless it wanted to be.

He finally arrived on the narrow street behind the cemetery. Vacant vendor stalls lined the path on his right, their shutters locked up tight for the night to protect the colorful trinkets and baubles inside. At the far end stood the embossed iron door leading to the interior.

Damek pulled the flashlight from his trenchcoat pocket and switched it on. The beam wavered slightly.

The cemetery was ancient. The Jewish community of Prague had buried their dead layer upon layer on this small plot of land from the first half of the 15th century until the year 1786.

Under the ghostly crescent moon, the throng of dilapidated grave markers crowded against each other like a gaping mouth full of broken, crooked teeth.

Damek sandwiched the flashlight between his left arm and his ribs, retrieving a small, leather kit from the front pocket of his trousers. With nimble fingers, he removed a set of lockpicks and deftly manipulated the mechanism of the heavy padlock that barred entry. The wrought-iron gate squealed in protest. Damek froze, but once the gate's screeching faded, the only sound he could hear was his own pulse thundering in his ears. After several anxious heartbeats, he slipped through the barely-opened gate and into the graveyard.

In that silent moment, a stiff, powerful wind engulfed him out of nowhere. His trench coat flapped around his knees. Dry, fallen leaves scuttled across the ground between the tombstones. The sudden gust snatched the gate from Damek's hands, slamming it shut. Panicked, he pressed himself flat against the cemetery's stone wall, searching the darkness with the beam of his flashlight. The bright cone of light danced across the crumbling headstones, casting spectral shadows that did nothing to soothe his mounting fear.

He braced himself.

The wind vanished.

After several heart-pounding moments, Damek peeled himself away from the stone wall and started into the graveyard. His steps were cautious as he scanned each marker with his flashlight, searching for one in particular. If his deeper examination of the diary was accurate, one of his ancestors – an heir of the Brotherhood – had left a clue hidden in plain sight somewhere in this vast maze of markers. This clue, the first of three, would ultimately lead to a safeguard: a weapon capable of defeating the sorcerer should he break free from his prison. Just his luck that after more than a thousand years, the responsibility would fall to him.

The wind returned in a fury, beating Damek back.

The old knight set his jaw and pushed on. With each step he battled forward, the wind howled against him, filling the air with detritus and dust, blinding him. Grabbing the runestone from his pocket, he thrust his arm out in front of himself, squeezed his eyes shut, and shouted a wordless shout.

The tempest stalled. The wall of wind he'd been pushing disappeared, causing Damek to stumble forward. As he regained his footing, a shrill whistle sounded from high above. He crooked his neck upward in the direction of the inhuman cry, eyes searching for his enemy through the twisted branches of the huge, primeval tree towering over him.

CRACK!

Damek's eyes widened as an enormous branch hurtled toward him.

He closed his eyes and thought of Anna, Nicholas, and Katarina.

55

Harris & Jones

CHAPTER SEVEN - A Gift From the Grave

Yellow light shone from the kitchen window as Nick wriggled back through the barbed wire fence – alone this time – and approached his house. The barbs tore several small gashes in his bare arms and legs, but he ignored them. The pain from the cuts paled in comparison to the hurt and humiliation gnawing at his insides.

Mom would be waiting to hear all about his adventures. It would take every bit of the acting skill he'd learned at the miserable summer acting camp when he was eight to convince her nothing was wrong.

He was back way too early. Slumping down against the garage door in the almost-dark, he scrubbed the involuntary tears from his eyes. *Just calm down and tell her it was great,* he coached himself. *Keep it simple or she'll be suspicious. Like last time.*

After his breathing steadied, he stood up and went inside.

"Mom?" He shut the front door behind him. "I'm back!" He winced at the audible crack in his voice.

No response.

Strange.

Pushing thoughts of his social ineptitude from his mind, he searched the main floor. Images of possible explanations swam around in his head: Mom slicing her finger while cutting an apple for Kat. Or Kat slipping down the stairs in her ridiculous fuzzy monster slippers. Or what if it was something worse? An intruder?

Nick's pulse spiked with worry. "Kat? Mom?"

Nothing.

Nick quickened his pace, hurrying up the stairs, his bad leg screaming at him in protest. *This is exactly why I need a cellphone!*

Past the open door to Kat's bedroom, Nick saw Mom and Kat asleep in Kat's bed, a book of fairytales lying open between them. Mom must have just nodded off in the middle of reading Kat a bedtime story.

Relief washed over him. Kat was okay. They were both okay.

A second later the relief disappeared, replaced by cringey memories of the creek. What a completely crap day.

Nick trudged down the hall to his bedroom. At least he wouldn't have to lie about having fun playing nightgames with his 'friends' tonight. Deep loneliness dragged at Nick as he entered his room. He was too tired to even brush his teeth. Kicking off his shoes, he fell straight into bed, not bothering to change out of his clothes.

"Just four more days," he whispered to Uncle Damek's photo on the nightstand. Then he switched off the light, turned over, and went to sleep.

* * *

Mist surrounded Nick like a boa constrictor trying to crush him, erasing all sight and sound.

Where am I?

Wait. He could hear something. Something alien, but familiar, too.

Pounding. Relentless pounding. Coming from somewhere nearby.

Suddenly, the ground under Nick's feet...shifted...and the pounding was right in front of him. Against his will, his feet dragged him forward one shaking, hesitant step at a time. After what could have been seconds - or hours as far as Nick could tell - the fog parted, revealing...

...Uncle Damek?

Yes. Damek stood right in front of Nick, back pressed against a heavy wooden door, feet digging into the rocky terrain as he struggled to keep whatever was pounding against the other side of the door from breaking through. Tremors passed through Damek's body with every impact from the avalanche of blows.

Determination and exhaustion painted Damek's face. His lips moved, but Nick couldn't hear what he was saying. Nick drew closer, straining his ears.

"...projde. Nicholas, rytíř i řádu, čas nést..."

"Damek!" Nick cried. "What's happening?"

Damek looked up, locking eyes with Nick.

"Be ready, young knight. I..."

The door blasted open. Damek sailed over Nick's head, landing with a heavy thud somewhere behind him in the mist.

"Damek!"

Frantically, Nick scanned the inky gray. He had to find Damek, to help him. But an impossible force weighed him down, gluing his feet to the spot where he stood.

A cackle like the splintering of ice froze Nick's blood in his veins. Slowly, he turned back to face where the door had been, heart jumping in his chest like a frightened mouse.

A tattered, inky shadow billowed out through the shattered doorway, completely obscuring whatever was on the other side. Hatred radiated from the darkness. Hatred for everything and everyone. Hatred for Nick, especially.

For one long, ominous moment, it lingered as if tasting the air. Then, all at once, it surged forward.

Instinct-quick, Nick raised his arms to shield his face.

Nothing happened.

Lowering his arms, Nick watched the shadow snake over his head, focused on something behind him.

Desperate, Nick followed the shadow's path with his eyes as it hurtled toward a small, long-haired figure standing alone in the mist.

"Kat!"

"Safeguard her, Dreamer. I pass the protection of the Brotherhood to you."

Nick woke, gasping. His head felt strange, groggy. Like he'd just woken up from a nap instead of a full night's sleep. Only the light filtering through the window told him it was morning.

Fragments of a dream drifted through his mind, fading as he reached for them. A shadow. A door. Cracking ice. And a strange incantation he didn't understand, spoken in a familiar voice: *"...projde. Nicholas, rytíři řádu, čas nést..."*

Whose voice? It was on the tip of his tongue, and then...gone.

He shook his head. Just a dream. Not surprising after such a crappy night. Then Nick smiled as he remembered: only four more days. That thought almost made everything better.

His clock read 7:09 A.M. Still early, even for Kat. But he knew he'd never be able to get back to sleep. Maybe he'd have time to eat a bowl of cereal in peace before anyone else woke up.

He paused on the stairs. Someone was crying. Not Kat. She didn't cry quietly. Not ever.

"Mom?" Nick kept his voice low enough that he wouldn't wake Kat. Nothing.

He continued down the stairs and rounded the corner into the kitchen. Gloomy, yellow light from the ceiling fan illuminated Mom's slouched form sitting alone at the table. Her phone lay next to her, but she wasn't looking at it. She stared blankly out the window, twisting her mother's ring around and around on her finger the way she always did when something bad happened. Like after Dad had gone.

"Mom? What is it?" Unease skittered in Nick's chest. "Where's Kat? What happened?"

Sorrow pooled beneath her eyes as she glanced up at him; her mouth drooped in a heartbroken frown. She didn't answer. Instead, she squeezed her eyes shut, lips quivering as tears streamed down her cheek.

Fear that felt like pain squeezed Nick's heart. "Mom?"

"Oh, honey." Mom wiped her face with her shirt sleeve and stood up, hurrying around the table and pulling Nick close. "Oh, Nicky. I'm so, so, sorry."

"Sorry why?" His head swam with anxiety. "Mom, please tell me what happened."

"I've just had a call from Mr. Zeman in the Czech Republic. I'm afraid Uncle Damek has been in some kind of accident..."

"Accident? What kind of accident? He's okay, though, right? He's still coming to visit, right?"

"I'm so sorry, Nick. Your uncle...he...I guess he was out walking in the dark, and...and he fell..."

Nick stiffened, pulling away. "Mom. What happened to Uncle Damek?"

"Nick, he... Your uncle has passed away."

Mom's lips kept moving, but Nick's brain had gone fuzzy, like it'd been stuffed with cotton. The only thing he could hear was the loud in-and-out of breath from his lungs and his pulse pounding in his ears.

* * *

Nick pushed down hard with his bad knee – not caring that it throbbed – on his suitcase to get it to zip shut. Three weeks was a long time to be away from home. Mom had given him an endless list of stuff to pack for the funeral, including his new orthotic dress shoes and an old suit he wore when they used to go to church. He didn't care that the suit pants hit well above his ankles, or that the tie was starting to fray around the edges. How could anything so trivial ever matter again?

The doorbell rang as he lugged his suitcase down the stairs, his overstuffed backpack bouncing against his shoulders with every heavy step.

"Nick, can you see who it is?" Mom called from up stairs.

Nick shuffled his way to the door, tired from another night without much sleep. His tears had dried up a few days ago, but his eye sockets ached. His whole body ached.

The mailman stood on the porch holding a brown, paper-wrapped package, along with a stack of junk mail and bills.

"Here, you go." The mailman handed everything to Nick. "Just a little too big to fit in your box!"

"Thanks." Nick didn't hear whether or not the mailman answered. He'd zoned out, staring down in disbelief at the writing on the package. In a daze, he wandered into the family room, sitting down hard on the couch.

Mom appeared at the top of the stair well. "Nick, you left the front door wide open! Who was it?"

Nick's tongue stuck to the top of his mouth. He couldn't answer. He could only stare, running his finger over the return address.

"Sweetheart, what are you doing? I need you to help Kat bring her suitcase down. The taxi will be here in 15 minutes. Who was at the door?"

"The mailman," Nick mumbled. "It's from Uncle Damek."

"What are you talking about?"

Nick held up the package wrapped in brown paper. "It's from Uncle Damek. It's postmarked the day after he died..."

"Oh, no." Mom sat down beside him on the couch and put her arm around his shoulder. "Damek must have mailed it before his accident."

"But why would he mail me something? He could have just brought it with him..."

"Let's open it and see what it is. But we'll have to be quick."

Carefully, Nick slid his finger under the taped edges of the brown butcher paper, pulling it back to reveal a large, hardback book and a small, ziplock bag containing what looked like a pendant of some sort, attached to a leather cord.

Examining the bag closer, Nick saw that the pendant was made from some kind of silver metal and shaped like a lion's head, mid-roar. He couldn't remember seeing Damek wear it before, but that didn't mean anything. He hadn't seen his uncle in several years.

The book, on the other hand, he recognized immediately. It was old and well-loved, as Damek would say. On the cover, a king dressed in rich gold and crimson robes stood with his counselor on a balcony overlooking his vast kingdom. Nick read the title under his breath: *The Legends of Old Bohemia.*

His eyes ached, but no tears came. Every night they'd been together, Damek had read him stories from this exact book. It was where Nick had first learned about many of the bohemian legends he loved so much, the same stories he told Kat when she struggled to sleep. He flipped through the pages, rediscovering the vivid illustrations that went with each tale.

"Uncle used to read stories to me from this same book," Mom said, "even before Grandma and Grandpa died and I went to live with him." Her voice sounded far away. She sat silently next to Nick as he thumbed through pictures.

A honking horn startled them both. Glancing up, Nick saw the taxi in the driveway through the open door.

"I'm not sure why he mailed this when he thought he'd be coming himself, but the important thing is that you know he was thinking of you. He loved you so much, Nick." She touched his face as if to wipe an invisible tear from his cheek before standing up. "Maybe bring the book with you if you have room in your backpack. You can look through it on the plane."

Eyes still fixed on the book, he nodded. Part of him wanted to never let it go. Another part wanted to hide it away somewhere he'd never have to see it again.

He was thinking of me.

The taxi driver honked again. Mom went to the door and waved. "Five minutes!" she yelled. Then she hurried back to her room calling, "Kat! It's time to go!"

Nick unzipped his bulging backpack, pulled out his laptop, and slipped the book and pendant in instead.

* * *

Dim light lit the main cabin. As far as Nick could tell, most of the passengers on the flight were sleeping. Including, thankfully, the fussy baby three rows back. Nick sat in seat 16B between Mom on the aisle and Kat by the window. Nick had actually been assigned the window seat, but it was only Kat's second flight, ever. Her first was a few hours ago on a smaller plane from Chicago's O'Hare International Airport to their connecting flight at Boston's Logan airport.

Now, according to the flight monitor on the seatback in front of him, they were halfway across the Atlantic ocean on their way to Prague.

During the first flight, Nick leaned over Kat's shoulder to stare out the small, plexiglass window as the plane climbed into the air, Chicago's massive skyscrapers turning into miniature towers as the ground quickly receded. Nick usually loved watching the buildings grow tiny below him. When they took off from Chicago, he couldn't seem to care less, except using it as a distraction. Since Damek had died, Nick avoided having nothing to do. Keeping busy meant less time being acutely aware that nothing mattered anymore.

I must be the only person left awake on the plane besides the pilot and crew.

He didn't like that thought. As happy as he was not to have to interact with anyone, being awake while everyone else slept felt...lonely.

He'd scrolled through all the movies and TV shows and live concerts and games available, but nothing interested him. Finally, desperate for a distraction that didn't make him want to claw his eyes out, he reached for his backpack and the book his uncle sent him.

His uncle's death more than a week ago left him spinning, a lot like the time he'd swum out into the Baltic Sea and been caught in a riptide. The violent current threw him upside down so many times, he couldn't orient himself. Every time he reached for the surface he grabbed fistfulls of sand from the seabed, and he knew he only had seconds before his lungs breathed in water whether he wanted them to or not.

Damek had pulled him to safety. But Damek couldn't help him anymore.

The Legends of Old Bohemia.

Nick let the book fall open to whatever random page it wanted.

His heart thudded in his chest.

Tucked between the pages was a small, torn slip of paper bearing one word written in his uncle's hand: *Nicholas.*

Pinpricks of anxious electricity surged through his fingers as he picked it up. Flipping it over, he found a message.

Dear Nicholas,

If you are reading this, it is because I am dead.

Touch the face of the lion to find the answers you seek.

Damek

Nick gripped the short note, hands shaking. His brow furrowed, his vision blurred.

"If you are reading this it is because I am dead."

Oh, I get it, Nick thought. *This is another dream. I'm just dreaming. Damek says dreaming runs in our family. When I wake up, there'll only be three days until Uncle Damek gets to Chicago!*

But if that was true, how come his eye sockets ached like a dried up creek bed? Why did his gut heave like being upside-down on a rollercoaster? Like he was starving, but everything he tasted made him want to puke.

No. This wasn't a dream. Damek wouldn't be anywhere in three days because he was dead.

And what did he mean, "...touch the face of the lion"? Did he mean the lion pendant he'd sent? That didn't make sense. He'd already touched it, and it certainly hadn't answered any questions.

All of this might be funny if it were a prank, but Damek didn't play pranks on people.

*Damek can't play pranks even if he **was** the kind of person who plays pranks on people because Damek is DEAD.*

Anger rose in Nick like a fire breathing dragon. Suddenly, he hated sitting in the middle seat. In fact, he hated the entire plane. He hated his ugly new shoes and he despised stupid riddles. He hated *everything,* and he only had one wish: *please let this anger last.*

For days after he'd learned about Damek's death, Nick had been angry – blindingly angry – at everyone and everything. He'd stomped around the house actually wanting his hip and knee to ache. He'd slammed doors and said mean things that made Mom cry and ripped up his favorite comic. He'd even almost shouted at Kat for looking through the photo album with sticky fingers, but Mom had whisked her away before he had time to erupt.

Then, out of nowhere, the anger had vanished and left Nick completely empty. Numb, like nothing. And sometimes nothing was nice, but most of the time it was terrifying, like being the only person awake on a jumbo jet halfway across the ocean.

Because, what if the nothing never ended and he was the only person awake forever?

So now, lonely and awake by himself, he tried to hang onto the anger because at least it was *some*thing. But how did being angry help him figure out why Damek had written him this weird note?

It didn't.

And just like that, his anger deflated like an untied balloon, leaving him empty again.

He couldn't tell anyone about the note. He didn't even want to tell anyone. Mom had enough to deal with and Kat wouldn't understand. Besides, for some reason he couldn't explain, he felt protective of the note. He wanted to keep it to himself, at least until he figured out what it meant.

He glanced around. Mom slept on his right, and Kat slumped against the window, holding her Grogu squishmallow on his left. They both looked so peaceful. Kat's long black lashes rested against the round curve of her cheek. Shame flared in his chest remembering how he'd almost lost his temper and yelled at her. Under the dim glow of his reading light, she almost didn't look real. It unnerved him to see her so pale and motionless. Instinctively, he reached out to touch her shoulder, just to make sure she was still breathing.

At his touch, Kat's eyes popped open. Nick recoiled in shock. His little sister stayed still, staring right through him.

"He's coming." Her voice was flat but urgent, her eyes unfocused as if she was in a trance.

"Who?" Nick whipped his head around to look up and down the aisle. It was empty.

Eyes wide as dinner plates, Kat reached out and grabbed his arm. "He's coming for you, Nick!"

WHOOSH!

Nick's heart dropped into his stomach as the plane plummeted.

Gasps and screams rang through the cabin as passengers woke, gripping their arm rests or their loved ones. Kat whimpered.

But the plane steadied almost as quickly as it had dropped. Kat closed her eyes, falling back to sleep almost immediately.

"Whoa," Mom exclaimed, pulling out one earplug and steadying her voice. "Are you okay, honey? Honestly, the pilot should have warned us." She readjusted her neck pillow, then turned back to Nick. "Nick? You look like you've seen a ghost!"

"I'm okay," he said, "just surprised."

"Try to get some sleep, son. You must be exhausted."

"Yeah, okay."

After Mom put her earplug back in and closed her eyes, Nick unclenched his fist and put Damek's note back inside the pages of *The Legends Old Bohemia*. Then, almost without thinking, he pulled out the ziploc bag containing the pendant, opened it, and slipped the odd bit of jewelry around his neck, tucking the leather cord under his shirt.

Okay, lion, answer my questions, Nick asked in his mind. *Why did Uncle Damek have to die, and why does my life suck so bad?*

Of course, he didn't expect an answer, and he didn't receive one. The silver lion rested against his skin and he decided he liked wearing something Damek had owned next to his heart.

He plugged his plane-issued headphones into the seatback entertainment system in front of him and selected a random cartoon from the kids' TV menu. Static distorted the characters' voices, but he didn't care. He figured if his brain had something meaningless to listen to, maybe it wouldn't make him think about Damek being dead and he could finally get some rest.

The last thing he remembered thinking before falling into a dreamless sleep was: *What's waiting for me in Prague?*

CHAPTER EIGHT – Th Old Squire

Mom, Kat, and Nick walked bleary-eyed through the halls of the Czech airport. Nick's leg and hip throbbed from sitting so long.

Nick looked over at Kat as they made their way through customs. She was tired, but other than being a little pale and quiet, she seemed fine.

What had happened on the plane, then? Nick shook his head, trying to knock the image of her blank stare and the sound of her flat voice from his memory. No luck. It remained stuck at the front of his brain.

Spooky.

Not to mention finding the weird note from Damek.

When Nick had been younger, sometimes Damek would make up riddles for him to solve with elaborate clues, kind of like a scavenger hunt. Now that he wasn't stuck in the middle seat on a long flight with a crowd of travelers bustled around him, the note seemed less ominous. Not a prank, maybe just one of Damek's games? Maybe it was just a tragic coincidence that he'd been in an accident and died before right after mailing the book.

Still seems like a messed up riddle, he thought.

He mulled it over as he limped past the last security checkpoint and out toward baggage claim a few steps behind Mom and Kat, towing his and Kat's carry-ons behind him. The airport was busy, with other arrivals streaming quickly past and plenty of friends, family, and taxi drivers waiting to receive them.

One man walking their way was holding a flower, the kind someone might try to sell to a tourist. Nick had never seen that in an airport, though. The man stood out like a sore thumb, dressed like it was mid-winter in a long wool coat and scarf.

"A flower for your lovely daughter?" The man approached them and proffered the flower, a deep red rose, to Mom instead of directly to Kat.

"No thank you." Mom tried to step past him. "Sorry, I don't have any cash on me."

The man walked backward, keeping pace with her. "No charge, Madame. Only trying to bring smiles and good cheer into people's days." He thrust the rose closer.

Something about the stranger bothered Nick, but he couldn't pinpoint what. His accent was Czech, but almost formal, the way someone might imitate a prince or king. And his smile kept slipping, like he had to remind himself not to scowl. Or maybe it was the slimy looks he kept shooting at Kat.

Kat hugged Grogu and stared at the strange man like she knew him, but couldn't quite remember his name.

"Would you like a flower, Kat?" Mom asked.

Nick could tell she was going to buy a flower just to get rid of him. It made him angry. "She said no thank you." Kat's suitcase wobbled a bit as he stepped between the stranger and Mom.

"Nick!" Mom sounded surprised. Before she could say anything else, they heard a deep booming voice from slightly behind them.

"My friends, the Gordons! You have arrived!"

Mom, Nick, and Kat all turned around at the same time. Nick recognized the voice instantly. It was Damek's attorney, Mr. Zeman. When

Nick looked back toward the man with the flower, he saw him walking briskly in the other direction.

All at once, the realization that Damek wasn't there to pick them up and that he'd never see Damek again hit Nick full across the face. Of course, he'd *known* that Damek wouldn't - *couldn't* - be there, but seeing the barrel-chested man Nick had met during his last visit to Prague made it real.

It had been seven years since he'd seen Mr. Zeman, before Kat had even been born. He remembered the attorney as a big, strong man with a warm smile and booming voice, not the older, stooped man he saw now. Mr. Zeman's large frame hunched over a small, wooden cane he held in his right hand. Nick watched him cough dryly into a handkerchief several times.

Mr. Zeman had been the one who called to tell Mom the news that Uncle Damek had passed away. It was his job to help her now that she was the executor of Damek's estate. From what Nick remembered, despite Damek being a couple decades older than Mr. Zeman, they had been more than attorney and client, they had been close friends.

Just then, Mr. Zeman glanced up, locking eyes with Nick. His brow creased ever so slightly, and the corners of his mouth trembled with what Nick thought might be pain. *Of course. He's grieving, too,* thought Nick. But then, a smile split the attorney's face.

"Welcome to my city!" Mr. Zeman spread his arms wide. "The most beautiful city in the world!"

Mr. Zeman's enthusiasm was contagious, and Nick found himself returning the smile as he shook his hand.

"You've grown tall since last I saw you, Nicholas," he said. Then he took Mom's small hands in both of his. "And you have grown more lovely, Anna. I am glad to see you two again. And to meet you, young lady," he said to Kat, who gripped Nick's hand and stared up at the attorney shyly. "You must be Katarina, yes? Master Nick's brave companion?"

Kat nodded, smiling. "I'm his bodyguard!"

"A lucky boy to have such a bold defender," Mr. Zeman said in his charming Czech accent. "Well met! I only wish it could be under better circumstances." His smile slipped, and his voice grew heavy. "My condolences to all of you. Your uncle was a dear friend and the best of men. His passing is a terrible tragedy."

"Thank you, Kyril," Mom said, placing her hand on his arm.

"Why do you have a walking-stick?" Kat asked. "Are your legs wrong like Nick's?"

Mom rounded on her. "Kat! That's not polite!"

Mr. Zeman let out a hearty chuckle that ended in another dry, raspy cough. "Hah! No, young lady. I took a bit of a tumble while spelunking recently. I'm afraid the old bones don't heal as quickly as they once did."

"Spahlunky...?" Kat tried sounding the word out.

"Spelunking," Nick corrected. "It means cave exploring."

"It does indeed. There are some fascinating caves not far from here," Mr. Zeman said as he helped everyone load their luggage from the carousel onto a cart. Despite walking with a cane, nothing seemed to be wrong with his arms.

They got lucky, too: their large bags were close to the first ones to come out on the carousel. Now more and more people were crowding in to get their luggage as Mr. Zeman led Nick, Kat, and Mom out of the airport and to a waiting car.

Nick stopped next to the trunk. "Damek said he'd gone spelunking when he called to let us know he was..." He stopped, realizing what he was saying. "Before he...uh..."

Mr. Zeman grasped Nick's shoulder with a large hand. "I know, my boy," he said, voice gentle. "It hurts. When there is time, I would love to share stories of my adventures with your uncle with you. Perhaps you would be willing to share your memories of him with me?"

Nick ducked his head, unsure how to answer. He'd been trying not to dwell too long on any Damek-memories because they hurt so much. "I...uh, sure, I guess." It's not like he could say no. That would be rude, and Mom would really flip out. He'd just have to try to avoid Mr. Zeman and deal with it if it ever came up.

But he couldn't avoid him now. Mr. Zeman was their ride to Damek's house.

* * *

The ride wasn't so bad. At least, not yet. Nick found himself listening attentively as Mr. Zeman narrated the sights on the drive. Mr. Zeman's accent wasn't heavy, and had a British lilt to it. Nick would bet he attended college abroad. Despite Mr. Zeman's raspy cough – no, he wasn't ill, the attorney assured Mom, his lungs had been slightly damaged due to smoke inhalation...nothing to worry about – his voice was pleasant to listen to, and he was a natural storyteller.

Even though she'd slept most of the flight from Boston, Kat somehow managed to fall asleep again, resting against Nick's shoulder. Nick didn't feel like sleeping. Instead, he focused on Mr. Zeman's words as the older man described the city around them. It was like having his own live audiobook narration to listen to. Nick didn't ask any questions, and Mr. Zeman didn't seem to mind. Nick's eyes followed where the attorney pointed, and in his head he imagined he'd slipped backward through time to the medieval age and was seeing the beautiful old buildings when they were new. For a moment, he let himself pretend he was gazing at the sparkling Vltava River through the windows of a horse drawn carriage instead of a minivan.

Before long, they were driving through the heart of the old city. Shops, libraries, restaurants, and apartments that looked as if they'd been built half a millennia ago blocked Nick's view of the skyline, ruining his daydream. Throngs of tourists and natives clogged the streets and sidewalks.

Just as unpleasant thoughts intruded his brain, Mr. Zeman interrupted, asking: "How much do you remember?"

The intensity of the man's piercing gaze caught Nick off guard. He looked over at Mom, but she was busy with a phone call. "Um, I don't know," he shrugged. Maybe if he stayed vague, Mr. Zeman would get the hint that he didn't feel like talking.

"Your uncle told me you are a lover of history," Mr. Zeman said. His voice didn't boom anymore. He spoke just above a whisper. "He said he taught you the myths and legends of old Bohemia. How much do you remember?"

Nick glanced at the back of Mom's head. She was still on the phone, not paying any attention to Mr. Zeman or Nick. Did Mr. Zeman know about the book?

"A lot, I guess," Nick finally answered. "I probably know more about the history and legends of Prague than I do about America."

"That's good. There's truth in legends, Nicholas, sometimes more truth than fiction. And that truth can be dangerous. Stay vigilant, young knight."

Nick's mouth fell open as he met Mr. Zeman's eyes in the rearview mirror. But before he could say anything, the car rounded a corner as Mom ended her call and gasped from the front passenger seat, pointing as Prague

Castle came into view. "It's more beautiful every time I see it! Do you remember any of this, Nicky? It's straight out of a fairy tale!"

"Nicky!? Really, Mom?"

"What? You let Kat call you that," Mom said, turning around. Then, after seeing the look on Nick's face, she put up her hands. "Sorry, sorry. There are just so many memories!"

When Nick looked back in the mirror, the lawyer had turned his eyes back to the road.

They neared St. Vitus Cathedral, where it stood towering over the rest of the castle complex and the Charles Bridge. Graceful spires topped stone turrets, and the soaring stained glass caught and reflected the daylight. Nick almost expected to see a chivalry of knights in full armor riding their noble steeds across the bridge.

"Isn't that church where King Wenceslas hid St. Vitus' arm?" The question was out of Nick's mouth before he realized he'd spoken.

"It is, indeed." Mr. Zeman locked eyes again with Nick in the mirror.

"Head's up!" Mom said.

Something landed in Nick's lap. He looked up to see her smiling over the seat in front of him. "Got you something. Open it!"

Nick could tell she was trying really hard to be cheerful. On the one hand it annoyed him that she was treating him carefully like he might break or something, but on the other hand, he was curious about what was in the bag. He opened it to find a small digital camera nestled inside. "This is really for me?"

"Yes, it's for you, silly," Mom said, "and the battery's fully charged. Do you think you can find anything to take a picture of?"

"Yeah. Thanks." It wasn't a phone, but it was still pretty cool. He'd wanted a camera for a long time.

"You're welcome," Mom smiled. "I expect you to take a lot of photos."

Mr. Zeman turned off the main road and drove up through narrow cobblestone streets. The buildings, each housing four or five tall, thin homes, squeezed tightly against one another. One car barely fit down the narrow through. Nick worried the door mirrors would scrape the brick facing on either side. Mr. Zeman didn't seem concerned, though. Before Nick knew it, the attorney had pulled up in front of a group of row houses and put the car in park.

They'd arrived.

"Hey, wake up." Nick gently shook his little sister. "Kat, it's time to wake up. We're here."

Kat yawned and stretched her little body. Other than that eerie moment on the plane, she'd been incredibly well-behaved so far, especially considering how long the trip had been.

While Mr. Zeman helped Mom unload her suitcase from the trunk, Nick took Kat's hand and led her to the narrow house second from the left. It wasn't that he instantly recognized the three-story home squeezed between two nearly identical houses. In fact, he couldn't put his finger on a single reason he was drawn to the building. Somehow, he just *knew* it was Uncle Damek's house. There was an odd...pulling sensation...that tugged him closer and closer until he and Kat stood hand in hand, staring at the front door.

Rough, oddly shaped figures decorated the wooden door frame. At first, Nick assumed it to be the work of vandals: graffiti written in Czech. But on closer inspection, he found that the carvings were too abstract to be letters. Etched lines looped and swirled, then transitioned into angular, geometric shapes. They looked vaguely familiar, like maybe he'd seen them in a book, but he knew for certain they hadn't been there on his last visit.

Hardly aware of what he was doing, Nick reached out and traced one of the symbols with his finger. A flock of goosebumps rose on his arms.

"So, you remember the house!" Mr. Zeman dragged a wheeled suitcase behind him as he joined Nick and Kat at the front door.

"What are these?" Nick indicated one of the patterns.

With a puzzled expression, Zeman leaned in closer to the spot Nick was pointing at. "Ah." The cheerful man's smile faltered a bit. "I believe these are protective runes. Your uncle had been studying them recently. I suppose he used his house for practice in replicating them."

Nick eyed Mr. Zeman skeptically. Damek didn't believe in anything superstitious like protective runes.

"Must make this house the safest place in Prague," the attorney winked, clapping Nick on the shoulder.

"Whew!" Mom joined them on the porch just as Mr. Zeman unlocked the front door, pushing it open. "That was a long trip. It's good to be back, even if..." She trailed off, as if she'd just remembered why they were there. She smiled awkwardly. "It's been ages. Your first time, Kat. Anyway. I can't wait to get unpacked and have a nice, long shower."

"I'm sure, I'm sure," Mr. Zeman said. "You must all be weary from your travels.

"Help your little sister get her bags, will you, Nick?" Mom followed the attorney inside.

Still holding Kat's hand, Nick led her back to the car to fetch their luggage.

As they reached the narrow cobblestone street, a shadow fell, plunging the bright day into sudden darkness. The hairs on Nick's arm stood straight on end. He glanced up to see that a lazy, gray thundercloud had moved in front of the sun.

Beside him, Kat raised her arm and pointed wordlessly toward the cloud, just above the building's red tiled roof.

"What is it?" Nick shuddered and glanced up, following the direction of her finger.

Kat didn't answer. Instead, she stood stock still, staring up at the sky. Her mouth hung open.

"Kat," he prodded when she didn't reply. "It's just a cloud. C'mon, let's get our suitcases so I can show you around inside." He tugged on her hand. Why were her fingers so cold?

She swayed slightly, but her eyes remained blank and locked on the cloud.

"...Kat?" Nick asked.

No response.

"Kat, answer me."

A sudden gust of wind sent Kat's long, brown hair streaming out behind her head, but the leaves on the trees lining the street remained still. Her head whipped up and she turned to face him, eyes locking on his, her hand gripping his tight enough to leave a bruise. Open-mouthed horror petrified her features.

"He's coming." Her voice came out like dried leaves scraping across stone.

Dread spilled over Nick like an ice bucket emptied on his head. It was the same way she'd looked when she'd said the exact same thing on the plane. Only now, she was pointing at the sky above the roof of Damek's house.

No. Not the sky, he realized. At a small window just beneath the eaves of the roof.

The next second, warm sunlight washed over the street again as the thundercloud broke apart and drifted away.

Kat's shoulders relaxed, as did the iron grip she'd had on Nick's hand.

She bobbed her head left to right. "We're finally here, Nicky," she said cheerfully, as if they'd only just arrived. "Can you believe it? We're really here in Prague! Except here, the houses are all touching each other. No yards!" She let go of Nick's hand and pulled her backpack from the car.

Nick shook himself as if waking from a bad dream. "Are you okay, Kat?"

"Will you get my suitcase for me?" Kat ignored his question. "It's too heavy."

After retrieving both his and Kat's suitcases, Nick closed the trunk and followed his sister up to the house. He couldn't shake the image of Kat pointing blankly up at the little window, or the hollow way her voice had sounded. She hadn't even been asleep this time.

He scanned his memory, trying to remember if she'd ever done anything similar before, but he couldn't think of anything. The closest would be what she did during her night terrors, but they'd stopped a while ago.

When did they stop, exactly? He concentrated. Right. Her last one was the night before Damek called to say he was coming to visit.

But since then, she's been fine. Up until the plane. *At least...* Nick hesitated. *At least, I **think** she's been fine. I guess I haven't really been paying attention the past couple weeks.*

Crap.

What if he'd been so lost in his own emotions that when Kat needed him he'd missed it? The thought of her feeling lonely and scared the way he'd felt on the plane when he'd been the only one asleep snapped the numbness and anger clean out of his body like the recoil of an industrial-sized rubber band.

He wouldn't let her down again.

CHAPTER NINE - The Lion's Face

Nick grabbed Kat's hand as they walked through the entry, leading her back to the kitchen. When they entered, Mom was pulling up window shades, speaking in low tones with Mr. Zeman. Motes of suspended dust danced in soft sunlight cast from windows on either side of Nick, painting the old, wooden floors with warmth.

The space seemed smaller than Nick remembered, almost like it was a set for a play. He kept waiting – *hoping* – for Damek's voice to enter from stage right and break the hush that filled the room. Mr. Zeman moved slowly, almost reverently, barely touching the tile floor with his cane.

With all the blinds raised, Mom brushed her hands off on her joggers and pulled Nick and Kat in for a hug. "It's been a long few weeks and this is hard, but it's going to be okay."

Nick wasn't so sure anything would ever be okay again. He shrugged awkwardly and stepped back a few inches.

Mom let him go, but kept her arm around Kat. "We're a team, right?" she asked. "We can do hard things."

Nick winced. Her forced cheer sounded too loud in the quiet room.

"Right?" Mom asked again, even louder. She locked eyes with Nick.

"Right," he said, just so she'd stop asking.

"Right, Kitty-Kat?" Mom jostled Kat's shoulder.

Kat nodded solemnly. "Yes, Mommy. I can do hard things."

Mom bent down and brushed her lips across her forehead. "Are you feeling okay, honey? No fever. Hmmm. In fact, you seem a little cold. Where's your sweater?"

Mom didn't give Kat time to answer any of her questions before fishing Kat's sweater out of her backpack.

"I'm okay, Mommy," Kat said while Mom maneuvered her arms into the knit sleeves, "just sleepy." She squeezed her eyes shut and yawned.

Nick had never heard Kat utter those words once in her entire life. Kat was *never* tired. Plus, she'd slept for hours on the plane and again on the drive from the airport. It bothered him to see her so pale and listless.

"Come on, Kat." He picked up her hand again and pulled her along after him out of the kitchen. "Time to explore. You've never seen the Maracek house before."

"Be careful you two," Mom called after them. "There are a lot of breakable objects in this house. It's practically a museum!"

Kat followed willingly. Much to Nick's relief, her 'ooohs' and 'ahhhhs' grew louder and more excited as he guided her from room to room. The sound of her wonder mixed with their footsteps.

She dropped his hand when they entered the sitting room, skipping off to peer into the built-in cabinets that lined the walls. Nick took his time to catch up, running his hands over the smooth, wood furniture. He compared his memories of the place with what he saw now, making mental notes of the statues, artwork, and objects he wanted to examine more closely later. His fingers left winding trails through the thin layer of dust that had settled on surfaces over the last couple weeks. A large, framed photo of Nick, Kat, and Mom hung over the mantelpiece.

Damek's oversized reading chair sat in front of the fireplace, just as Nick remembered. Whenever they talked on the phone, this is where he always pictured his uncle sitting.

A closed door sat at the end of a narrow hallway behind the stairs to the second level: Damek's study.

Nick paused, remembering the hours he'd poured over maps, listening to Damek recounting myths and legends, tracing the trails of legendary heroes, retracing the paths his uncle had followed on his famous digs. Together, he and Damek had stayed up long into the night after Mom and Dad had gone to bed, sitting at the mahogany desk beneath the yellow lamp glow.

Nobody had ever believed in him like Damek had. More than anything, he wished that he could open the door to Damek's study and find his uncle there sitting behind his desk, waiting to greet Nick in person.

"Where the real adventure begins."

"What?" Kat asked.

Nick startled, not realizing he'd spoken out loud. "Oh. Nothing. Find anything cool?"

"Lots! But now I wanna go upstairs!"

"Sure," he said, relieved she didn't know about Damek's study, or she'd for sure want to go in. He wasn't ready to open that door just yet. Too many memories. Plus, he didn't want his grief or anger to infect Kat, and he didn't want to zone out. Kat's eyes were bright and eager again, and that's what mattered most. "One sec." He shrugged out of his heavy backpack, retrieved his new camera, and slipped its strap around his neck. "Okay, now I'm ready. Wanna lead the way?"

"Yes!" Kat exclaimed, grabbing his hand and tugging him toward the staircase.

The hallways and stairs were much taller and narrower than Nick remembered. It was as if the builders had to squeeze and stretch to make everything fit. At the first landing hung a more recent photo of him, Kat, and Mom. Dim sunlight filtered through the curtained windows in the cramped, wood-panelled hallway. The staircase continued to the third floor, but narrowed even more tightly as it rose.

Kat dropped Nick's hand and scampered off down the hallway to the right.

"Nicky! I found my room! Come see!"

Following Kat's voice, Nick found her in a cheerful, yellow-painted bedroom at the end of the hall. She'd already pulled back the curtains, swirling up dust that filtered around her in soft beams of late afternoon sunshine. A baby cradle sat in one corner in front of a painting of a little girl on a swing.

A pretty little bed, carved and painted with flowers and leaves, stood in the center of the room. If Nick's memory was right, this had been Mom's room when she moved in with Damek after her parents' accident. Kat jumped up on the bed and spread out across the coverlet. She looked like a princess from a fairytale with her hair fanned out around her head in a halo. Nick aimed his new camera and snapped a picture.

"I want this room!" Kat said.

"It's perfect for you," Nick agreed. "Wanna help me find mine?"

"Yes!" She slipped down off the bed and followed Nick out the door. As she left, turned and blew a kiss over her shoulder. "I'll be back, room!"

Kat's returning enthusiasm was contagious; Nick's spirits lifted just watching her skip down the hall. Maybe nothing all that strange was going on with her. Maybe her grief about Uncle Damek's death just showed differently.

Maybe she hadn't been sleeping great either. Jetlag was tough for anyone, and she was only six years old.

"Let's check the third floor," Nick said.

Kat scrambled up the steep, narrow staircase ahead of him. Together, their shoes squeaked on the polished, wooden floorboards as they moved down the third floor hallway. Kat paused at a closed door, but Nick kept going. All the other doors had been open.

"Wait, Nick," Kat called. "This is your room."

He turned around. "How do you know it's mine?"

"Well, since Mom is sleeping downstairs in Uncle's room, this one has to be yours. It's the only one left."

Nick glanced down the hall, realizing there were no more doors. On previous visits, he'd wanted to be near his parents and uncle, so they'd made him a bed on the couch in Damek's study. He barely remembered coming up to the third floor.

Shrugging, he opened the door into utter darkness. He reached inside, felt around for the light switch, and switched it on...

...revealing the ugliest room he'd ever seen.

Frog-green and puke-brown flowered wallpaper covered the walls. A plain, wooden bed frame with a saggy mattress sat in the middle sat at the center of the windowless room.

"Ew. Your room is *gross*," Kat said.

Nick leaned against the doorframe, suddenly a lot less excited. *Oh well,* he thought, *it's not like I'll be staying here forever.*

"Nicky, look!" Kat pointed. "What's that?"

He followed her finger, peering back into the hallway. What *was* that?

The light from the bedroom illuminated the end of the hallway, where a wooden ladder had been built into the wall. Looking up, Nick saw a trap door in the ceiling directly above him.

"Must go to an attic," he mused. Kat already had her feet on the bottom rung. "Here," Nick said, "let me go first."

As he climbed, the memory of Kat standing next to the car pointing up to a tiny window under the eaves popped into Nick's head. Maybe there *was* an attic, and if so, maybe that's what she'd been pointing to. A chill spread across the back of his neck.

He paused with his hands on the top rung. "By the way, Kat," he called down, "have you had any more bad dreams lately?"

"Nope." She shook her head. "Hurry up!"

The trapdoor swung open easily as Nick pushed against it with his shoulder, though the hinges definitely needed some oil. He poked his head up, silently surveying the room.

"Well?" Kat demanded.. "What's up there?"

Nick grinned down at her "My room."

He climbed the rest of the way up, his smile growing wider and wider. The room wasn't very big, and it had odd, slanted ceiling angles, but its contents more than made up for its size and shape.

Treasures filled the space. A large, antique map of the city of Prague covered the far wall. Trunks, knickknacks, and pieces of furniture crowded the small floorspace, some draped in sheets like he'd seen in old horror movies. Except, instead of creepy or neglected vibes, this attic had a sense of lived-in, coziness.

Nick's heart skipped a beat. Uncle Damek's workbench nestled into a smallish alcove kitty corner from a tall, four-poster bed. Last time Nick had seen it, the bench had been in a small room off Damek's study. He didn't even notice the creaking floorboards as he walked reverently over to his uncle's workspace.

"Hey, no fair," Kat said, having scrambled up the ladder on her own. "Your room has a trap door and way cooler stuff than mine!"

Nick barely heard her. He was too busy running his fingers over the hand-made puppets that hung above the workbench in various stages of completion. The faint scent of pine wood and varnish reminded him of Damek. Everything in this space reminded him of his uncle.

"I can see the whole world from here!" Kat exclaimed.

Nick turned to see her kneeling up high on the bed, gazing out the window they'd seen from down below on the street. Climbing up beside her, he gasped as he took in the astonishing view of the city. Red-tiled rooftops extended in every direction. A small strip of the Vltava River gleamed in the afternoon sun.

Unlatching the lock, he pushed the window open and leaned out a little way, turning to glimpse the spires of St. Vitus Cathedral in the distance.

Kat slid down from the bed and made her way to the workbench. She reached up to jiggle each hanging puppet to see how it moved.

"Nicky," she said. "Let's make a deal, 'kay? You can play in my room whenever you want, and I can play in your room whenever I want."

"Oh, sure," Nick replied, *"now* you want to share!"

"Look, Nicky!" Kat pulled a dust sheet from a huge globe in the center of the room. "Show me where we live!"

Nick smiled to himself as he stepped off the bed to join her by the globe. He showed her where their suburb would be, just a fingertip away from Chicago in the outline of Illinois. Then they traced the path their plane took to Boston, and finally to Prague.

Next, Nick uncovered the trunk at the foot of the bed. He lifted the heavy top, securing it open on a moving lever.

"Nick, come see this!" Kat shouted before he'd barely started looking through the trunk.

He abandoned his search and hurried over to where Kat stood beneath the big map of Prague, staring down at an intricate, looping, crisscrossing maze of wooden chutes and tracks.

A wooden marble run. No. WAY. He gasped and leaned in for a closer look.

It stood two feet tall and was made of dark, polished wood. Nick's eye followed the path of the smooth, wide track. At the bottom of the first incline was a tight corkscrew, followed by a procession of marionette dolls that made a tunnel over the chute with their arms. Dozens more loops, turns, and sheer drops led past toy soldiers, metal chimes, wooden dolls, and carved creatures Nick recognized from Czech folklore. At the end, a marionette of a puppeteer stood at the top of a final corkscrew, posed as if manipulating a menacing Noon Witch, a creature from Czech mythology famous for luring naughty children and farmers alike away from to their chores in the midday heat, at the bottom where the marble would come to rest.

"Whoa," Nick whispered. Instinctively, he knew Damek had made this. Probably for him and Kat.

"How do you make it go?" Kat asked.

Nick turned back to the first incline. A carved, roaring lion stood at the top, its front claws clasped around a big, green-glass marble poised at the apex of a steep hill.

Touch the face of the lion to find the answers you seek.

Would this lion answer his questions if he touched its face? What answers did he seek, anyway? The only question he had at that moment was why Damek had written him such a strange note in the first place. Why had he said: "If you are reading this it is because I am dead"? Which meant he knew that whatever he was doing was dangerous enough to get him killed, and if that were true, he likely didn't die in some accident. Except, if Damek thought he might die, why wouldn't he go to the cops or something? Why hadn't he at least called Nick?

Nick had more questions than he'd realized. With one finger, Nick reached out and gently brushed the lion's face. Its head clicked back, and its arms stretched out wide, releasing a green glass marble down the chute.

The marble sped along the amazing contraption with a slick, satisfying sound, passing through hand-carved spirals and loop-de-loops. It raced along its track, ringing the delicate chimes and neatly changing directions along zigzag turns until it finally plunked out into the tiny basin beneath the Noon Witch.

"Again!" Kat said.

Brow furrowed, Nick paused. The puppeteer manipulating the witch was posed wrong. Its hands stretched out to mirror the witch's, but Nick knew its posture should be more relaxed. When Damek taught Nick about marionettes, Nick's first instinct was to hold his arms perfectly straight in front of himself – just like the puppeteer was posed now. Damek had explained that his arms would grow tired too fast if he held them like that. No way would Damek pose the puppeteer incorrectly when he'd spent so much time making everything else perfect.

Gently, Nick corrected the doll's posture, just like his uncle had corrected his. Then, satisfied, he placed the marble back at the top, pressed the lion's face, and let it run down again. Kat clapped and giggled as the green-glass marble once again descended through the handcrafted maze.

When it reached the incline before the final corkscrew, it bumped into the puppeteer's left arm, jumped the edge of the chute, and plonked onto the wooden floor.

"Crap." He should have known better than to mess with his uncle's handiwork. The marble sped along a groove in the floorboard Nick hadn't noticed before, continuing until it reached the far wall. But even then, it didn't stop. It turned at a 90 degree angle, continuing along the baseboard...

...and suddenly disappeared from sight through a hole in the floor.

CHAPTER TEN - Hidden Treasure

"Whoa." Nick and Kat said in unison. The way the marble moved had been too precise to be accidental. Is this what the note was about?

A low rumble of anticipation built in Nick's chest, but he pushed it down. *Knock it off,* he told himself, *you're being stupid. It was another riddle game to play when he got to Chicago, not a message from the grave.* Still... "Did you see another marble?"

Instead of answering, Kat scrambled over to the beginning of the run, eyes wide. She shook her head.

Without speaking, they both hurried over to where the marble had disappeared. Nick laid down on the floor, peering with one eye into the tiny hole. It was pitch black.

"Can you see it?" Kat asked.

"Nope." It was a small hole, only big enough for two fingers. Nick reached in but couldn't feel the bottom or anything on either side, just the back of the wall.

As he pulled his fingers out, the floorboard shifted ever so slightly. "Back up a little," he said. "This board is loose."

He pulled at the underside with his two hooked fingers, but nothing happened. He tugged harder. Still nothing. Pushing up to his knees for better leverage, Nick yanked as hard as he could.

The entire foot-long section of floorboard popped out, sending Nick tumbling backward onto his butt.

"Are you okay?"

But Nick had already picked himself up and pried the board from his fingers. He nodded and stooped forward.

Side by side, Nick and Kat knelt over the secret compartment, peering inside. The opening was deep and dark. Kat inched back and stood up. "Be careful, Nicky. There might be spiders."

Spiders or no, Nick *needed* to know what was inside. Reaching into the compartment, Nick's fingertips grazed something hard and leathery. He grasped at it. Whatever it was fit comfortably in his palm. Something metallic lined both edges of the object, and Nick's eyes widened with sudden realization..

"What is it?" Kat crouched back down as Nick slowly pulled the object from between the floorboards.

A dagger sheathed in a beautifully decorated scabbard lay in his hand. Graceful silver filigree danced across the hand-and-a-half hilt and spiraled out into the two bars of the handguard.

No way. Slowly, Nick drew the blade from the scabbard. Despite looking ancient, the metal gleamed so bright that he could almost see his reflection. Nick had never seen a dagger like this before. He gripped the hilt with both hands and found it fit comfortably. But the strange blade measured about the same length as the hilt, and one edge was notched three quarters of the way up from the base to the tip – almost like an uneven staircase – while the other edge was smooth.

He ran his index finger along the smoother edge, then quickly drew away. A small bead of blood welled from a papercut-thin wound.

Kat put out her hand to touch it, but Nick quickly re-sheathed the blade. "Don't touch it, Kat," he said. "It's super sharp."

"Can I hold it at least?" she begged.

"Yes, just don't take it out of the sheeth."

Nick handed the dagger to Kat and watched for a moment as she turned it over in her hands to inspect the raised embossing on the scabbard. Then he bent down again, fishing into the compartment for the marble. Instead, his hand closed around a book. He pulled that out as well.

It looked old. The aged, brittle spine cracked slightly as he opened the cover, and a musty smell clung to the paper. It appeared to be some sort of handwritten journal.

Flipping through the first couple of pages, Nick discovered that not only was it written in Czech, it was also absolutely ancient, even more than he'd guessed by looking at the cover. The ink on the pages was so faded, Nick had to flip past the first handful before he could even tell it wasn't written in English. The first page was especially tattered and hard to read. It looked like some sort of poem written in four stanzas, each two lines long. Nick guessed it was some form of Bohemian because the alphabet was Latin, not Cyrillic, and he recognized what might be the háček, čárka, and kroužck accent marks. Maybe. His modern Czech wasn't even that good.

Out of the corner of his eye, Nick watched Kat set down the dagger and inch closer to the secret compartment. She knelt down to peer inside.

"There's nothing else in there, Kat," he said, not bothering to look up from the diary.

Kat startled a little at the sound of his voice. Jumping back, she slipped something into her pants' pocket.

"What was that?" Nick asked. "Did you find the marble?"

"Yep!" Kat brushed back the hair that had slipped forward onto her face and held out her hand to show the round, clear green sphere resting on her palm.

"Good eyes!" Only, there was something shady about her expression, and she still had her other hand in her pocket. "What else did you find?"

Reluctantly, Kat pulled a small, wooden box from her pocket. It was about the size of one of the fancy pen cases the pens Damek collected came in, only this one looked very old, at least as old as the journal. Nick realized that every inch of the box was covered in the same strange runes Damek had carved around his front door.

"What's inside?" he asked.

Kat tried to pry it open, then shrugged. "Can't open it." Nick held his hand out. Reluctantly, she placed it on his palm.

The attic dimmed as if a cloud had moved in front of the sun. All the color faded from the room.

For a moment, the box simply balanced on Nick's palm. It was heavier than he'd expected. Entranced, Nick ran his fingers over the carved runes, turning the box this way and that. Finally, he found a tiny keyhole near the corner on one side. Some kind of figure had been burned beneath the hole, but he couldn't quite make it out. He leaned in close and squinted, recognizing it with a start.

A blood-red eagle. Like the one he'd see painted on the stone wall above the locked door in his dream.

A sound like a distant gong rung in Nick's ears.

"Give it back." Kat stepped in front of him, hand thrust out. The corners of her mouth turned down in a sullen pout.

"I don't think so, Kat." Nick shook his head, eyes still on the box. "Uncle Damek hid these things under the floor for a reason. We better put everything back."

"Give. It. BACK." Kat stamped her foot. "I found it. It's MINE!"

Her voice scraped out rough and dry from her throat, like she had a bad sore throat. Or like how she sounded outside on the sidewalk when she'd said, "He's coming!"

But more than her voice, it was her words that shocked Nick. Kat had never tried to boss him around before.

That decided it. The box was bad news. "I said I'm putting it back."

"No!" She stomped her foot again. Harder. Red-faced, she glared at Nick, pure hatred in her eyes. "You always keep everything for yourself! You never let me have anything! Selfish, selfISH SELFISH!"

CRASH!

The window over the bed blasted open, slamming against the wall. A screaming wind lashed at the attic, setting the hanging puppets in motion and whipping Kat's long brown hair around her face and shoulders as she continued yelling at the top of her lungs, fists clenched at her sides.

"IT'S MINE. I WANT IT! GIVE IT TO ME. RIGHT. NOW!"

Rage roared out of her small body, mingling with the howling gale, slamming into Nick like an open-handed slap. He clamped his hands over his ears and stumbled to the bed. Scrambling up, he wrestled with the windowpanes, forcing them closed inch by inch. Pinning the panes shut with one shoulder, he was finally able to close the latch and lock it.

Breathing heavy, he rested his head against the glass, catching his breath. That's when he noticed: protective runes had been chiseled into the window frame, top to bottom.

A chill prickled the hairs on the back of his neck. How had he not noticed when he opened the window before...?

Kat's screams had gone from bewildering accusations and demands to a wordless wail. She stood stiff as a board in the middle of the attic floor, eyes bulging, tendons tight in her neck, staring and screaming at nothing.

Adrenaline raced through Nick as he threw himself off the bed. In an instant he had Kat by the shoulders, shaking her gently, turning her face so he could look her in the eye. "Kat! Shhh, Kat, listen. Can you hear me, Kat?"

Kat's body went limp. Her screams stopped. Nick caught her as she sagged against him. Stooping, he hooked his arm under her knees and picked her up.

Upper body strength wasn't a problem, but Nick groaned as he shuffled on his bad leg to the bed where he laid Kat down. He touched her forehead with the back of her hand...something Mom always did when he or Kat didn't feel well. Kat wasn't warm. If anything, her skin left his hand cold.

"Are you okay?" Nick asked.

Kat shook her head, searching his eyes as if looking for something she'd lost. "I don't know, Nicky," she said in a small, hoarse voice. "I feel kind of funny. What happened?"

"It's been a long couple of days, that's all. You're just tired." With an effort, Nick kept the unease out of his voice. What was he going to say? *"You acted like a possessed person and screamed bloody murder at me for taking a box you've never seen before?"*

Instead, he asked, "Won't it be nice to sleep in that princess bed tonight?"

"Yes!" She sat up, eyes eager, voice normal, no traces of anger anywhere. She threw her arms around Nick and gave him a quick squeeze. "I want to show Mommy my new room!"

"I think she's seen it before," Nick said, voice light like everything was normal. "She used to live here, remember?"

"Oh yeah!" She hopped down from the bed. "Nicky, how did you make those shapes on the window glow? Is there a button? Do you think the shapes around my window will glow, too?"

Nick paused. "You...have shapes around your window, too? Like these ones?"

"Mmhmm," she answered. "All the windows I've seen have them."

"Hmm. Well, I didn't push anything," Nick said, "and I didn't see them glow. Maybe you just saw light reflecting off the glass or something? These windows are really old. See how the glass is thick and kind of wavy? It's pretty sunny today."

"Maybe." Kat skipped to the top of the ladder and waited. After a second she said, "Aren't you coming?"

"You go on ahead. I'm going to lay down for a minute and rest my leg. It's a little sore."

"Okay!" And with that, she climbed down the ladder as if nothing terrifying had happened at all.

Nick didn't like lying to Kat, but what good would it do to tell her he'd seen them, too? Especially if he couldn't explain how it had happened.

Maybe Kat had somehow transferred her nightmares to him and all of this was just one, long trick his unconscious mind had decided to play on him?

What is going on?

CHAPTER ELEVEN - Psychic Powers

Touching the face of the lion raised a lot more questions than it answered.

Leaning in to look closer at the window frame, Nick's eyes traced the strange angular shapes and loops completely covering the wood. Mr. Zeman said these were protective runes – or at least that the ones down on the door were – and these ones looked pretty similar as far as Nick could tell.

And for the briefest moment, right after the window had blown open, it really *had* looked like they started to glow a bright blue.

"I've got to find out what these mean," he muttered. But that could wait. For now, he just wanted some fresh air.

Opening the window, he poked his head out, breathing in deeply.

The afternoon was perfectly still. There wasn't even a breeze, which was strange considering it had been blowing hard enough during Kat's tantrum to blast the window open. The cloud that had darkened the room had also vanished, leaving only a clear, blue sky.

If only the neighbor's stupid roof wasn't in the way. If it weren't for the slightly taller roof of the row house next door on the corner, his view of the city would be completely unobstructed.

Nick surveyed Damek's roof. It sloped, but not too much If he could even just get over by the chimney...

On impulse, he pushed the window open as wide as it would go and boosted himself up. Then, after some minor wriggling, he was out on top of the roof. Using his stiff leg as a sort of brake to keep from slipping, he made his way to the chimney. He could see clearly in every direction. His new camera still hung around his neck, so with one hand against the chimney for balance, he started snapping pictures. After a while, he inched closer to the edge of the roof to get a better angle of the river.

"Hey, Nick."

Nick'stiff leg nearly buckled. Adrenaline zapped through him.

Reaching back, his arms wheeled as he grabbed for the chimney bricks. If he fell forward, gravity would pull him over the edge.

But his legs held firm, or just firm enough at least. Panting, he finally managed to steady himself after a few seconds that had felt like a whole minute.

"Whoa," the accented voice said. "Nice reflexes!"

Nick's mouth had gone dry. Still clinging tight to the chimney, he looked over his shoulder toward the voice.

A girl sat on the neighbor's roof, casually leaning back against what must be her own attic window. At first glance, she seemed to be about Nick's age, except he'd never seen a girl his age with hair like that: shaved above her ear on one side and long on the other. She wore jeans, a Depeche Mode t-shirt, and black and white checkerboard high tops. A cross earring dangled from her ear on the shaved side, along with several small hoop and stud piercings that curved all the way up to the top of her ear.

Nick's face flamed with embarrassment.

"You scared the crap out of me!" he said, once he'd worked up enough spit in his mouth to talk.

"Yeah, I noticed." She winced. "Sorry about that."

"Who are you?" Nick's heartbeat slowly returned to normal. "How long have you been there? How did you know my name?"

"I have psychic powers," she winked. Her English was excellent, with only a slight Czech accent.

"Right." *Stupid question,* he told himself. *She lives next door to Damek, you doofus. Please at least **pretend** to be cool.* "So, come here often?" His inner voice groaned in abject humiliation and all the color drained from his face in an instant.

"Smooth," she chuckled. Standing up, she walked confidently to the edge of her slightly-sloped roof and casually jumped across the gap between their buildings.

"No!" Nick cried, images of the rope swing and the creek flashing in his mind. But she'd already landed. "Are you insane?" he sputtered. "You could have fallen and broken your neck!"

"You sound like my dad," she laughed. She continued forward. When she'd made it to where he stood by the chimney, she reached out and gently touched his cheek. "Thanks for caring. You're sweet. But I do it all the time."

A dizzy spell hit Nick as his soul tried to escape his body and find somewhere to hide. He couldn't think. Or speak.

The girl sat down against Damek's attic window. She patted the space next to her on the roof. "Come sit," she said. "You look out of it. Jet lag?"

Nick couldn't tell if her question was serious or just she was just being very polite, but he didn't really care at the moment because he *definitely* needed to sit down. He landed a little heavier than he'd intended. When he glanced over to see if she was laughing at him, he was shocked to see shame on her face.

"Damek told me about you."

"You knew my uncle?" Nick's voice caught in his throat.

"Yeah," the girl said simply. "He was great. He put on awesome puppet shows for all the kids on our street, and he told the best stories. He even started tutoring me after my dad told him I was interested in becoming a linguist."

She sniffled, and Nick thought he saw her wipe away a tear. Or maybe she was just rubbing her eyes.

"I'm so sorry for your loss," she continued. "Everyone who knew Damek loved him. I miss him. The whole neighborhood does."

Nick looked out across the city. "He was supposed to come visit us in Chicago last week."

"He talked about you a lot," the girl said. "He kept a photo of you and your mom and your little sister in his wallet. He was so proud of you."

Nick fiddled with the strap of his camera. He could tell she was trying not to sound too sad, or cry. He could tell because she sounded like he did when he tried to do the exact same thing.

Here he was sitting on a roof, in a city halfway across the world from home, talking to a girl he'd never met who knew a lot more about him – and maybe his uncle – than he did about her, which was exactly zilch. He could at least do something about that.

"So, what's your name?" he asked.

"Oh wow, where are my manners?" She blushed. "I'm Helena. Helena Olbrycht."

Nick grinned. She seemed at least as awkward as he felt, which was crazy because she looked so cool. "Hi Helena. I'm..." he started, before stopping himself. "Oh. Wow. Ha. You already know that."

Helena laughed, and Nick could tell she thought he'd made a joke. He wasn't about to admit otherwise. Helena leaned back against the chimney and sighed. They gazed at the view for a few moments together, in silence.

"Thanks for not being angry at me," Helena finally said, still looking out across the city. "And for making me laugh. You just might be as great as your uncle was always telling me."

"You're lucky I have cat-like reflexes."

Helena laughed again, Nick was grateful to his brain for giving him a semi-normal response for once. "So, how is your English so good?" he asked.

"You think it's good?" she asked, sounding embarrassed. "I was afraid you wouldn't be able to understand me. My accent is so thick."

"Oh, wow, no not at all," Nick assured her. "Honestly, I thought you must study abroad or something."

"Really?" She glanced over at him.

"Really," he nodded.

"Well, to be fair, I go to an English school. Plus, my father works for the Ministry of Regional Development. *And,* I'm a tour guide."

"Yeah, right," Nick laughed, sure she was joking.

"No, really," Helena insisted. "I had to pass a test and everything. My English is good because I speak to tourists all the time."

He tried not to gawk. *Who even is this girl?* "So, I guess that means you know about all the architecture and history, right?" He arched an eyebrow. "And legends and lore?"

"I'm not joking. Besides, anything I didn't learn in school, your uncle taught me. I told you, my dad hired Damek as a private tutor to teach me the history of the Czech language, remember? And, as he would say: 'language was invented to create the myths that explain humankind to themselves.'" She spread her arms, indicating all the buildings of the city sprawled out below them. "Quiz me! Ask me about anything."

Nick pointed to the spires poking up behind the building across the river. "What's that tower over there?"

She rolled her eyes. "As *everyone* knows," she said, her voice starting to sound like an airline attendant from the safety videos they show you before take-off, "those spires belong to St. Vitus Cathedral, an excellent example of gothic architecture. The building you see is actually the third church dedicated to St. Vitus that stood on that spot, and it's part of the palace complex. King Wenceslas, the patron saint of Prague, commissioned the first church in the year 930 AD. In order to accommodate the growing congregations of faithful, a larger cathedral was built in the same spot in 1060 AD. Finally, construction of the existing structure began in 1344 AD. The Cathedral is located entirely within Prague Castle, and contains the tombs of many Bohemian Kings and Holy Roman emperors."

"Okay, okay," Nick chuckled. "I believe you! Besides, you could make it up and I probably wouldn't know."

"I'm the best tour guide in Prague," Helena lifted her chin. "And people always tip enthusiastic young scholars, so I make pretty good money." She smiled at Nick, then pointed at the thick sole of his right shoe. "What's wrong with your foot?"

Nick raised his eyebrows, surprised, but not offended. "Wow. Are all Czechs so blunt?"

"Blunt?"

"Most people don't ask me about it. They usually just stare and then act all embarrassed when I notice them staring." *Or throw rocks and call me names.*

"That's dumb," she said. "How is anyone supposed to learn anything if they don't ask questions?"

"Good point," he said. "I have proximal focal femoral deficiency."

"Maybe my English isn't as good as I thought," Helena joked. "I didn't understand any of that!"

"Wait, you mean they didn't teach you about PFFD at your fancy English school?" Nick grinned "There's nothing wrong with my foot. It's a problem with my hips. They're twisted in a way that makes my right leg shorter than my left. The thick shoe just evens things out."

"Does it hurt?"

"Sometimes," Nick said, "but usually not too bad. Mostly after I walk a lot. Or sit for too long. I've had to have a few surgeries, and that sucked, but now I just move kind of funny. I won't be running in the Olympics any time soon."

"I don't think it's funny," Helena said. "And I like your shoe. Maybe you will be the cool American and start a new trend. All across the Czech Republic, kids will be wearing them!"

Nick smiled at the thought, suddenly realizing sitting here on the roof with Helena was the best he'd felt in days, if not weeks.

With that thought, everything that had happened before with Kat in the attic and on the plane and the whole reason he was there in the first place came crashing in around him. With a barely audible groan, he let his head fall back against the window frame.

"Are you okay?" Helena sounded worried. "Was that a bad joke?"

"No, no," he said, sitting up. "I just... It's been a really long day. It was a great joke." He paused, then asked, "By the way, were you out here a while ago when that crazy wind came out of nowhere? It blew the window wide open."

"Crazy wind?" Helena asked. "No, it's just been breezy since I came out half an hour ago. I'd just assumed you opened your window yourself."

"So creepy," Nick said, almost to himself, remembering the stiff way Kat had stood, screaming. Then to Helena: "Sorry. It's nothing. I'm probably just tired."

Helena sat up eagerly. "You said 'creepy,' I heard you. Please tell me? I love creepy things! What happened?"

Nick hesitated. What was he supposed to say? That his little sister had been acting like she was possessed and throwing tantrums? That his uncle had sent him a book and a clue about a marble run? That there was a weird box hidden beneath in a secret compartment under the floor in the attic?

No way was he saying any of that.

He shrugged. "No, really, it's nothing. This weird wind blew the window open and it spooked my little sister. She's never been here. No big deal, really."

Helena looked at him as if trying to decide whether or not to believe him. "Hmm," she said. "I don't know. I think there's something you're not telling me."

"Nick?" Mom's voice called from somewhere inside. "Nick, are you up there?"

"That's my mom," Nick said. "I'd better go." He used the window frame to pull himself up. "It was really nice meeting you, Helena. I'm glad I didn't plunge to my death."

She grinned and ducked her head. "Yeah. Me too."

"Nick?" Mom called again. It sounded like she was climbing up the ladder to the attic.

"Coming, Mom!"

"Hey," Helena said, covering his hand on the windowsill with hers. "At least let me know if you want a tour of the city. I know this really amazing tour guide."

Nick turned back to look at her. "Really? That would be great!"

"Yes, really," Helena laughed. "And if you tell me your creepy story, I might even give you a discount."

"Nick?"

"Sorry, gotta go!" Nick said as he climbed over the window ledge backward and dropped down onto the bed. A second later, he poked his head back through the frame. "I can't wait for my personalized tour," he said, before closing the window and disappearing.

CHAPTER TWELVE - The Knight's Tale

That night, Nick lay in the attic bed, several pillows propped under his head. The *Legends of Old Bohemia* lay open against his knees, but he wasn't reading. Instead, he gazed at the moon through the latched window, exhausted but too wound up to sleep.

After he'd climbed back through the attic window, he and Mom and Kat went to find street food for dinner and essentials from the local market, which included chocolate chips for cookies, according to Kat.

Wenceslas Square had a bunch of street vendors to choose from, and Nick had been hungrier than he'd realized. Kat had a fried cheese sandwich while Nick munched on a Czech hotdog, and Mom chose some sort of soup called halušky: the dish Damek made for her after her mom and dad passed the December she'd turned eleven and moved in with him.

"Hot soup in the summer is weird," Kat proclaimed.

"You're wearing a sweatshirt," Nick pointed out.

"Because I'm cold." Kat scrunched her nose. "It smells like cabbage."

"Your sweatshirt or the soup?" Nick asked.

"It tastes like Christmas," Mom sighed.

"Clothes don't taste like Christmas," Kat hooted. They all chuckled.

As they'd walked and shopped, Kat babbled about her new room, and Mom pointed out familiar places. She wore a smile, but Nick wasn't fooled. He pretended not to notice tears sliding down her cheek.

When they got back to Damek's house, after putting Kat to bed, Mom lit a small fire in the grate.

"How's your head, Mom?" Nick asked.

"It's okay, honey. It's just…hard being here without him."

Nick sat with her for a while pretending to look through a book titled *The Art of Looking Up* that featured famous ancient ceilings from around the world. He wished he could think of something to say that would cheer her up, like chatting with Helena had cheered him up.

That's stupid, he told himself. *As soon as I go to bed, all the bad stuff will just come back.* How could he comfort her when he didn't even know how to make himself feel better? He couldn't, so he'd said good night and gone up to bed, hurting for Mom and for himself.

That morning, he'd woken up in his bed in Chicago in an entirely different world. A world where he had a hole in his heart because he'd lost his hero, but only because of an unfortunate accident. Now he was on the other side of the planet in a world where Kat was having waking nightmare-tantrums and couldn't seem to get warm, and Mom – who always tried to hide her stress and sadness from them – was falling to pieces in front of his eyes and there was nothing he could do about it.

Even with all that, sitting here in bed with his Uncle's book open on his knees, only one thing repeated on a loop in his mind: *"If you are reading this, it is because I am dead."*

No matter how he tried to spin it in his head, Nick could only interpret Damek's message one way: he'd known he was going to die. Which meant he hadn't died because of some 'unfortunate accident'.

Pulling the duvet cover up under his chin, he tried to push that line of thinking away. But the intense quiet of nighttime surrounding him in his late uncle's house creeped him out. He didn't even have schoolwork or something else boring he could think about to distract himself into sleeping. No white noise from Mom's fan down the hall like at home, either. Not even traffic from congested Chicago expressways. Here at the top of Damek's house, two floors up from her room Nick doubted he would even hear Kat if she screamed.

Light from a full moon spilled in from the window above the bed. *Good grief, I'm gonna get moonburn*, he thought. Standing up on the mattress, Nick adjusted the curtains, but they were too thin to block out much of the light.

Instead of laying back down, he gazed out over the rooftops, desperate to give his brain anything else to think of than Damek's cryptic note. Had he written a note to Mom, too? *No way. If she even just* thought *Damek's death wasn't an accident, she'd be flipping out like I am.* But why would his great uncle send the message to him? *I'm just a 13-year-old kid! What am I supposed to do?*

Faint mist crept through the narrow street below, glowing snake-like beneath the streetlamps. In the distance, he almost thought he heard a faint clattering and clacking, like horses galloping through the streets of Prague.

That made him smile. He laid back down and draped his forearm across his eyes. The sound of hoofbeats had woken him the other time he visited Prague. His parents told him it was part of a dream. *"Horses don't run through the streets of Prague at night,"* Dad had said. But Damek disagreed.

"You heard the Knights of Blaník," he'd said, a knowing twinkle in his eye. *"They sleep in a tomb beneath the mountain with Wenceslas the First, their king. But sometimes, when peril threatens their city or her people, the knights and King Wenceslas awaken and ride, shrouded in mist, weapons drawn."*

Wait. A tomb beneath a mountain? Could that have anything to do with why Damek had gone spelunking?

No. Lots of legends involved tombs and underground caves. No reason to think his random childhood memory about hoofbeats had anything to do with Uncle Damek.

Creeeeak!

Nick's breath froze in his lungs. The sound had come from somewhere close. Somewhere in the attic. Holding absolutely still, he counted to ten, listening.

Nothing.

Old houses make strange noises, he reassured himself. *Chill out.* But what if it was a rat?

Creeeeaaaak!

Louder this time.

Slowly, he sat up and scanned the room. It seemed much darker now. "Who's there?" His voice barely reached a whisper.

No answer. Nothing moved.

"I said who's there! Mom? Kat?"

The trap door lifted open...

...and Kat's head popped through. "Shhhh!" she shushed. "You'll wake up Mom!"

Nick's muscles untensed. "Kat, you nearly gave me a heart attack! What are you doing? Why aren't you in bed?"

"I had a funny feeling in my tummy." Kat stared up at him from the ladder with her big, brown puppy-dog eyes. "I couldn't sleep. "

Nick's irritation evaporated."Come on up," he said. "Tell me about this funny feeling. Too much fried cheese?"

She didn't answer. She seemed distracted as she climbed the rest of the way up the ladder. As soon as she reached the attic, she made a beeline to the hidden compartment at the far end of the room.

"Kat?" A stone of dread dropped in Nick's gut. "What are you doing?"

"I just want to see it again," she said. "I didn't even get to see if there was anything inside!"

The box. She'd snuck up here to see the box.

"No, Kat." His voice came out louder and harsher than he'd meant for it to. "It was hidden for a reason. We shouldn't have been snooping around in the first place."

She stopped in her tracks at his command. "Please? I just want to say good night to it. I'll put it right back!"

"I said no, Kat."

Her little hands curled into fists, her eyes narrowing. "It's not yours," she spat, "and you're not the boss of me!" Her voice rose in pitch and volume with every word. "I'm the one who found it. Finders keepers!"

Nick slid out of bed, wincing as his bad foot hit the ground a little too hard. "Kat," he said, keeping his voice reasonable as he hurried over to her, "you don't want to wake Mom, remember?" He placed his hand on her shoulder as soon as he reached her, crouching until they were eye to eye.

When his hand touched her, the anger drained from her face and her fists uncurled. She blinked, and her puppy-dog eyes returned.

"I'm so tired," she yawned. Then she took his hand and tugged him back toward the bed. "Will you read me a story from this?" she asked, gently tracing the golden scrollwork spelling out *The Legends of Old Bohemia*.

"Sure," Nick said, relieved she'd calmed down so quickly. "You might not remember because you were too little, but Damek has read us stories from this book before. He brought it with him the last time he visited us in Chicago. It's got all the legends and myths about Prague in it from a long, long time ago."

"Like the ones you read to me at home?"

"Exactly like those." Nick opened the book, flipping through the colorful pages with his thumb.

"I want this one." Kat slipped her hand inside the book. "This one, with the dragons and the lion!"

"You already know this one. It's about Bruncvik. Don't you want to hear a new one?"

"Nope!"

"Then Bruncvik it is."

Kat snuggled in next to him, leaning her head against his arm. He began: "Beyond seven mountain ranges, beyond seven rivers, there was a brave knight named Bruncvik and his beautiful wife Neomenia. One day, Bruncvik told Neomenia, 'I must prove myself worthy of your love by overcoming danger and hardship. I must go on an adventure.'"

Kat's shoulders shook with silent laughter at the way Nick made his voice deep and dramatic for Bruncvik.

Nick continued, "'Neomenia didn't want Bruncvik to go, but she knew his mind was made up. 'Oh, my handsome husband, how I shall miss you!'" Nick read in a high, love-struck voice. "'When will you return?' Neomenia asked. 'I will return after I have slain many scary beasts!' Bruncvik said, and gave her a tender kiss.'"

"Ew, kissing," Kat said. "Gross."

"Bruncvik took his wife's ring and wore it on a leather cord around his neck so it would rest next to his heart. He said he would bring it back to her, but that if he didn't return within seven years, that meant he was dead and that she should re-marry." Nick paraphrased now, realizing Kat wouldn't recognize some of the words in this version of the story.

"He left for seven years?" Kat asked. "That's older than me!"

"I know." Nick tousled her hair.

"Hey, look!" Kat said, pointing at the illustration of Queen Neomenia's ring dangling from a leather cord. "This ring is like Mommy's ring. The one that she got from her mommy after she died."

Nick studied the picture. Queen Neomenia's ring in the book was a large, round, black stone mounted on a thick, braided-gold band. Set in the stone was some kind of scarlet bird with its wings raised. "Kind of? Except Mom's ring is smaller and doesn't have a black stone like that, or a bird. And the band is different."

"It does have a black stone," Kat insisted. "Mommy lets me wear it when we play dress up sometimes. She said she'll give it to me one day, but it's too big right now."

"That's cool." Nick didn't see the point in arguing that the round part of Mom's ring was gold inlaid with black enamel and not a stone at all. Why not let her pretend? He continued the story. "One day, Bruncvik stumbled upon a huge lion fighting an evil dragon with *nine* heads. He watched them battle for hours. The lion fought like crazy, but every time he got hold of one of the dragon's heads, another would come after him. Bruncvik could see that the lion was getting tired and was about to be dragon-food. The dragon came in for the kill, but at the last moment, Bruncvik jumped in and helped the lion defeat the dragon. Except while he was fighting, Bruncvik accidentally sliced the lion's tail with his sword. That's why the Czech lion has two tails!"

"That must have hurt," Kat said. "Then what?"

"Well, Bruncvik and the lion went on adventures together, and in one of them, Bruncvik discovered a sword that had magical powers."

"Magical how?" Kat asked, even though she knew the legend by heart.

"It was *undefeatable*." Nick closed the book and set it down so he could unsheath an imaginary sword for his sister. "When Bruncvik held the sword in his hand, all he had to do was swing it and yell 'Blade. Heads off!' and the head of his enemy would fall to the ground, even if the sword didn't touch their necks." He swung the invisible sword at the shadows on the far end of the room, making swooshing sounds to complete the effect.

Kat clapped, then grabbed for the book. "Is there a picture of the heads?"

"That's gross," Nick chuckled. "You can look at the pictures, but you have to be gentle, okay? This book is really old. And I'll tell you part of the legend you probably don't already know, but then you have to go to bed. Pinky promise?"

"Pinky promise!" Kat said, hooking her pinky around his.

Nick laid the book flat, revealing a watercolor illustration of Bruncvik, the two-tailed lion, and the magical sword.

"Legend says that Bruncvik gave the sword to his son, and from his son to his son's son, until it passed into the hands of King Charles IV, who buried it somewhere in the Charles Bridge when it was being built. Czechs believe that when things are at their worst for Prague, the Good King Wenceslas will return from the dead, retrieve the sword from the bridge, and save the city."

"I've seen that sword before," Kat said matter-of-factly.

"I know. I told you Uncle Damek read this book to you when you were little."

Kat shook her head. "Not from the book. From a dream. The soldiers used it to chop up the puppet-man." She hunched up her shoulders and wiggled her elbow, a menacing leer taking over her face. "The soldiers came to his house because he'd done something bad. And the puppet-man didn't even try to run away. He just stood outside his little house laughing, and the soldiers chopped his head right off."

Nick stared at her for a moment before slowly closing the book. No wonder she woke up screaming from her dreams. "It's time for bed now," he said. "We can read some more tomorrow night.."

"Okay," Kat did a big, theatrical yawn. "I'm just going to say good night to the box first."

"No, Kat. You aren't."

Kat's body went rigid, her lower lip extending in a pout.

"You promised, Kat, remember?" As calmly as he could, Nick slid out of the tall four poster bed and held out his hand.

Kat didn't take it right away. Instead, she cocked her head to the side as if she could hear something Nick couldn't.

"Kat...?"

At the sound of his voice, Kat's muscles relaxed. She took Nick's hand and let him lead her to the trapdoor.

When they reached the top of the ladder, Kat threw her arms around Nick's middle, squeezing tight. "Thank you, Nicky."

"Night, Kat." He hugged her back.

Nick watched until she reached the floor below and blew him a kiss, then he closed the trap door and moved his still unpacked suitcase on top of it. There'd be no more unexpected guests in the attic if he had anything to do with it.

CHAPTER THIRTEEN - New Neighbor

...something wrapped in brown packing paper weighed heavily in his hands...

BLINK.

"Remember Nicholas."

...the air was chilly. He ran his fingers over the rune stone in his pocket to...

BLINK.

"The protection of the Brotherhood."

...turned, and then was open. A field of oddly crooked stones standing upright splayed out before him...

BLINK.

"Guards this house."

...heard the snap from up above, but he barely had time to look up before...

...Nick snapped awake, gasping. The afterimage of his dream refused to fade as he came to full consciousness. He sat up, rubbing his eyes.

What the heck was that?

He wiped sweat from his forehead. It was probably nothing. Just more bad dreams brought on by stress.

The scattered images faded into his subconsciousness, leaving behind remnants of dread and anxiety. Like he'd forgotten something important he was supposed to do.

But layered on top of the confusion and anxiety, a warm presence surrounded Nick.

Damek's presence.

Nick couldn't remember dreaming about his uncle, but the feeling was undeniable. He clung to it, wanting it to stay.

It didn't. It faded quickly, leaving him empty, sad, and scared.

He couldn't remember ever experiencing anything so strong before, even when awake. The absence of Damek's presence hurt him physically, like waking up after one of his surgeries when the meds wore off.

He remembered all the times he'd told Kat that dreams couldn't hurt you. Maybe he'd been wrong.

Nick forced the dream and loss and fear to the back of his mind. He had to drag his suitcase off the trapdoor and then climb down the ladder, limping stiffly downstairs to the kitchen where he found Kat and Mom. Mom was at the stove preparing a French toast feast; sausage sizzled in a pan on the stove.

"How'd you sleep?" Mom asked as Nick grabbed two slices from the stack at the kitchen table.

"Okay, I guess. Eventually." He winked at Kat, whose strawberry jam-covered face grinned back at him from across the kitchen table. "Leg's a little stiff this morning."

"From sitting so long on the plane, I bet," Mom said. "Did you do your stretches this...?"

A knock sounded at the front door. Everyone looked at each other in surprise.

"Who on earth could that be?" Mom set down the pan, heading for the entryway.

Nick and Kat listened as Mom answered the door. "Good morning. Can I help you?"

"Good morning, Ms. Gordon. I'm here to see Nick."

No way, Helena! Nick looked down at his rumpled pajamas, then ran his hand through his bedhead-hair with a burst of panic.

"You want to see Nick?" Mom sounded confused. "What's your name, dear?"

"I'm Helena Olbrycht," Helena replied. "I live next door."

Nick jumped from his chair and bolted to the foot of the stairs as fast as his stiff leg could carry him. "I told Nick I'd take him on a tour of the city."

"Oooooh, who's that, Nicky?" Kat's loud voice followed him up the stairs. She'd gotten up from the table to peek around the corner into the entryway. "Is that your girrrlllllfriend?"

"No!" Nick whispered back. "Be quiet!" He started up the two flights of stairs as quickly and quietly as he could. As he climbed, snippets of conversation from below floated up to him.

"It's nice to meet you, Helena. What a pretty name," Mom said. "I'm Anna, Nick's mom, and this is his little sister, Katarina."

"Kat," Kat said, "like a lion. Are you Nick's girlfriend?"

"Hush, Kat!"

At least Mom has the decency to be embarrassed about something, Nick thought.

"Nick must be getting dressed," Mom continued. "I've just made some french toast. Are you hungry?"

"I'd love a piece," Helena replied. "It smells lovely."

"Nick!" Mom called. "You have a visitor!"

"There in a sec!" Nick called back from the third floor landing. He scrambled up the ladder and rifled through his suitcase for something cool to wear.

Get a grip, doofus, he told himself. *You wouldn't know cool if it bit you on the butt.* He threw on shorts and a solid black t-shirt and climbed down the ladder, racing to the bathroom on the second floor to comb his hair and brush his teeth.

"On the roof?" Mom's raised voice easily reached Nick's ears. "What on earth was he doing on the roof!?"

Nick groaned and spit out his toothpaste. He almost forgot to wipe off his mouth before he hurried down the last flight of stairs, practically sliding off the last step. "Hey, Mom, do you mind if Helena shows me around the city this morning? She's a tour guide."

"She mentioned that." Mom gave him an amused look that scared him a little bit. "I've known Helena's father since I was a little girl. We haven't kept in touch, but I've heard he has a very respectable position in the government. Is that right, Helena?"

"Yes, Ms. Gordon," Helena nodded. "He's the Minister of the Interior."

Nick had no idea what that meant, but Mom seemed impressed.

"You can call me Anna," Mom said, glancing back at Nick with the same slightly amused smile. "Where were you planning on taking Nick?"

Nick winced. *Why is she smiling like that?*

"Oh, not far," Helena replied. "I thought we'd explore the Jewish Quarter, since we're so close. I have a cell phone, if you'd like me to write down my number for you. That way, if you need Nick for anything, you can call and we'll come right back."

"Perfect!" Mom pulled her cell phone out of her purse lying on the counter and typed in Helena's number. "I'll text you if I need anything. I should have thought about getting Nick a phone for our trip, but honestly I didn't imagine he'd need one. Nick, sweetheart," she turned, "you'll want your camera. And get the sunscreen from my bedroom – it's supposed to be sunny today."

"Oh, don't worry, Mrs. Gordon," Helena smiled, patting the leather travel bag slung over her chest. "I always have extra sunscreen with me. You wouldn't believe how many tourists forget."

"*Anna*, dear," Mom reminded her. "How wonderful Nick has such a *responsible* new friend."

Nick left to trek back up to the attic to get his camera, praying Mom wouldn't whip out her phone and start showing Helena his baby pictures while he was out of the room. Still, he couldn't help grinning at how smoothly that had gone, minus all the weird looks from Mom. Was it about the piercings and the hair?

Probably not. Mom was always trying to get him to do something 'adventurous' with his hair and clothes. She didn't get that standing out was the opposite of what he wanted.

He decided it would be a waste of time to try and figure Mom out. Instead, he focused on the fact that Helena had walked straight up to the front door, introduced herself and then announced she was taking Nick on a tour of Prague.

Today was off to an excellent start.

* * *

Outside, sunlight danced over the cobblestone streets, casting a golden glow on everything it touched. This was the perfect distraction. Touring around the Jewish Quarter with a new friend – who also happened to be a cool girl – Nick wouldn't have time to think about Damek's death and his weird message or Kat and her creepy-ass behavior.

"I didn't know you were coming over this morning." He glanced at Helena out of the corner of his eye.

"I was going to wait a day or two," she shrugged, then hesitated, "but after last night..."

Nick stopped in his tracks at the stress in Helena's voice. The smile she'd been wearing while talking to Mom had entirely disappeared.

"What do you mean, 'after last night'?"

Helena stopped too, looking up at the red tile roofs and the gap between her building and Damek's. "I..." She shuddered, then shook her head. "You're going to think I'm crazy. We need to find someplace we can sit and talk. Somewhere away from...here." She nodded up at the dark space between her building and his.

Maybe this wouldn't be the distraction Nick wanted after all.

CHAPTER FOURTEEN - A Sidewalk Cafe

Nick limped after Helena down the narrow, winding streets of Prague as quickly as he could. His mind spun. Why did she need to talk to him? They'd just met; they didn't know each other at all. Helena must have friends she could talk to if something bad had happened, right? Or her dad, at least?

After several minutes, the crowd of buildings surrounding them seemed to step back. The street broadened all at once, and Nick realized they'd reached a small, open square.

The piercing sky dazzled behind the pale yellows, blues, and greens of the ancient buildings, all wearing their fresh, pastel paint. A sparkling fountain topped with statues of golden angels and a large, two-tailed lion splashed in one corner of the square, surrounded by ornate ironwork.

Amidst it all, a sidewalk café was just opening for business. Waiters brought out large umbrellas, opening them over tables where their customers could seek shelter from the sun. Flower boxes packed with pink blossoms surrounded the outdoor seating area, and a slender white vase sat in the center of each table, each holding a single rosebud.

Without waiting for anyone to seat them, Helena walked straight up to a small bistro table close to the street and took a seat. Nick followed suit, in awe of Helena's boldness. He'd never been out to eat without one of his parents.

They were the first customers of the day. A waiter arrived before they'd even tucked in their chairs. He asked a question in Czech.

"Rádi bychom pomerančový džus, prosím," Helena responded. She looked at Nick. "Do you like fresh-squeezed orange juice?"

"Um, yeah, sure." He couldn't remember if he'd ever even had fresh-squeezed orange juice. But that wasn't what was important right now. As soon as the waiter left, he asked: "Are you going to tell me what's going on? What happened last night?"

Helena leaned in close. "Okay, remember when I said I like creepy things?"

"Yeah...?"

"Well, after you went back inside yesterday, things got too creepy, even for me." She stopped speaking, her gaze weighing him, as if she were deciding whether she could trust him or not.

"You're freaking me out," Nick said after the silence dragged on for several seconds. "What happened?"

"I..." Again she hesitated, glancing around like she was afraid someone might be eavesdropping. "This is so stupid," she muttered almost under her breath. "I'm not a scaredy-cat, and I'm not bonkers, I promise. But..."

"I promise I'm not going to think you're a scaredy-cat or bonkers," he assured her. "Just tell me."

"Okay, but don't say I didn't warn you." She shook her head like she couldn't believe what she was about to say. "So, last night, after you went inside, something tried to...to *push* me off the roof."

Nick's mouth fell open. "Someone pushed you?"

"Some*thing*. I swear I'm not making it up." She took a deep breath and continued in a rush, staring down at the table. "I've jumped the gap between my roof and Damek's a thousand times. I could travel the whole neighborhood by rooftop in my sleep if I wanted. But this...*wind*...came out of nowhere, and I..." She sighed. "I don't know. I guess maybe I slipped?"

She shook her head, as if she was arguing with herself. "No," she said, finally looking up and locking eyes with Nick. "I *didn't* slip. One second I was standing, getting ready to jump, and the next, my legs were dangling over the edge. You have to believe me! I've never been so scared in my life."

"I believe you, Helena. Don't you remember? Yesterday – right before my mom started calling for me – I asked if you'd been on the roof when the cra..."

"...crazy wind came through!" Helena interrupted, finishing his sentence. She smacked her forehead with the palm of her hand. "That's right? How did I forget that?"

A weird energy filled Nick. He knew exactly how it felt to nearly fall off that roof. Terrifying. But hearing Helena's experience felt strangely validating, too. He *hadn't* imagined all that stuff. Then a thought occurred to him: Helena had spent more time with Damek than he had. Maybe she could help him figure out what his note meant.

Or, she could call up a psychiatrist and have me committed to an insane asylum.

Except, if she was getting spooked by weird things too, maybe he didn't have to worry about that after all.

"Uzivat, si." The waiter returned, placing two tall glasses of orange juice and a small basket of pastries on the table.

"Uh, thanks," Nick said. The waiter smiled and went back inside.

Helena leaned closer and whispered urgently. "Was the wind one of the creepy things you said had been happening?"

He nodded.

"You need to tell me what's going on."

Nick stirred the straw around in his glass, watching the pulp swirl in a tiny circle. Helena was right. He needed to tell her. She was part of this now.

Except, part of what? An evil wind – possibly summoned by his six-year-old sister – had...what?...tried to get in the house but couldn't because his uncle had carved protective runes around the doors and window, so instead it tried to push Helena off the roof?

Yep. Pretty much. But you CANNOT say that! he told himself. Even if she thought the wind had been weird, all of that at once would probably be too much for her. But when he looked up into Helena's eyes, the look of fearful pleading he saw changed his mind. He sighed. *Get ready for your straight jacket, doofus.*

"So, my little sister and I found a secret compartment under the floor. Inside were a dagger, a really old book, and..."

Before he could finish his sentence, a sudden, stiff breeze rattled the table's umbrella. The little vase with its single rose toppled over, and the napkin on Helena's lap was snatched up into the air, where it twirled briefly before darting off across the square.

Helena jumped to her feet, but the breeze settled.

Nick righted the vase and put the rose back, even though all the water had spilled out.

"Sorry," Helena said, sounding embarrassed. She sat back down. "Guess I'm a little jumpy."

As if on queue, a strong, cold gust of air sent the vase flying off the table. It smashed to bits on the cobblestones.

Nick and Helena stared open-mouthed at each other.

Before either of them could say anything, the gust became a shrieking howl that rose all around everyone else seated at the café. Every vase on every table careened to the ground, where they all exploded, littering the dining area with shards of broken glass. The tablecloths flapped and the umbrellas rattled in their stands as the gale ripped at them. Several chairs at other tables pitched over.

"Inside!" Nick shouted.

Ducking their heads, they ran for the door as the wind screamed like an angry wildcat behind them.

Nick threw a look over his shoulder just in time to see the umbrella from their table lift from its stand and fly straight toward them like a javelin.

Without stopping to think, Nick pushed Helena against the side of the building, then shielded her body with his. He braced for impact.

But instead of pain, all he felt was a brief slap as the umbrella's fabric grazed his back. With a loud *CRUNCH,* the heavy metal pole embedded itself in the cafe's plateglass window. A thick spiderweb crack splintered outward from the point of entry.

Then, silence.

Huddled against the brick, the two of them panted as if they'd run a marathon. Helena whispered, "I think... I think the wind's stopped."

Nick raised his head, wary. A waiter stood in the open door, mouth hanging open in horrified disbelief. Small bits of glass tinkled to the ground from the huge, spiderweb crack forming around the entry point of the pole. But the air around them remained mercifully still.

Nick stood slowly, stooping to help Helena to her feet as the waiter babbled, apologizing in English and Czech.

Adrenaline rushed through Nick's system, his reflexes on high alert, but his mind remained strangely calm. *I should be freaking out,* he thought. *Why am I not freaking out?*

"Thank you, Nick." Helena gazed at him with grateful, forest-green eyes, face stunned.

Nick's cheeks flushed red.

"At least we don't need to waste any more time worrying that one of us will think the other's bonkers for saying that an evil wind is trying to kill us. Come on."

Nodding at the waiter, Helena grabbed Nick's hand and led him into the cafe. Nick followed her to a booth in the back as far away from any windows as possible.

The waiter brought napkins, a fresh basket of pastries, and new glasses of orange juice, repeatedly apologizing for the 'upset outside,' as if the wind had been his fault.

"You said you found a secret compartment?" Helena asked when they were alone again.

He nodded. "Yesterday. In the attic."

"Like, you were just exploring the attic and tripped over it or something like that?" Helena asked.

"No," Nick said, "not like that." He paused. The adrenaline coursing through him had faded, leaving him drained. He'd give anything to not have to think about the events of the past couple of weeks – and the past 24 hours specifically – let alone talk about them. But the wind had just tried to skewer them with an umbrella pole like a shish kebab in public in broad daylight, so he didn't really feel like he had another choice. "I don't even know where to start," he admitted.

"Start with whatever happened that made the wind come alive and try to kill me," Helena said, then held up two fingers. "Twice."

Nick leaned his elbows on the table and rested his head in his hands. He'd been pushing so many thoughts and emotions down so he wouldn't have to think of them. Now he searched his memory, looking for connections, speaking out loud as he worked through the most plausible story.

"Okay, so, just before we left for the airport to come here, the mailman dropped off a package from Damek. It was a book. And in the book was a note. It said: 'Touch the face of the lion to find the answers you seek.'"

"So, he mailed the book to you before his accident? But he was coming to see you, right? That *is* a little weird."

"There's more." Nick fished out the note that he'd stashed in his pocket. Silently, he handed it to Helena.

"'Touch the face of the lion to find the answers you seek,'" she read. Her eyes widened as she flipped it over and read the other side. "No way. Is this some kind of joke?"

"I wondered that, too, except it's not funny. And Damek is dead."

Helena muttered something in Czech that Nick was pretty sure was a swear word. "You think this note – and your uncle's death – are somehow connected to the secret compartment you found, yes?"

"Yes."

"That makes sense," she said to herself. "If he knew he was going to die, it couldn't have been an accident..." She leaned against the back of the booth and crossed her arms over her chest. Her eyes darted back and forth as she stared into the middle distance, as if she was reading something written in the air slightly above Nick's shoulder. "But why send a note if you couldn't do anything about it? Hmmm..."

She narrowed her eyes and chewed the inside of her cheek. Nick didn't want to interrupt, especially if she was already getting to the same conclusions he landed on.

"So I'm guessing you found the lion and touched its face," Helena mused, "and that's what led you to the secret compartment. But what does that have to do with a killer wind?"

'I don't know,' was on the tip of Nick's tongue, but before he could say it, Helena sat up straight and stared at him.

"Oh my gosh, Nick! A *killer* wind!"

Thoughts spun in Nick's brain. "Are you saying the wind killed my uncle?"

"I honestly have no idea what I'm saying," Helena said. "But something is going on and we need to figure it out. Come on!" She stood up.

"Where are we going?" Nick followed her, completely confused.

"I want to see the lion and the secret compartment. You said there was a book and a dagger and a box, right?"

They'd reached the entrance. A policewoman stood outside asking their waiter questions and taking notes. Another crouched beside the umbrella sticking out of the glass.

"Yeah, but there's more," Nick said. "I think the box did something to my little sister. She's been having these night terrors, and yesterday..."

Helena's face was grim. "Tell me on the way."

CHAPTER FIFTEEN - An Imaginary Friend

Kat's head slowly emerged through the trap door as she reached the top of the ladder. The attic was dead quiet. Nothing moved except tiny dust motes floating in slanted beams of pale sunlight from the window above the bed. Stepping gingerly from the top rung, she tiptoed across the room to the floorboard with the small hole carved out. Then, placing her little fingers in the hole, she tugged the floorboard away. It creaked slightly, and Kat froze, checking over her shoulder to make sure she was alone.

When Kat snuck up to the attic, Mom had been unpacking her suitcase on the first floor. Nick and Helena had gone out to look at the neighborhood, and Mom said they wouldn't be back for a while. Mom also said that if Kat would play quietly with the dollhouse in her new princess room for 30 minutes, they could make cookies together. Normally, fresh cookies would be all Kat could think about. Not now. Now was the perfect time to finally visit her new friend.

She didn't like to think of it all alone in the dark little compartment under the floor.

Slowly reaching in, Kat pulled the tiny box out of its resting place. She turned it over, examining it closely. Now that it was in her hands, she smiled and relaxed. It seemed like weeks since she'd held it, not just a day!

She replaced the floorboard, stood, and slipped the thin wooden box into her pocket. Then, she tiptoed back to the ladder and pulled the trap door closed above her as she climbed down.

Back in her room on the second floor, Kat sat in the corner by the dollhouse. Soft light streamed through the window, turning the pale yellow of the walls a creamy buttercup. Next to her on the hooked-rug sat an antique doll cradle that Mom said her Grandpa had made. Kat wrapped the wooden box snugly in a silk scarf she'd borrowed from Mom's suitcase and laid it on a pillow in the cradle next to Grogu.

"Of course I want to meet you!" Worry creased Kat's eyebrows. She rocked the cradle gently with one hand while leaning down a little closer, as if to listen. "Yes, I do, I promise!" she insisted. "I just don't know where the key is. If you tell me where it is, I'll..."

"Kat?" Mom stepped into the sunny bedroom, searching every corner with curious eyes. "Who are you talking to, honey?"

Kat hastily covered the box with the scarf and turned around. "Oh, hi, Mommy." Her face brightened. "I'm just talking to my friend. He's a magician!"

"Oh? That's nice. Does your friend talk back to you, sweetie?" Mom picked Kat's pajamas up off the floor and put them in a hamper at the end of the bed. Then she started unpacking Kat's suitcase, arranging her clothes neatly in the bureau drawers.

"Of course he does, silly," Kat giggled. "But not like Jenny Penny used to talk to me. I know *she* wasn't real."

Mom paused. "What kind of things does your magician friend tell you?"

"He said he's lonely and tired of being locked up in the dark with no one to talk to. But as soon as I let him out, we'll be friends and he won't be lonely anymore!"

Mom dropped the pair of socks she'd been folding back into the suitcase and knelt down next to Kat. "Oh, honey, it's been a rough few weeks, hasn't it?" She pushed a strand of Kat's long hair back behind her ear. "I'm sorry if you've been feeling lonely. Why don't we go downstairs and make those cookies now?"

"It's okay, Mommy," Kat said. *"I'm* not lonely, Horymir is. He's tired of being stuck in this stupid old box." Kat pulled the scarf back, revealing the box in the cradle.

"Where did you get this from, Kat?" The concern on Mom's face deepened. "It looks ancient. Have you been poking around in your uncle's cabinets? I told you those were off limits."

"I haven't been, I promise!" Kat covered the box back up, avoiding Mom's eyes. "It was in the attic. Nick said I could have it."

"I think I'll hold onto it until I check with Mr. Zeman to see if it's valuable." Mom fished the box out of the cradle, still wrapped in the silk scarf.

"No!" Kat hissed, grabbing for the box.

Mom recoiled, shocked, but before she could respond, the anger vanished from Kat's face. Kat leaned her head to one side for a moment, as if listening to something. She straightened, nodding. Then, she did a little bounce in place, and asked, "Can we put M&Ms in the cookies, Mommy?"

* * *

Nick burst through the back door and into the kitchen, Helena hot on his heels.

Mom, wearing an apron, and Kat, who had a large dish towel wrapped around her waist, turned from the stove, startled.

"Whoa, slow down you two!" Mom wiped her hands on her apron, setting her wooden spoon on the counter in front of Kat. "I wasn't expecting you back so early. What's the rush?"

"You scared me!" Kat chimed in. "I almost fell off my stool!"

"Sorry, Kitty-Kat." Nick stopped on his way to the stairs, exchanging glances with Helena. They hadn't thought about an explanation as to why they'd returned so quickly. "Hey, it smells good in here! What are you guys making?"

"Cookies," Mom replied. "Would you like to help?"

"No!" Nick blurted. "I mean...uh, we can't. It's just that...we're in a hurry. I need... I mean, is there, like, a...a notebook I could use? You know, to take notes about stuff we see. For when I have to write an essay about it in school this fall."

Mom looked at him suspiciously, but nodded toward her purse that was hanging from a hook by the door. "There's a notebook in my purse. It's my to-do list, but it has plenty of blank pages."

"Nick was telling me about Damek's workshop in the attic," Helena said, completely composed. "He used to put puppet shows on for the kids in the neighborhood during festival days. Would it be alright if Nick showed me?"

Mom's eyes went soft. "I didn't know he put on puppet shows for you," she said faintly. "That's just like him."

"He was a wonderful man," Helena said. "Everyone who knew him loved him. I'm so sorry."

"Thank you, Helena," Mom said, eyes wet with unshed tears. "Of course you can show her the attic," she said to Nick. "The cookies should be done before you leave again."

But just as Nick reached the stairs, Mom stopped them. "Oh, Nick, I almost forgot..."

A strange undertone in her voice made Nick turn and give her his full attention. She sounded worried. "Yeah?"

"Your sister was telling me about her friend, the magician," Mom said. "I was wondering if you've ever met him? Kat says he lives in a box she found in the attic that you said she could play with it. She said his name was Horymir or something like that?"

Nick watched Kat while Mom spoke. She hadn't stopped stirring, but he could have sworn her shoulders stiffened. Her ears had definitely perked up at the mention of the box.

"Kat must have misheard me, Mom." Nick kept his tone light. "I told her the box looked old and might be valuable, and that she *shouldn't* play with it. I put it back where we found it and told her to leave it alone."

"I see." Mom put her hands on her hips. "What do you have to say for yourself, Katarina?"

"I'm sorry, Mommy." Kat's lip trembled as she stared down at the mixing bowl. "I couldn't find a doll for the cradle. I just wanted someone to play with."

Mom sighed and wrapped her arms around Kat. "Nevermind about the box. I've got it tucked away someplace safe." She patted her apron pocket. "But Kat, it isn't nice to lie."

"I know, Mommy."

A bit of guilt for leaving Kat alone in the big house tugged at Nick's heart as Kat returned Mom's hug.

"And I want you to listen to what your brother says, okay?" Mom said. "He's always looking out for you."

"I know Mommy. I will."

"We'll be back down in a bit," Nick said, starting up the stairs. Throwing one last glance back, he saw that Kat still had her arms wrapped around

Mom's waist in a tight hug. But the shame had vanished from his little sister's face, and her lips curved up in a triumphant smile.

135

CHAPTER SIXTEEN - Creepy Things

"Thanks for the save back there," Nick said as he climbed the ladder and opened the trap door. "How are you so good at talking to adults? I always get nervous and say something dumb."

"Lot's of practice," Helena said. "Tour guide, remember?" She reached the top of the ladder and surveyed the attic. "Whoa."

"Right?"

"So, the box your mom took from Kat. It's the same one you found in the secret compartment, right? And she threw a tantrum when you took it away from her, and that's what you think made the wind crash the window open."

Nick scratched the back of his head. "Yeah, well, when you say it like that, it sounds insane."

"Um, hello?" Helena arched her eyebrow at him. "Rooftop? Umbrella pole? It's real whether it sounds insane or not. Let's make a deal. From now on, we don't worry about sounding crazy, okay? We just say what we think."

He nodded. "Deal. I only held the box for a few seconds, but it gives me the creeps. I'm glad my mom took it away from Kat."

Helena walked over to Damek's workbench and picked up a chisel. Nick could see her biting the inside of her cheek again. She glanced at the big map of Prague hanging on the wall and then gasped and pointed. "The lion!" She hurried over to the marble maze. "Oh my gosh, this is incredible!"

Nick followed her to the beginning chute. "Go ahead. Touch its face."

Helena reached out with one finger and pressed back the roaring head. The beast's front legs rotated just like they had before, releasing the marble over the edge of the polished chute with a quiet *click.*

Together, they watched the marble plonking off the chute and rolling across the ground to the hole in the floorboard.

"No way," Helena whispered.

Nick followed the path of the marble again, retrieving the dagger and diary from their spot under the loose floorboard to show Helena.

"May I?" She reached eagerly for the book.

Nick handed it to her, keeping the strange dagger. Helena absent-mindedly wandered to Nick's bed, where she sat to examine the book with better light from the window.

"This is amazing," she breathed.

"Can you read it?" Nick asked. "I know a little Czech, but those don't even look like real words to me."

"Not these early parts. I'm not even sure what language they're in. They're way too old and worn for me to piece together." She flipped through more pages. "But here, look. Near the middle I can pick out a few words."

"What does it say?" Nick sat down beside her.

"See this?" Helena pointed to some spidery writing in black ink on one of the pages toward the middle of the book. "This was written by Sir Arnošt of Pardubic."

She started reading:

I, Arnošt of Pardubic, recovered the cursed box, the dagger, and this journal from the sole remaining acolyte who attacked and killed my father.

"A cursed box," Nick muttered. "I knew that thing was bad news."

"Hush," Helena said. She continued:

I do swear on this day to take up my father's stewardship. Furthermore, I vow to safeguard the secrets of the Brotherhood and protect the relics with my very life if need be as my father did.

Let posterity witness that Ernst of Hostinka, Knight Commander of the Order of the Red Eagle was cut down in the act of defending these relics. He dispatched seven acolytes who attacked him unawares before surrendering his life. I vow to hunt down the last acolyte and avenge my father's death.

The task of finding a new resting place for the weapon falls to me, as does the responsibility of rewriting the ciphers.

I shall take a squire, as my ancestors did before me and as my heirs ever shall. This burden is too great for one soul to bear. Together, we will secure the weapon, hopefully for all time.

A warning to the heir: when awakened, the prisoner will seek to betray you. Protect your dreams.

June 21, Anno Domini 1310.

"Damek called about two weeks before he died, he said he had a story to tell me about a cursed heirloom." Nick lowered his head to his hands. "I didn't think he meant *our* family's cursed heirloom!"

"Do you have any other aunts or uncles or cousins? Did Damek ever marry or have any children?"

"No," Nick whispered. "His sister – my mom's mom – passed away before I was born. My mom was only eleven."

"You're going to wear a hole in the floor," Helena said.

He stopped pacing. He hadn't even realized he'd stood up and started. "If there was a cursed heirloom we were all supposed to watch over, why didn't Mom tell me about it?" He paced again, his bad right foot landing slightly louder than the left, like the uneven rhythm of a racing heartbeat.

Helena, who had flipped to something near the back of the book, stood and walked to Nick, placing her hands on his shoulders. "He must have thought you could do something, or he wouldn't have sent you the book and the note. He wanted *you* to find these things, Nick, not your mom. Have you even read what he wrote?" She held up the journal.

"I don't. Read. CZECH!" he snapped.

Surprise registered on Helena's face.

"Oh, wow," he said, raking his fingers through his hair. "I didn't mean to shout. I'm so sorry."

"I understand," Helena said. "I'm freaking out, too. I can't imagine how you must feel. But Nick. You don't have to do this alone. For whatever reason, the wind attacked me, too. So whether you like it or not, we're a team. Got it?"

He just looked at her. Today, instead of the cross, a little cluster of stars dangled from her pierced ear. *This girl I just met yesterday wants to be my friend.*

"Got it?" Helena asked.

"Yeah, yes! I got it. And I like it."

"So smooth," she smiled. "I like it, too. Except for the curse part."

Nick died a little inside.

"Now if you will finally listen to what I'm saying, I think you'll find that you can, in fact, read this." She shoved the journal into his hands.

He looked down and saw a message. To him. Written in English. By Uncle Damek.

In a daze, Nick sat down on the bed next to Helena. She handed him the journal. He pictured his uncle sitting at the desk in his study with a fountain pen gripped in his hand. He could hear his uncle's voice in his head.

"Will you read it outloud?" Helena asked.

Nick cleared his throat and began:

Dear Nicholas,

I apologize for all this secrecy, and for not being able to tell you the truth about our lineage in person. Prague, the Golden City, is in great jeopardy. Truth be told, the whole world is in jeopardy. A great evil has awakened. It seeks to enslave all of humankind.

Nick and Helena exchanged wide-eyed glances before Nick continued reading.

Upon my father's death, I became the steward of ancient artifacts that our ancestors have been charged with guarding for over a thousand years. Upon my death, the stewardship of this Brotherhood will pass to you.

Unfortunately, this responsibility involves more than simply caring for family heirlooms. It comes with grave peril as well, one I had hoped to protect you from entirely. But, if you discover this message, it is because I have failed.

Blood rushed through Nick's ears. *It's a joke. It's a joke,* he repeated weakly in his mind, wanting it to be true. But the crunch of the metal umbrella pole skewering the window after barely missing his head drowned out any other thought.

Our ancestors — and those in the Brotherhood who serve as our squires — have gone to great lengths to prevent the return of the ancient, evil sorcerer whose soul was sealed within the wooden box you found with this journal and the blade beneath the floor.

Young knight, I am solely to blame for the danger you now find yourself in. With all my education and experience, I believed myself capable of doing what none of our ancestors had dared before: ending this burden once and for all. Now, as the very air stalks me night and day, it is clear that my attempt to destroy the sorcerer's body has instead awakened his soul for the first time in centuries.

From the corner of his eye, Nick saw Helena's mouth fall open. She jumped to her feet and started to pace. Nick continued reading aloud:

In this journal our ancestors have left clues that lead to a weapon, the last safeguard against the sorcerer should he return. It appears that the clues have been changed a handful of times in the past centuries as deemed necessary by the Brotherhood. In my haste after decades of disbelief, I failed to compile and interpret their words correctly.

However, if you are reading this, it is likely because I am on the right track. Our adversary will do anything he can to stop the heir from retrieving the weapon before he has returned to full power and can wield it himself.

This means your time will be short in which to decipher the clues. My personal notebook contains what I finally believe to be a correct translation. Find it.

Nicholas, I have seen you act with courage, determination, and resourcefulness in the face of the trials you have encountered thus far in your life. It is because of these strengths that I know you will succeed in this task. I am so proud of you, young knight.

You know I have never believed in superstition or magical powers. But when the scientific mind is presented with irrefutable proof, it must adapt. The danger is now undeniable, as fantastical as it may seem. I believe your young mind will see solutions I was blind to. Use it to unravel the riddles my mind was too stubborn to solve.

"Holy crap." Helena raced back to the bed. "Is that the end?"

"'*The very air itself...*'" Nick recited to himself. Then, to Helena, "There's a little left." His voice trembled slightly as he read the last words Damek Maracek had ever written:

One last note, Nicholas: beware of dreams. They can be powerful, wonderful, dangerous things. Stay vigilant. Protect your mother and sister. Protect our beautiful city. Protect the world from Horymir's revenge.

Damek

Helena froze. "Horymir? Isn't that..."

"Yep." Nick's entire body was numb with disbelief. "The name of Kat's new imaginary friend."

CHAPTER SEVENTEEN - An Antiques Shop

"That nechutný chlap," Helena cursed, "what a disgusting creep! Some evil ghost has been trying to turn your sister into what, a servant?"

"A puppet." Nick stared at the noon witch on the marble run, still posed like a puppeteer.

"I can see the gears turning in your head," Helena said. "Tell me what you're thinking."

"It's all jumbled up. But here." He grabbed the to-do list and pencil he'd taken from Mom's purse and made a list, which he narrated as he wrote:

Dreams

1. Night terror #1. A crooked man who did a puppet show wrote my name in the snow.

"It wasn't the first night terror," Nick explained to Helena, who was watching over his shoulder, "but it's the first one I remember her mentioning a puppeteer in."

2. Same night, my dream: red eagle + door in mountain.

3. Damek: dreaming runs in family

4. Dream #2, night terror? Crooked man + itsy-bitsy spider. Kat rips head off marionette.

"Okay," Helena murmured, "not terrifying at all."

5. Dream #3? Plane: Kat: He's coming.

6. (Waking) dream #4 sidewalk, Kat: He's coming.

7.   ??? tantrum/dream #5: murder wind/runes.

"What runes? Ohhh...wait!" Helena's eyes darted to the window. "I wondered what those were for! I saw them around the door when I came over this morning. They're new, by the way, but Damek showed me a rune bone the first time we met for tutoring."

"A bone? So you know what those runes say?" Nick asked, excited by the animated way Helena was talking.

"No. I mean...no." She deflated a bit. "It was just a picture in a book, not an actual bone. He showed me because archeologists found a rune bone inscribed with Elder Futhark runes in Lány, Czechia, which is a Slavic settlement that existed before any known contact with Germanic tribes..." She trailed off at the overwhelmed expression on Nick's face. "Anyway, his point was that languages are complex and interconnected with history. But I'm pretty sure he didn't carve these runes for educational purposes. Nowadays, a lot of people associate runes with occult powers – like witches and warlocks."

"Mr. Zeman told me they're for protection," Nick said, "that Damek had been studying them. I saw them work with my own eyes. When Kat freaked out at me taking the box away yesterday, this wind came out of nowhere and blasted the window open, but it couldn't get in the house."

"So it tried to get me instead?"

"But why? What does any of this have to do with you? You're Damek's neighbor, not his family member."

"Maybe that's enough," Helena said, her voice so quiet Nick almost didn't hear. "I went off once about sexism in history and he smiled and said we should change it. He called me 'Squire Helena Olbrycht of Prague.' I thought it was just a joke, but..."

"I don't think it was a joke." Despite how overwhelmed he was, Nick couldn't help thinking that Damek had great taste. "Besides, why would

Horymir care about him calling his neighbor a squire? How would he even know in the first place?"

Helena shrugged. "I mean, if we're dealing with an undead, evil sorcerer or whatever Damek said, would it need a *good* excuse to hurt someone? All the more reason we need to find the weapon Damek mentioned. But how do we do that if we're stuck in this house forever?"

Nick jumped up, holding the dagger out in front of him. He looked down at it, studying each curve and embellishment. "Do you think this is the weapon they're talking about?"

"No," Helena sighed. "I wondered that, too, but they wouldn't have to make clues and go to all this trouble if they already had the weapon. And even if that's just meant to protect us, I don't really feel comfortable going out in public waving a dagger around. Do you?"

"Oh, crap." Nick grabbed the notepad and pen from where he'd left them on the bed and wrote quickly.

"What?" Helena asked. "What's wrong?"

"I forgot a dream!" Nick said, still scribbling.

"Kat had another dream?"

"No. I did. The night Damek died. And it was really weird. The thing...Horymir, I guess...broke through a door in the side of a mountain, and Damek was there. He said something about protection? And he told me to keep Kat safe. He said to safeguard her. That part I remember for sure."

Helena sat heavily on the bed beside him, staring at him with a look that was half awe, half pity. "He talked to you in your dream right before..."

"Nick!" Mom's voice rose up from the floor below. "Could you and Helena come down here for a second?"

"Shoot," Helena whispered, glancing at her phone. "We lost track of time. We've been up here for almost half an hour!"

"Coming, Mom!" Nick called down. Helena followed him over to the secret compartment, handing him the book, which he put back along with the dagger before replacing the floorboard. Then they scrambled down the ladder.

When they got to the kitchen, Mom was wiping the counter and Kat sat at the table dunking a cookie into a glass of milk.

"Sorry to interrupt you two," Mom said, "but Kat has something she'd like to ask."

"What's up, Kat?" Nick started toward the table, but stopped as a vague uneasiness welled up in his chest. *If all of this is real,* an anxious voice in his head thought, *wouldn't that mean Kat is like...possessed or something?* He looked her up and down cautiously. She was just Kat. His six-year-old-little sister. *Except she's not,* the same voice whispered. *You know she's not.*

"Will you and Helena take me to Wenceyslos Square?" Kat asked, licking a bit of chocolate off her fingers. "Mom said there are pretty statues that come out of it soon and dance around."

Mom laughed. "I didn't say they danced, Katarina. They don't dance."

"You mean the clock tower?" Nick raised an eyebrow. "Uhm, well, I'd like to, but..."

"And so would I," Helena cut in cheerfully, nudging Nick with her elbow. "I've led tour groups there. I can tell you everything you want to know. And some stuff you probably don't care about!"

"Yay!" Kat hopped down from her chair.

Actually not a bad idea, Nick thought. *What better way to keep an eye on Kat?*

"We've got to get going quick, though," Helena said. "The statues come out at noon, and it's already 11:46 A.M."

"Hurry, Mommy!" Kat ran over to the sink. "Wash me! I don't wanna be late!"

* * *

Helena and Nick walked down the cobblestone street with Kat between them, each holding one of her hands. Kat wore a red-hooded sweatshirt and a huge smile.

"Your hands are really cold," Helena said to Kat. "Like ice."

"That's weird, 'cuz I'm super warm." Kat said matter-of-factly. "'Specially with this sweatshirt, see?"

Nick eyed her suspiciously. Out in the sun, he noticed how pale she was, how her lips were tinged slightly blue. "Do you feel okay?"

Kat smiled. "I feel great!"

"Well maybe you're just a lizard." Helena said. "Do you know a lot about lizards, Katarina?"

Kat shook her head.

"Lizard's are always cold. That's just how their bodies work – especially when they're growing, like you!"

"Or if they have a circulation problem," Nick mumbled.

Helena shot him a look.

Nick kept quiet, but couldn't shake his worry about his little sister. Once, about a year ago, Kat got in trouble for playing with some of Mom's nice earrings and then losing them. She wouldn't admit to Mom that she'd taken them, but she'd confessed to Nick. She knew lying was wrong, and as far as he could tell, she'd never kept secrets from him.

Until now.

More than that, he remembered the first time he'd noticed her being cold like this. It was after she'd broken the head off her spider puppet. Damek had called, but Mom had said Kat couldn't talk on the phone because she wasn't feeling well, and that she'd put her in the bath to warm her up.

"I like your hair," Kat smiled up at Helena. "One side is pointy and the other is soft."

Nick groaned.

"Both sides are pretty soft," Helena laughed. "Wanna feel?" She crouched down next to Kat, who rubbed her hand across the buzz cut-side of Helena's head.

"Fuzzy!" she smiled.

"What about my hair?" Nick took Helena's cue. It wouldn't help to upset Kat. It's not like she'd turned evil. Horymir was obviously tricking her. He wondered if she even realized what was happening.

"You'd look silly with long hair," Kat said.

Helena laughed. "At least Nick and I don't have to worry too much about our hair getting all tangled up when we sleep."

"Yeah!" Kat said. "I always have to brush my hair for so long in the morning, and it hurts!"

"Oh, I'm sure," Helena replied. "If my hair were long, it would probably get super tangled because I have nightmares sometimes and roll around in my sleep a lot. What about you, Kat? Do you have nightmares sometimes?"

Oh? Nick raised an eyebrow. Had Helena been planning this all along? Kat usually wasn't very shy – she might open up to Helena about her night terrors if she thought Helena was just being friendly.

"Nope," Kat declared. "I sleep good!"

"Huh?" Nick blurted out. "Kat, you have nightmares all the time!"

"I used to," she said, rolling her eyes, "but that was before."

"Before what?" Nick asked.

"Look! I think we're here!"

They rounded one last corner and walked into a large square absolutely packed with people. Nick instinctively tightened his hold on Kat's hand. He'd never lost her in a crowd before, and he definitely wasn't going to start now.

"Whoa!" Kat's eyes filled with wonder.

On an old brick building across the way was an enormous clock. But it wasn't just the size that seemed to stop everyone in their tracks. It was the color and the gears and the carvings and the sheer *complexity* of the face.

"Right?" Nick asked, completely entranced. This wasn't the first time he'd seen the clock. He'd visited this same spot several times with Damek on his last trip to Prague, but his memories from all those years ago didn't come close to the actual magnificence of the Prague Orloj.

"If I saw it every day for a thousand years, I'd never get tired of it," Helena said.

Not only did the Prague Orloj and its astronomical dial show the time at different locations on Earth, it also showed a zodiac calendar, the movement of the planets, and the positions of the Sun and Moon. The various shapes and models were framed by four rotating rings of vibrant orange and gold set against a sky of gradient turquoise. Below the astronomical dial was a calendar plate, featuring a wheel listing 365 saints along with fixed holidays. That wheel surrounded the first inner circle – each symbolic of a specific month – which in turn surrounded smaller circles depicting the zodiac. The innermost circle was a view of Prague Tower.

A chime rang, and a pair of wooden panels flanking a statue of an angel at the clock's top slid open. Behind each panel, a procession of colorful statues rotated in and out of view. Each had a distinct appearance, and some of them even had props like swords and trumpets clutched in their wooden arms.

Kat pointed up, delighted. "Look!"

Helena knelt beside her. "Those are the Twelve Apostles. And now Death is ringing his bell." On queue, a grinning skeleton held out an hourglass in one hand and a small chime in the other, which it continued to ring as the apostles moved above it.

Including the skeleton, there were four statues on this level of the massive clock, flanking the face in the middle in pairs.

"What are the other ones?" Kat asked.

"On the right, next to Death, is the Turk playing his flute. On the left is the Miser with his bag of money, and next to him is Vanity looking at himself in a mirror," Helena explained.

Too soon, the chiming finished, the panels slid shut again, and the skeleton turned the hourglass over in its hand. Finally, a deeper bell struck out the hours.

The crowd thinned as the clock's hourly procession finished. A lonely breeze swirled around the stragglers' ankles, as if hurrying them out of the square. Nick took a moment to appreciate the cool air against his skin.

The wind intensified, kicking up dust around them and tugging at Kat's long hair.

Nick panicked. "Let's get out of here!" He grabbed Kat's hand.

"Come on, into the museum!" Helena grabbed Kat's other hand to lead the way, but Kat had gone stiff.

"Hurry, Kat," Nick urged. But Kat's eyes had glazed over. She cocked her head to one side as if she was listening to something. Only, Nick didn't hear anything but the wind and the crowd.

He squeezed her hand a little harder. "Kat, can you hear me?"

Kat looked up, but her eyes stared straight through him. Again, she seemed to be listening to something above her. After several seconds, she slowly nodded her head.

"Kat." Nick did his best to stay calm. "Kat, I need you to listen to me." He let go of her hand and crouched in front of her, hands on her shoulders. He shook her slightly. "Are you listening?"

Kat nodded again. "Yes." But her voice was empty. Hollow. She didn't sound like Kat at all. "I hear you. I'm coming."

"She isn't talking to you, Nick." Helena's eyes held all the fear Nick sensed closing in around him.

Before Nick could do anything else, Kat bolted. Nick grabbed a fistfull of her red hoodie, but she wrenched away.

Stumbling over his own feet, he landed hard on the ground. Kat darted out of the square faster than he'd ever seen her move.

Helena sprang into action, following Kat as Nick picked himself up. He hurried after them as fast as he could on his bad leg, keeping Helena in sight and trusting her to keep her eyes on Kat. He lost sight of Helena as she intersected a group of tourists snapping photos and listening to a tour guide who was pointing up at the State Opera House.

Up ahead, Kat's small figure weaved in and out of the people on the streets, her red sweatshirt standing out clearly in the mob of people.

Silently cursing his bad leg, Nick kept his arms out in front of him, issuing a steady stream of apologies as he plowed through the startled crowd. After several minutes, Helena slowed, and Nick caught up to her, panting, just in time to see Kat approach a small shop about halfway down the block.

"Kat, stop!" Nick cried. But she already had her hand on the doorknob.

Nick and Helena hurried after her, pulling the door open not long after it had swung shut behind Kat. They found themselves in a quaint, brightly-lit antique shop. A tall window behind the cash register was open to let in the pleasant afternoon breeze.

The pale shopkeeper glared at them through one eye, the other hid behind a shock of greasy hair. "No children without adults," he snarled.

There was something eerily familiar about the man, but after his initial glance, Nick ignored him. While he scanned the aisles for Kat, he heard Helena explaining they'd just come in to fetch their little sister.

"Did you hear what I said?" The shop keeper nearly growled. "There are no children allowed. Now get out!"

"That's her, just over there," Helena said politely. "I'll just get her and we'll leave."

Nick's eyes followed where Helena pointed. Kat stood in front of a display near the center of the shop. An old, opened, scrolltop desk covered in music boxes, jewelry stands, and figurines.

With stiff, jerky movements, Kat reached into her sweatshirt pocket and pulled out a small, wooden object.

"NO!" Adrenaline zapped Nick's legs. Mom had said she'd taken the box!

Beside him, Helena lunged into action.

"Stop!" the shop keeper yelled, knocking over his stool as he leapt from behind the counter.

Kat reached out with arms stiff like wooden planks and picked up a tiny, ancient-looking key on a thin leather strap from the desk.

The world slowed, moving like a video playing a frame per second. With all his might, Nick struggled to reach his little sister. He jumped with both feet. Something ice-cold latched around his ankle. He sprawled forward onto the floor.

Kat inserted the key into the tiny keyhole in the box. It turned with a silver *CLINK* that echoed throughout the entire shop.

Suspended in mid air, Nick watched in horror as Kat dumped the contents of the box into her hand to reveal a small lock of hair.

Outside, darkness swallowed the sun.

The window behind the front desk shattered. The shop door crashed open as gale-force winds attacked from all sides.

A cyclone twisted through the shop, whipping papers into the air, knocking crystal vases and ceramics from the shelves, ripping paintings from the walls. An enormous mirror smashed to the ground. Porcelain and canvas rained down like hail.

Customers fell to their knees, covering their heads with their arms like in an earthquake drill, their frantic cries drowned by the maelstrom.

A visible torrent of dust, glass, and shredded paper spun toward Kat and paused, pulsing. Then it...*stooped,* and reached for the contents of the box in Kat's open hands.

"Get away from my sister!"

Finally able to control his body again, Nick lunged forward.

Then, all at once, it dispersed, rushing out the window, vanishing as quickly as it had appeared.

A high-pitched cackle behind Nick repeated as if on a loop, chanting: "It is done! You are too late! He is free!"

Nick looked behind him. The shopkeeper, still cackling, clung to his ankle with both bony hands.

Repulsed, Nick kicked, but the man held on tight. Nick crawled forward, desperate to get away, to free himself from the deranged shopkeeper's clutch. With one final, violent kick he freed himself, smacking into something with his shoulder. He turned and looked up.

Kat smiled down sweetly at him. "I found the key."

He stared up at her, chest tight with horror. "Kat..."

"Come on." Helena was there, reaching down for his hand, pulling him to his feet. "We've got to get away from here. Hurry!" She yanked him forward.

Nick glanced back over his shoulder. The shopkeeper no longer seemed angry. He was...smiling? Maybe more like snarling...

Helena didn't stop dragging Nick and Helena behind her until they reached the opposite side of the street. She let go of Nick, who panted, hands on knees, but kept a tight grip on Kat's arm.

"Ow, let go!" Kat whined. "You're hurting my arm."

"Sorry," Helena said, letting go.

"No!" Nick stood up straight and grabbed her arm. He shook her. "What was that, Katarina? Why did you think it was okay to run off like that?"

"Nick, stop," Helena said quietly. "Horymir made her do it."

"Why are you being so mean to Horymir?" Kat demanded, stomping her foot. "He's my friend! He whispered to me in my head! He made my nightmares stop, and he told me where the key was so I could let him out of that box he was stuck in for so long! Wouldn't you want to let me out if I was trapped in a box like that?"

Around them on the street, Nick saw shoppers and tourists eyeing them warily, crossing to the other side of the road to put more distance between them and the little girl throwing a tantrum.

The stress and fear and anxiety that had been brewing inside Nick steamed up. *Don't lose your temper. You've never lost your temper with her.* He'd promised himself he'd never yell at her the way their dad had yelled at him and Mom. Inhaling sharply, he counted to five before letting the air out of his lungs. He loosened his grip on Kat's arm.

"Kat. Horymir isn't your friend. Friends don't ask us to lie or to take things that don't belong to us." He pulled Kat closer for a hug.

A sudden gust whipped Kat's hair across her face. She stiffened. "You shut up!" she shouted. "Horymir IS my friend!"

Nick's temper boiled over. "Well your 'friend' killed Uncle Damek!"

Kat gasped and dropped the box she'd been hiding behind her back. She stumbled away from Nick as if he'd slapped her. Helena scooped the box off the ground and put it in her backpack.

"You're lying." Kat's voice trembled. "Mommy said a tree fell on him. It was an accident..."

Nick's anger vanished at the shocked horror on Kat's face, replaced instantly by guilt. "I'm really sorry, Kat. I shouldn't have said that. But..."

Kat took off running.

"Kat!" Nick limped after her, his stomach in knots. There was no way he could catch up to her on his bad leg.

"I'll get her." Helena caught up to Kat right before she ran around a corner down the street. Gratitude pumped through Nick as he watched Helena crouch down in front of his little sister, comforting her.

"...he's lying, he...he..." Nick heard when he finally caught up.

Nick knelt down next to Helena. "Kat, I'm sorry."

Kat turned away from him.

In all the years since becoming her older brother, he'd seen her upset, but never like this. Never at him.

"I think we're all a little tired," Helena said. "Maybe we should head back to the house and get some rest, yes? Maybe a cookie and some milk?"

"I... Yeah, you're probably right," Nick said, standing back up. "Let's head home. Kat?"

Kat slipped her hand in Helena's and walked with her down the street, acting as if Nick didn't even exist.

Ouch. He shouldn't have lost his temper. He shouldn't have told Kat that Damek had been murdered, but he wouldn't pretend that nothing was wrong, either. Horymir was on the loose, and Kat was in more danger than ever.

* * *

An unnatural wind gusted through an empty alleyway. It rattled window latches and tugged at bin lids, snatching up small bits of trash and dust from the dirty street. It howled, swirling as it increased in intensity. Little by little, it gathered more debris, growing taller and wider until it resembled the raging funnel of a tornado, navigating between discarded furniture and bags of junk to a hidden place behind two dumpsters. There, it coalesced further, taking the shape of a crooked little man with his arms spread wide. His feet hovered above the ground, his bald head thrown back in triumph. Only when the figure lowered his arms and opened his eyes did the whirlwind dissipate.

He was free.

The figure's bare, insubstantial feet hovered inches above the filthy street in the empty alley, the trash bins and broken furniture clearly visible through the transparent outline of his body. He glanced up at a streetlamp nearby and narrowed his eyes. Instantly, the fluorescent bulb buzzed with a bright crackle before sparking out.

Horymir cackled in delight. He was stronger than he had dared to anticipate. Even without his body, he could access more power than he ever had before he'd been imprisoned in the wooden box.

But it wasn't enough; he wanted more. And for that, he would need a true body again. As foolish as the old knight had been in immolating the sorcerer's resting place, it had reduced Horymir's old body to ash. He could fashion a new one from almost anything, given the right amount of time. And what was any amount of time compared to how long he had spent imprisoned?

And yet, with his newfound freedom came a newfound sense of impatience. The ash of his old body had only succumbed to the flames a matter of weeks ago. Certainly, some of Horymir's essence would be lingering still. With enough effort, it could be reformed. Until then...

A twitchy-looking man with longish, greasy hair rounded a nearby corner. His gloves, scarf, and long, wool coat belied the warm summer day. Yet, the man held his coat tight around him, scarf pulled up over his nose, and he shivered with cold. He approached Horymir's form, uncautiously, and kneeled.

"Master," he intoned, pulling his scarf down. Reverence battled with ecstasy in his voice. "You are here at last! I have done everything you asked. The little girl..."

"Quiet!" Horymir demanded. "You will speak when spoken to."

The man bowed his head, averting his eyes. "Yes, master," he said.

"You have served me well." Horymir's tone softened. "I have one more use for you before you gain your everlasting reward.

"Anything, master!"

"Your clothing."

"My...clothing?" The man lifted his gaze, expression puzzled.

"A bit rough around the edges," Horymir's form encircled the acolyte, "but well made. Yes. They will do nicely until others can be procured."

"I don't understand, Master. What do you want with my clothes?"

"TO WEAR THEM, OBVIOUSLY! STAND UP, YOU SIMPLETON!"

"Yes, Master," he stammered, stumbling to his feet. His nervous hands fumbled at the buttons of his coat.

"Not here, you fool!" Horymir hissed. Then he crooked his wrist, beckoning with one hand while the fingers of the other wriggled as if controlling the strings of a marionette. The man's one visible eye glazed over. As if in a trance, he followed Horymir silently back into the alleyway and out of sight. And when his life began to drain from his body, he didn't even scream.

CHAPTER EIGHTEEN - The Study

Kat stomped through the kitchen door and right up the stairs to her room.

Nick winced when she slammed her door.

"What was all that about?" Mom poked her head in the kitchen from the hall.

"Kat's mad at me because she ran off in the square and I yelled at her," Nick said. "She's not speaking to me now."

"She ran off?" Mom asked. "That's not like her. I'm sorry Nick. All this..." she waved her hands around, indicating everything and nothing, "...has been too much for her. I'm sure she just needs to calm down."

"I dunno," Nick said. "She wouldn't even look at me on the way back."

"She loves you," Mom said. "Thank you for watching out for her. And, you'll still babysit tonight for me, won't you? Mr. Zeman will be here to pick me up at 7:00 P.M."

He nodded. "We're just going to hang out until then, if that's okay," he said, indicating Helena, who stood behind him, not saying a word.

"Of course. I have a stack of time-sensitive papers to get through for the bank, but in a few days it will all be sorted and we'll be able to spend time together as a family."

Once Mom had gone back to her room, Helena went to a cupboard and took out a canister. She filled the teapot with water from the sink and turned on the stove, all the while biting the inside of her cheek.

"What are you doing?" Nick asked.

"Making tea, obviously," Helena spoke quickly and quietly, her voice full of nervous energy. "It's what I do when I'm anxious. And right now I'm *extremely* anxious." She took two cups and saucers from another cupboard and set them down firmly on the table, then looked at Nick. "I can't help but notice you seem disturbingly calm."

"Trust me," Nick said, "I'm one hundred percent freaked out." He slumped into a kitchen chair and let his head fall on the table. He felt radioactive with dread. "I don't think I've been okay since Damek died."

"Do you take sugar with your tea?" Helena chewed the inside of her cheek while rifling through the pantry. "Where is the sugar? It's always right here."

Nick sat up. "Helena, stop. I don't drink tea. It's gross."

She glared at him. The tea kettle whistled. She turned the stove off and the whistle turned to a hiss.

"Sorry," she said, bringing a cup of tea to the table and sitting across from Nick. "I just... That was *so* creepy. That shopkeeper... it was like he didn't want you to stop Kat. He didn't even seem to care about the wind tearing up his shop..."

"I'm such an idiot!" Nick slapped his hand to his forehead.

"What?"

"I just remembered where I'd seen him before. The shopkeeper! He was at the airport, Helena. When we got off the plane. He tried to give Kat a flower!"

"Oh no, no, no," Helena moaned, lowering her head into her hands. "Nick, what are we supposed to do? How many other people does Horymir have working for him?"

"It probably doesn't even matter now that Kat's unlocked the box."

Helena groaned.

"Kat's never been mad at me like this. I mean, sometimes she pretends to be mad, but *never* like this. Helena, Kat ran away and set Horymir free 20 minutes after I read Damek's note and swore I'd never let her out of my sight. What if I can't fix this? What if I've failed? What if she's not my little sister anymore?" Leaning on his elbows, he covered his face with both hands.

Helena lifted her head and pulled his hands away from his face. "Listen. She's still your little sister. I'm sure of it. You haven't failed."

"How do you know?"

"Well, for one thing, Damek believed in you, and that's really saying something. He's very skeptical and super scientific, and that's on top of being the smartest person I've ever known. Plus, there's a failsafe, remember? Horymir may be out of his box, but that doesn't mean this is over. Last time I checked, Prague is still standing. Until he's taken over the city or whatever else he's plotting to do, we can still do something. And as for Kat, maybe it's like you said: maybe he doesn't need her any more now that he's free. Please, Nick. We don't have time for this. We've got to find Damek's notebook."

Nick breathed in relief. "You're right," he said. "We don't. Thank you, I needed that."

"You're welcome. Besides, I think it should be a rule that only one of us can break down at a time, and I'd already started. Now, where should we look?"

* * *

Nick pushed the door to Damek's study open. A wave of emotion washed through him as he stepped into the room. This room represented everything Nick loved best about his uncle. The scent – a mixture of book dust, antique varnish, and clove – startled him with its familiarity. Damek's absence was like the ache of a phantom limb. There was nothing he could do to make it go away.

Silently, he walked over to the leather chair and ran his fingers over the tall back. A memory sprang up in his mind: he'd been standing right next to Damek – who'd been sitting in this very chair – begging him to take him on his next dig...or, as Nick had called them back then, treasure hunts.

"The real hunt begins here." Damek gestured around his study. "All good adventures begin with learning."

"You have treasure in here?" Nick jumped up from where he'd been kneeling on the armchair next to his uncle, eyes wide with excitement.

"The very best kind of treasure," Damek nodded.

"Where? A secret passage?" Nick ran to the far wall and knocked, ear pressed against the surface.

"No, no, nothing like that, though that would, indeed, be incredibly cool," Damek chuckled. "The treasure I'm referring to is in here." He slid a thick, gold-embossed volume of history toward Nick. "And here," the older man tapped a stack of loose documents near his inkwell, "and there." He pointed to the built-in bookshelves that practically groaned beneath the weight of countless books.

*Nick slumped. "Not boring old books. I mean **real** treasure!"*

Another chuckle. "I know it may not seem like it now, but in time you will understand that the very best treasure is not at the end of a map, but in here," he tapped Nick's forehead with his index finger, "and in here," he touched Nick's chest, above his heart.

"This place is incredible!" Helena said, pulling him out of his memory. "Have you been in here before? I bet he has more books than the Klementinum!"

"Haven't you?" Nick asked. "I figured you'd have done tutoring in here."

"Uh-uh. We either met at the cafe I took you to this morning, or walked to the library. Probably for the better, though. This would have been way too distracting."

"I've never seen it like this," Nick said, taking in the disorganized mess. "It was always so clean and tidy."

"He was searching for clues, though, right?" Helena mused. "He tried to get rid of Horymir's body and realized he'd somehow made him stronger, and the wind had him trapped in the house – so he was pulling books off the shelves and digging through maps, trying to figure out where he'd gone wrong." Her eyes wandered around the room. "At least, that's what I would have done."

"Yeah, but how are we supposed to figure out something he couldn't? Like you said, he was the smartest scholar, the best researcher. He was a famous archeologist. And now he's gone."

"You read what he said," Helena shrugged, "find his notebook and use our imaginations. Well, your imagination specifically, but mine's pretty spectacular, too. Now let's not waste time. I call dibs on that pile!" She pointed to a sheath of loose parchments and rolled up maps stacked up on one of the armchairs.

His eyes settled on the large, ornately framed painting directly behind Damek's chair. In the painting, a warm sun shone brightly on a lone man wearing a breastplate and holding a sword, head bowed as he knelt on the Charles Bridge beneath a simple wooden cross.

His uncle had taken him to the Charles Bridge – maybe even to the same spot in the painting, right there in front of the big cross that loomed over passersby and the pristine water below – the last time Nick had visited Prague.

"...but I doubt *that's* gonna help us out at all," Helena was saying. "Still, it *is* about dreams, and it must be important, or he wouldn't have underlined it. Nick! Are you even listening to me?"

"Oh, I...sorry," he said, gesturing toward the painting. "Just remembering the last time my uncle took me to the Charles Bridge. "

Helena's eyes softened. She turned to face the painting. "He really loved that bridge," she said. "I mean, he loved all the historical spots in the city, but I think the Charles Bridge was his favorite."

Nick stayed silent.

"He'd show up during my tours sometimes," Helena continued. "I take tourists up and down the bridge all the time, of course, and sometimes your uncle would just be walking along, see me with a group, and stop to tell them about whichever statue we were standing closest to. There are thirty statues on the bridge now, not like hundreds of years ago when this painting was done. I only know the stories behind the more important ones, but your uncle could give an hours-long lecture on every single one of them."

"I'd give anything to hear one of his lectures again," Nick said. "I don't remember what he said about this one. Or even its name."

"It's the Crucifix and Calvary," Helena said. "The original wooden crucifix was erected in 1361 A.D., but it's been destroyed and replaced several times. It's considered a very holy place by the people of Prague. You see people kneeling at its foot in prayer all the time – sometimes even people from my tour groups join in. But Nick, check this out. Damek was reading this book the day before he passed."

"The day before?" Nick's legs trembled unsteadily, as if the world had lurched suddenly sideways. "How do you know when he was reading it?"

Silently, Helena held out what Nick had mistaken for a bookmark, but was actually a folded up piece of newspaper. In the top right corner, the date read: June 3rd of this year. Two days before Damek called him for the last time.

Stunned, Nick took the book.

"The title is A History of Dreaming in Prague," Helena said.

"This is definitely a clue!" Nick's excitement mounted as he opened it to the page with the newspaper clipping. The chapter heading had been underlined three times. "What does this say?" He pointed to the chapter heading.

"'The Legacy of Libuše.'"

"I've heard of her," Nick said. "She was the youngest daughter of some famous guy named Kronk or something, right?"

"Krok," Helena laughed.

"Like the shoes?"

Helena rolled her eyes and swatted at Nick.

"It was a joke!" Nick grinned. "Libuše and her two older sisters each had different powers. One was a healer, one was a powerful magician..."

"And Libuše," Helena cut in, "was a powerful dreamer. She had visions, including one that told where the city of Prague should be built." She looked up at Nick. "I'm impressed," she said. "Libuše isn't common knowledge, even for Czechs."

"Damek must have taught me things he thought might be useful one day. It's kinda funny, though. He didn't believe in 'magic,' but he was always saying dreaming runs in the family."

"Funny you should mention that, actually." Helena pulled the book closer. "This part, here," she pointed to a paragraph that was underlined, "it says the same thing: the ability to dream runs in certain families."

"But he already knew that." Nick shook his head. "That can't be why he marked this chapter with the newspaper.

"Maybe he didn't underline it for *himself,* genius. Maybe he underlined it for *you.*" She continued to read to herself, mumbling in Czech, when suddenly she punched him hard in the shoulder.

"Ow!" he cried, grabbing his arm. "What was that for?"

"Sorry! Shoot, I'm so sorry, but listen to this: 'Arnošt of Pardubic was the first archbishop of Prague, as well as the last bishop. Additionally, he was a special advisor to Karl of Luxembourg, who would later become the Holy Roman Emperor, King Charles the Fourth'!"

Nick's mouth fell all the way open. "Arnošt of Pardubic as in *the* Arnošt - *my ancestor* Arnošt from the diary? He was an advisor to King Charles as in *the* King Charles, the Holy Roman Emperor who hid Brunkvic's magic sword in the Charles bridge?"

"Yes!" Helena grabbed Nick's shoulder and shook him. "And listen: 'Arnošt of Pardubic was a direct descendant of Libuše. In 1346 A.D., while serving as a special advisor to Charles, the ruling King of Bohemia, Arnošt learnt of a threat to the king and to Prague. Partisans from a rival house engaged a Dominican monk who was loyal to their cause and practiced black magic to infect the dreams of Charles' inner circle by means of witchcraft. Once they had infiltrated the dreams of his advisors', they planned to incite a coup and end Charles' life.'"

Nick held up a hand. "Whoa, slow down, that was a lot. So, you're saying..."

Helena rolled her eyes. "Basically, the book says that a bunch of Germans wanted their own king and tried to get rid of King Charles by getting his advisors and guards to kill him by using magic."

"Wait," Nick said, "that's kind of like how King Wenceslas' brother – Boleslaus – tried to take the throne by having Wenceslas' guards kill him, right? Because one of his advisors brainwashed him or something?"

"Yes, kind of. But none of this magic stuff is true, you know that, right? Including the part about King Charles hiding Bruncvik's magic sword in the Charles Bridge. That's just a myth."

"I thought a lot of things were 'just myths' before today," Nick said. "What else does it say?"

"That Arnošt took it seriously. He apprehended the priest – the book uses the word černokněžník, a dark priest – himself before any dreams were 'infected'. Apparently, Arnošt insisted that all the knights and advisors wear a medallion in the shape of the Bohemian lion to protect them. It became a symbol of loyalty to the crown for a while, though. I guess people were more superstitious back then. What are you doing?"

Nick had jumped to his feet as soon as Helena mentioned the medallion. Fishing the pendant out from under his t-shirt, he held it up.

Helena gasped. "Nick. Where did you get that?"

"He sent it to me," Nick said, in a daze. "Damek sent it to me with *The Legends of Old Bohemia* book..."

"No way," Helena cut him off.

"He really did," Nick said. "Remember? I told you that the mailman showed up right before we left for the airport..."

"No, not that, I remember that," Helena said. "Here: Damek wrote something in the margin!"

Eagerly, Nick leaned close, reading his uncle's words: **Sometimes dreams cannot be avoided.**

"This fits in with what Arnošt said in the diary about protecting your dreams, and..." Helena said, but Nick was already halfway to the door.

"Nick, wait! Where are you going? We still haven't found the notebook!"

"Come on!" he urged. "We've got to talk to Kat!"

CHAPTER NINETEEN - The Big Bad Wolf

"Nick, What are you talking about?" Helena followed him out of the study and up the wooden staircase.

"The last time I talked to him, Damek told me that he was going to bring something when he visited that would protect Kat's dreams 'from crooked men,'" Nick explained, wishing he could take the stairs two at a time. "He had to be talking about this pendant!"

"Wait!" Helena grabbed Nick's arm as he reached the second floor landing.. "I know you want to protect Kat, but *you* need the pendant. You're the one who has to defeat Horymir!"

Nick turned to face her. "Kat's the one he's been messing with. I've had a few weird dreams, but Horymir has never tried to talk to me."

"That doesn't mean he won't," Helena argued.

"You saw what Damek wrote in the book: sometimes dreams can't be avoided. He said kind of the same thing the last time I ever talked to him on the phone. He told me that sometimes messages in dreams can help you solve problems in the waking world." Nick focused on the conversation in his memory. "He said Kat was too young to understand, but for people like...oh wow... Damek said, "for people like you and me..." That's what he meant, it has to be! He was telling me my dreams might help us figure this out! What if I can't have those kinds of dreams if I wear the pendant?"

Helena covered her face with her hands for a second. "Okay," she finally said, taking them away. "I hate to admit this because I would *not* be okay with an evil sorcerer poking around in my dreams, but that makes sense. Besides, I guess you have the Brotherhood's protection or whatever, and hopefully that counts for *something*."

"Exactly!" Nick didn't even hesitate. "That creep's not getting anywhere near Kat's dreams again if I have anything to do with it. Besides, maybe Horymir won't even try getting in my dreams. Maybe I'll be the one poking around in his."

Helena looked him in the eyes for a long minute, like she was looking each inch of his brain up and down. Then she nodded, and gave him a little shove. "Well," she said, "don't just stand there all day. Let's go talk to Kat!"

He rolled his eyes, then continued down the hall to Kat's room and knocked softly at her door.

No answer.

Not surprising, really. Kat could hold a grudge. She'd given Mom the silent treatment for almost two days straight one time Mom forgot she'd promised to bring home donuts. He pressed his forehead against the door and tapped with one finger. "Kat, it's me. Can I come in?"

"Go away."

"Kat, I'm sorry for shouting at you. Will you please forgive me?"

Nothing.

"Any ideas?" Nick asked Helena.

"I'll be right back," she whispered, and ran back down the halls and then down the stairs.

Nick closed his eyes, suddenly exhausted. It felt like weeks had passed since he'd woken up in Prague that morning.

"Hey Kat," Helena said, startling Nick. He hadn't even heard her come back. "I found a book of fairytales down in your uncle's study. Do you want to read it with me?"

The lock clicked, and the door swung open a moment later to reveal a teary-eyed Kat in her Baby Yoda pajamas. "*You* can come in, but not *him*." She pointed to Nick.

Ouch.

Helena nodded, not even glancing at Nick. She followed Kat to her bed and sat down next to her, opening the book on her lap.

Kat immediately began flipping through the pages, pausing to gaze at the colorful illustrations. "Look how big the Big Bad Wolf is," she exclaimed, swiping her cheek dry with her pajama sleeve. "He doesn't even look like a grandma! Red Riding Hood wasn't very smart."

"I don't know," Helena shrugged. "Kids are taught to listen to adults, right? And she *was* suspicious. Red was lucky to have the woodsman to protect her."

"Yeah, I guess," Kat said, staring at the page in front of her.

"You know," Helena said, "not all the scary things in the world look like big bad wolves. Sometimes they even pretend to be our friends to get us to trust them."

"Ugh," Kat groaned and flopped backward against her bed. "You're on *his* side." She pointed at the door.

"Nick loves you more than anything," Helena said gently. "I know, because he told me. I wish I had a big brother who loved me as much as he loves you."

"Hmph," Kat hmphed, turning her back to Helena.

"Has Nick ever done anything to hurt you before? Does he ever call you names or take your toys or pinch you?"

Kat covered her head with her arms and said nothing.

Standing in the doorway, Nick shuffled his feet. It was weird to hear this tough-looking girl say such nice things about him.

"Has he ever asked you to do something you knew was wrong?"

"Ugh" came Kat's muffled response.

"I know you said Horymir was your friend, but do you think he might have been trying to trick you? Sort of like how the wolf dressed up as Red's grandma to trick her?"

Kat began to sniffle. "But he seemed so lonely." Her body curled up in a tight, little ball. "I'm sorry. I'm sorry I let him out of his box."

Nick hated hearing the pain in his little sister's voice. He hurried to sit next to Kat on the bed.

"Hey," he said, patting her back. "It's okay. I know you know not to talk to strangers, or go with someone you don't know. This was different. Horymir didn't just trick you, Kat. He..." Nick paused, looking at Helena, unsure what to say. *I can't tell my little sister that a magician put a spell on her! She'll never trust anyone again!*

"Nick said that when you dream about Horymir it makes you really scared, right?" Helena asked Kat

Kat sat up, nodding.

"He pretended to be nice to you, but he made you feel bad, didn't he?

Kat nodded again, brushing her hair off her damp cheeks. "There was a hole in the sky. It sucked away all the light, like this," she twirled her finger around and around in the air very fast.

"Like a whirlpool?" Nick asked. She knew what a whirlpool was. He'd shown her how to make one in a bucket in the backyard last summer.

"Yes, like a whirlpool! And then everything got sucked into the hole, like trees and buses and even Mommy."

Nick pulled Kat close. "I'm sorry, Kat. That sounds really scary. But I have something that will make him leave you alone." He pulled out the lion pendant and unlooped it from his neck.

"Where did you get that?" Kat asked, clearly impressed.

"From Uncle Damek," Nick took Kat's hand and put the necklace in it, "It's for you. It's been in our family for a long, long time, and it protects against bad magic and bad people like Horymir."

"He looks mad," Kat used the blanket on her bed to polish the lion's face. "I read about lions in a library book. Did you know you can hear a girl lion roar from eight miles away?"

"Really?" Nick asked, impressed.

"Yes," Kat said. "This is a boy lion, though, see his mane? He looks like Bruncvik's lion from the book. I wonder how many tails he has?" She turned the pendant over. "No tails."

"In Czechoslovakia, lions are a symbol of protection," Helena added. "If you wear this, Horymir won't be able to whisper in your head or give you bad dreams."

"But what about you, Nicky? Don't you need a lion, too?"

"Nah," he said, ruffling her hair. "I've already got you, Kitty Kat!"

"Rahhhrrrr!" Kat growled, making fierce claws with her hands. Then, without warning, she flung her arms around Nick.

"Woah there, you're gonna squeeze the life out of me!" Nick coughed and sputtered like he couldn't breathe

Kat giggled and squeezed even harder before finally easing up. "I love you, Nicky."

"I love you, too. And I'm sorry I yelled at you. I know you won't run off like that again right? And you'll tell me if anything strange happens, even if it seems silly, promise?" Nick held up his pinky.

She hooked her pinky around his. "Pinky promise."

CHAPTER TWENTY - A Knock at the Door

"Nick! Kat? Will you please come down here?" Mom walked out of her room wearing a simple navy dress, fastening the back of a pearl earring. "Oh!" she said, startled to find Nick, Kat, and Helena already standing in the entry hall. She smiled. "Look at you all, getting along again." She knelt down next to Kat. "Are you feeling better?"

Kat nodded. "Uhhuh. I'm hungry, though. And tired."

"You look tired." Mom pressed her lips against Kat's head. "You're so cold, Katarina. Are you sure you're warm enough? Maybe run up and get your sweater."

"Nu-uh," Kat shook her head. "It's too hot in here."

"Hmmm." Mom didn't sound convinced.

From the front window, Nick saw a car pull up in front of the house. Mr. Zeman got out and started up to the door.

"Don't worry, Mom. I'll take care of her," Nick said.

"I can stay and help look after Kat if you'd like, Mrs. Gordon," Helena said. "I have experience in childcare, and my CPR certificate."

"Nick?" Mom asked, hope in her voice. "Would that be okay with you?"

"Sure," Nick said, trying not to sound too relieved, "I guess that'd be okay."

"Yay!" Kat sat down on the couch, drooping just a little bit.

"Maybe I shouldn't go…" Mom said just as Mr. Zeman knocked at the door.

"We'll call if she says she doesn't feel well," Helena said. Nick opened the door, and Mr. Zeman stepped inside.

"Hello, young knight!" Zeman greeted Nick. "And miss Helena. I hope you've been keeping our guests out of trouble."

Helena grinned. "Of course, Mr. Zeman. I've only been showing the best of Prague's hospitality."

The older man rolled his eyes in an exaggerated huff. "Always with the 'Mr. Zeman.' Like I haven't known you almost your whole life."

Nick's eyes darted between the two. "Oh, duh," he said, mostly to himself. "I should have figured you two had met."

"Now," Mr. Zeman clapped his hands, "perhaps we can catch up after your mother and I return. We do have a reservation to catch."

Nick nodded and waved goodbye. He still didn't know much about his uncle's attorney, but he felt better about talking to him now. He had more to worry about than awkward conversations. And it helped that Helena seemed to like him.

As he and Mom walked out through the front door, Zeman paused and turned back. "Be sure to lock and bolt the door after us," he instructed, "and don't open it for anyone until your mother returns."

Mom looked up at Mr. Zeman, alarm showing on her face. "Are you worried someone might try to get in?"

"Worried?" Mr. Zeman shrugged. "Not worried, so much. Cautious, perhaps." He splayed his hands wide. "There have been some reports of vagrants in the area pestering people, tourists especially, asking for money and food. They've even grown bold enough to walk right up to people's doors, apparently. They're mostly harmless, but still, better safe than sorry. It's always good policy not to answer the door unless you're expecting someone."

* * *

"Tell me about your friends in Chicago." Helena sat on the couch with Kat cross-legged on the floor in front of her. She was braiding Kat's hair.

"Janey and Zach are my best friends at school." Besides seeming a little low energy, Kat chatted away like nothing weird had happened that day. "Most of the kids in my class are nice, but Tabitha picks her nose and eats it!"

"Ew! Gross!" Helena wrinkled her nose in disgust.

"Yeah, one time she wiped a booger right on her desk. It was green. I almost threw up."

Helena made a barfing sound and Kat giggled.

Nick almost pointed out that Kat used to pick her nose when she was younger, but then he realized there were plenty of embarrassing things she could reveal to Helena about him, so he kept his mouth shut.

"Are you excited to go back to school and see your friends in the fall?" Helena asked.

"Yes," Kat said. "I like school!"
"Hey, maybe we're twins," Helena said. "I like school, too. Especially history. Sometimes I get bored in the summer. My friends are always traveling with their families, but my dad works for the government, so we never get to go on vacation. That's why I'm extra glad you and Nick showed up!"

"Ahh," Nick said, nodding. "You have a death wish. That explains so much."

"Haha." Helena stuck her tongue out at him.

Nick grinned. It was bizarre, sitting here enjoying himself after the day they'd had. But it wasn't all bad. They were alive, Kat's mind was protected from Horymir, they were safe in this house, and Prague still stood. That was a lot to be happy about.

There was a knock at the door. They all jumped.

"Mommy's back," Kat cried, climbing to her feet.

"No. Kat! Wait." Nick grabbed her arm.

Helena flipped open her phone. "It's only 8:30," she said. "It hasn't even been an hour."

"And Mom has a key." Nick exchanged glances with Helena.

Another knock. Louder this time. The sound echoed through the house. Kat whimpered, tucking herself behind Nick.

"It's okay, Kat." His voice sounded oddly brave in his own ears. "I'm not going to let anyone hurt you."

Pounding rattled the hinges of the door.

Helena took Kat's hand. Her wide eyes stared unblinking in the direction of the noise.

"You two stay here," Nick said as he walked to the entry hall.

It had gotten dark since Mom and Mr. Zeman left. Nick flipped the entry hall light off before opening the shuttered slats of the narrow window next to the door and flicking the porch light on.

The darkness outside shrank slightly, the single bulb casting a yellow glow over – or through, rather – a face that was barely there.

The 'man' standing outside wore a long wool coat over a vest over a nondescript button-up and black trousers – the same coat the antiques shop owner had been wearing, Nick was sure of it. But his clothes couldn't hide the fact that Nick could clearly see the row houses across the street through his head.

"What do you want, Horymir?" Nick asked loudly through the door.

"Ah, Master Nicholas." Even without a tangible body, Horymir's teeth gleamed pointed and yellow in the moonlight. "You already know my name, as I know yours, even though we have yet to become formally acquainted." His smile was sharp, eyes cutting into Nick's skull like hot wires. "But introductions will have to wait. I have come to retrieve an item in your possession that belongs to me. Be a good lad and open the door."

"Not in a million years," Nick said.

A hate-filled scowl passed over Horymir's face, but was quickly replaced with a wicked smile. "Oh, Katarina," he called. "Katarina, your brother is keeping a sharp little blade upstairs beneath the attic floor. Will you please bring it to me, dear?"

"Don't listen to him Kat," Nick said over his shoulder.

"Katarina, dear, remember the promise I made to you? I only need to retrieve some items from upstairs to finish the potion to cure your nightmares." The sorcerer's voice curled like a vine through the keyhole, sickly sweet. "Your brother must not know we are friends."

Nick looked over his shoulder at his little sister. She stood, fists clenched, with more color in her cheeks than he'd seen in weeks.

"You're *not* my friend!" Kat charged forward to stand beside Nick. Helena flanked her. "You're a creepy old man!"

All pretense of friendliness vanished from Horymir's features. "Shut up and do as you are told, you sniveling little brat!"

A gleam of silver from the edge of the lion pendant beneath Kat's pajama top caught Nick's eye. He grabbed her hand and said: "Kat, show him your pendant!"

Kat pulled the medallion out and held it up on its leather cord.

Rage gathered on Horymir's transparent face. He hissed, lunging forward, grappling at the doorknob, but it slipped through his fingers.

The phantom figure glowered at the door, but then he pulled his lips back from his yellowed fangs in a mocking smile. "That pathetic sigil may ward your little sister's dreams," Horymir spat at Nick, "but will it save her waking body? I think not."

Anger coursed through Nick. "There is nothing here that belongs to you."

"I am Horymir the Immortal!" the sorcerer seethed. "Open this door at once, I command you!"

Nick squared his shoulder, staring through the glass straight into Horymir's eyes. "The protection of the Brotherhood guards this house. You will *never* enter here!"

The words had flickered into Nick's mind from somewhere in his memory he couldn't place. One second, Horymir shouted his command and Nick stared back at him through the glass, unsure what to do or say, and the next second, the words were on his tongue – along with a surge of confidence he'd never experienced before. .

And as Nick spoke the words, the entire front doorway *glowed.*

Bluish white energy crackled as the runes sparked to life, beaming from where Damek had carved them.

The night outside illuminated so brightly that Nick had to shade his eyes. In that brief moment, he saw Horymir make another futile grab for the doorknob.

The sorcerer yanked back his hand as if burned. Smoke rose from his spectral form and the air around him sizzled like sparkles spitting tiny flames.

At that moment, headlights shone onto the porch as a car pulled up the street.

"When I return to my full strength, you will all kneel before me!" Horymir's words howled in a sudden gust of wind that shook the shutters furiously on their hinges, but it disappeared as quickly as it had come.

The sorcerer was gone.

"Nick!"

He turned at the urgency in Helena's voice, just in time to see Kat lose consciousness and collapse into Helena's arms.

Ignoring the pinpricks of adrenaline stabbing at his mouth and fingers, Nick rushed to Helena's side, helping her half carry, half drag Kat back to the couch and lay her down.

KNOCK KNOCK KNOCK

Nick nearly jumped out of his skin at the new sound at the door. He whipped around, fists raised, ready to punch Horymir in his immortal face, but lowered his arms as he recognized the sound of a key turning in the lock.

* * *

Mr. Zeman had helped them bundle Kat up and carried her to her room. Then he'd made a phone call.

His physician – an English woman named Dr. Smithe – had driven straight over. She put Kat on an IV drip of antibiotics and fluids. She'd pursed her lips at Kat's thready pulse and insisted on bed rest for at least the next two days. No exceptions.

Mom had wanted Kat to stay in her room so she could keep a close eye on her, but Kat begged to sleep in her princess bed, and Nick volunteered to sleep on a blow-up mattress Helena brought over from her house next door.

Kat, who'd woken up while Mr. Zeman carried her up to bed, dutifully agreed she'd rest after the doctor warned her she'd have to be admitted to the hospital otherwise.

Dr. Smithe told Mom that despite Kat's extremities being cold, her temperature was only slightly below normal. Her vital signs showed she was under stress, which the doctor attributed to Damek's death, international travel, and jet lag.

"We'll keep a close watch on her," the bespectacled doctor said, scribbling on her notepad. "Check her pulse, oxygen levels, and temperature every four hours. I'll be back after my rounds tomorrow, but you can call me with any concerns."

When the doctor had unbuttoned Kat's pajama shirt to listen to her heart, Mom gasped. "Kat, where did you get that? I told you not to handle your uncle's things!"

"It's okay, Mom," Nick said. "That's the pendant Damek sent with the book, remember? He left a note saying he wanted Kat to have it."

"Well, I suppose it's all right, then," Mom said, reaching for the leather cord. "But let's put it on the nightstand, sweetheart. It looks heavy, and I'd rather you not sleep with it on."

Nick's mind raced to come up with an excuse for her to keep it on, but before he could think of anything, Mr. Zeman, who'd been standing in the doorway, spoke up, directing his words at Kat: "You know, *davenka*, the Bohemian lion is a symbol of protection. Your uncle told me of this medallion. It has been in your family for centuries. He wore it to bed when he was young, to protect against bad dreams."

Mom sighed and withdrew her hand. "I suppose it wouldn't hurt if you wore it. Unless you think she shouldn't, Dr. Smithe?"

"I'd say let her keep it if it's of comfort," the doctor said in her clipped accent. "The cord is too long to become wrapped around her neck, and the medallion too large to be a choking hazard."

Now, everyone had gone and Nick lay on the air mattress pushed up against the princess bed listening to his little sister's steady breath. He could just see the thin, blue vein where Dr. Smithe had inserted the needle for the IV. His thoughts spun as he tried to process everything that had happened since Helena had knocked on Damek's door that morning.

The umbrella pole at the cafe.

Finding his uncle's message in the diary.

Kat fitting the key into the tiny lock and opening the wooden box.

Horymir knocking on the door and the glowing runes.

Kat collapsing.

Too many things in a year, let alone a day. But the thing Nick's mind kept going back to was that after Mr. Zeman convinced Mom to let Kat keep the medallion, he'd glanced at Nick, and winked.

CHAPTER TWENTY-ONE - The Legacy of Libuše

Nick floated above the street looking down past his own feet to see that it wasn't just any street he was floating above: it was Damek's.

Blink.

He hovered weightless in the air, but now he was right outside the window of Damek's study.

Nick knew he was dreaming; he knew it wasn't real. But if he hadn't known, Nick would have sworn he could float through the window and his uncle would wrap his arms around him in one of his famous bear hugs.

Blink.

Damek! He was there, peering out the same window Nick peered in!

His uncle's eyelids sagged with exhaustion. His body seemed thinner, more angular than Nick remembered.

Damek surveyed the street, but his focus seemed more inward, like some sort of enormous weight pinned him to the spot.

Blink.

Now, Nick stood in the study, gazing out the window at the street through eyes that didn't feel like his, his mind swimming with thoughts and worries that weren't his own. Next door, the lights shone in his neighbors' windows.

"That cursed wind has died down at last."

*Nick jumped at the sound of his uncle's sonorous voice before realizing it was coming from **his** mouth.*

Nick knew he was dreaming. But he also knew it was more than a dream. It was the kind of dreaming that ran in his family. The kind Damek said could help him figure out problems in the real world. So, could he control it? Or should he just go where the dream took him and observe?

Blink.

He didn't dare hope the evil in the wind had given up. But what if he'd confused it by transferring the protection of the Brotherhood to Nick? Maybe it no longer considered him a threat?

He must act quickly.

Moonlight spilled into his study. He retrieved the wrapped, rectangular package from the chaos of books, maps, and papers on his desk, examining its carefully taped edges. The parcel was addressed to Nicholas Damek Gordon in Park Ridge, Illinois.

Securing the bottom seam with one more piece of packing tape, he placed the package under his left arm and a flashlight in the deep front pocket of his trench coat. Then he walked through the corridor to the kitchen, turning off lights before opening the door and stepping into the night.

His tense shoulders relaxed a bit when he saw the streets were still empty.

Blink

Beneath the ghostly crescent moon, the crumbling markers grinned up at him like broken, crooked teeth crowding together in a gaping mouth.

The dry scuttle of fallen leaves racing toward him from between the tombstones was his only warning.

A supernaturally strong gust of wind snatched the gate from his hand, slamming it shut. Panicked, he pressed himself flat against the cemetery's stone wall, searching the darkness with the beam of his flashlight. The bright cone of light jerked crazily across the headstones, casting spectral shadows that did nothing to soothe his mounting fear.

But the wind died as quickly as it had arrived.

Breathing hard with both hope and dread, he peeled himself away from the stone wall, and stole into the graveyard.

The wind returned.

It did not touch him, but its howls intensified with every step he took, swirling a whirlwind of dirt and debris so thick around him, it nearly blinded him. He thrust his hands out in front of him, clutching the rune in one as if to shield himself from the attack. Again, the tempest faltered, and went still.

Dead leaves and small rocks rained down around him, no longer supported by the wind. He straightened his shoulders and blinked his eyes. He'd nearly reached the mausoleum.

A soft, sighing breeze whistled upward through the twisted branches of a huge, ancient tree growing along the cemetery walls.

CRACK!

His head whipped up. The tortured groan of heavy, gnarled wood splitting apart filled the night. He had just enough time to process the sight of an enormous branch plummeting toward him before it struck.

"Nicholas, he is coming!"

A voice called his name, but he couldn't tell where it was coming from. The pain in his head throbbed as if it might split in two. Disoriented, he stumbled backward.

"Nick, can you hear me?"

NICHOLAS. I AM HERE.

Nick shook his aching head, hoping to clear his vision, but the movement sent a wave of dizziness through him. His foot caught on an exposed root and...

Nick snapped awake, gasping.

For seconds that passed into minutes he sat on the air mattress, hugging his knees to his chest, trembling and rocking back and forth.

The afterimage of his dreams refused to fade as he came to consciousness...

Damek's presence that had been so strong in the dream left an empty ache in its absence. Horymir's voice echoed in Nick's ears; his yellow, jeering smile leered at him from a gaping black hole imprinted on the back of Nick's eyelids. He needed to make it stop. He needed to make it go away...

"Nick, honey? Can you hear me? I said Helena is here!"

CHAPTER TWENTY-TWO - Wenceslas Square

Much of Prague still slept when Helena set out from home in the early hours of the morning. But plenty of tourists filled Wenceslas Square to take in the famed sights of the picturesque city.

She stalked the perimeter of the growing crowds nervously, eyes darting in every direction. The space took up several blocks, featuring beautiful architecture, shops, and restaurants. The opera house and train station were just around the corner, and the Vltava River, with its ancient bridges, was only a short walk away. Even after hundreds – if not thousands – of times, the sight of it all rarely failed to bring a smile to Helena's face.

Today was an exception.

She hadn't slept well. Every time she'd closed her eyes, she'd seen Horymir's furious, translucent face leering at Nick, his bony fingers reaching for the doorknob. After hours of tossing and turning, she'd slid from her bed well before dawn, full of restless energy.

Horymir's threat that they would kneel before him boomed in her head. Every now and then as she walked, she glanced over her shoulder, sure she'd find someone – or some *thing* – sneaking up on her.

Subconsciously, her hand rubbed a small block of wood in her pocket, tracing the rune Nick had hastily carved into it before she left last night. He'd mimicked one of the symbols lining his window on each of the four sides. Hopefully, it would be better than nothing.

Realizing she was just going in circles, she set off for the rendezvous point for her first tour group's walk through the historical district. Slipping off her backpack, she sat next to it on the steps surrounding the Wenceslas statue in front of the museum. All the familiar scents and sounds filled the air as the shops opened up and down the streets.

A dust-devil kicked up at the edge of the square. Helena jumped to her feet, every muscle tensed and ready to flee as the dust steadily swirled closer and closer. It snaked its way across the sunbaked stones of the square until it was only a few yards from where Helena stood.

It disappeared. She let out a shaky breath and sat back down.

"Do you ever tire of all these filthy foreigners, my pet?" a soft voice spoke near Helena's ear. A cold breeze lifted the fine hairs on the back of her neck.

Whipping around, Helena saw a thin, crooked man in a black suit sitting on the step above her, a sinister smile tugging at the corners of his pale lips.

Her breath caught in her throat.

Here, in the light of the sun, Horymir's form looked...*wrong*. The too-large trench coat covered his frame like a thin sweater on a wire hanger. His gnarled hands stuck out from the sleeves like knotted branches of a diseased tree.

Helena scooted back to the edge of her step and scrambled to her feet. She reached into her pocket for the small block of wood.

It was gone.

"Now, Helena. Is that any way to greet a fellow Bohemian?" he mocked, reproach on his transparent face.

"I have no business with you," Helena said, unable to hide the tremble in her voice. "Leave me alone!" Furtively, she checked her other back pocket and found...

...a hole.

"Did you lose something, pet?" Horymir's cruel eyes narrowed. Then, without raising his voice he uttered a single command: "Sit."

Completely without her permission, her muscles moved to obey. Her legs folded, lowering her to the step. Her hands positioned themselves politely on her lap, mimicking Horymir's exactly.

"No!" she screamed, but the air stuck in her lungs, and her voice was a whisper.

"Shut your mouth and bite your tongue."

Helena's jaws locked, her teeth clamping down. Hard. The iron taste of blood slid across her tongue, filling her mouth.

With a flick of his wrist, Horymir tipped back her head and released her throat. She could swallow, blink, and move her eyes, but nothing more.

Eyes straining to follow his movements, Helena watched as Horymir leaned forward and beckoned with his fingers. Her backpack rose in the air and drifted to his feet. Another pantomime, and the front pocket unzipped itself.

In a slow, helicopter spin, the rune-covered wooden box rose from the bag, hovering in the space between them.

Helena blinked back tears. In all the chaos since they'd left the antiques shop, she'd completely forgotten she'd picked up the box after Kat dropped it in the street and put it in her bag.

"Did you really think you and your little friend playing knights and squires could thwart me, pet?" The sorcerer leaned in close, speaking in a low, intimate voice. "I am Horymir the Immortal, the greatest sorcerer who has ever lived. I knew at some point they would deduce who was actually responsible for the king's death. I knew they would come to cut me down. And so I prepared. *They* did not separate my body from my soul. *They* did not seal me in a box. I did. I placed myself in the resting place I had prepared and I have been waiting. I have been watching and listening for the right time. That time is now."

He only has the box, Helena told herself. *The book and the dagger are protected.*

"The book?" Horymir sneered. "What use have I of books?"

Horymir could hear her thoughts. There was nowhere to hide.

The sorcerer grinned, a cat toying with a terrified mouse. "As for the blade, all in good time, my pet." He waved his not-quite-solid fingers over a pigeon's's feather lying on the step next to Helena. It rose into the air as if tugged by a breeze and swayed back and forth, drifting and twirling wherever the sorcerer's hands moved. "I know you love Prague as much as I do."

Horymir's voice became gentle and rhythmic, almost hypnotic. "I have heard the tenderness and awe with which you speak of her history. You cannot imagine what it was like to walk these streets when the city was in its prime – when it was under *proper* rulership. Your modern rulers are no better than common pickpockets and thieves elected by other pickpockets and thieves to protect their interests."

Helena followed the motion of the feather, unable to resist the sorcerer's lulling voice. But at the mention of pickpockets, her eyes narrowed.

You're the filthy pickpocket, she spat mentally. *All you have is childish tricks. You don't even have a body. You're just a crooked old spook in a smelly trenchcoat!*

"Childish tricks?" The feather dropped to the ground. Horymir's mouth drooped, his thin lips quivering like a toddler who'd just been scolded. Then a sneer replaced his mock-sorrow. He raised his hand and pointed at Helena's shoulders with two of his fingers, which he slowly raised into the air.

Instantly, Helena was on her feet. The puppet master made little stepping motions around the palm of one hand with the fingers of the other, then flattened them. He cackled delightedly as she turned in a tight circle and sat down again. "Is it not easier like this, my pet? Dancing to someone else's tune? You need not ever worry yourself again with any thought at all. Once I have regained my strength, I ensure all your future thoughts will only be to please me and obey."

You and what army? Helena mentally shouted.

The wizened ghost leaned back as if reclining on an invisible throne. "Perhaps you've heard the tale of Rabbi Loew? You see, I did not merely slumber during my confinement. I learned much of happenings in the mortal world through the thoughts and dreams of my acolytes?"

The skin on Helena's legs crawled as if swarming with beetles. She'd told the story of Rabbi Loew – who could give life to inanimate objects – to a ghost tour group just last week.

The tale of Rabbi Loew isn't real. It's just a legend.

"Perhaps," Horymir's voice turned silky smooth and rhythmic again. "Though all legends contain some truth. There are many powers in this world, my pet. The blade – or dagger, as you call it – is but a part of one object of power, and it *will* be mine. And once I retrieve it, the army I will raise shall be undefeatable. The greatest the world has ever known. And I will control it just as easily as I now control you."

As he spoke, the box spinning slowly between them sped up, rotating faster and faster until it was a blur. In a sudden flash of purple lightning, it winked out of existence. Eyes stinging, Helena blinked rapidly, blinded by a bright yellow afterimage.

"As for my body," Horymir purred, hunger on his sallow face, "thanks to you, I now possess the tools to remake my flesh and blood from the ash it was reduced to by that wretched old knight and his squire. Once I am whole, nothing will be able to stop me."

The glee in his voice twisted Helena's stomach. She gathered her strength and hurled it against the invisible bonds controlling her limbs. She willed her arms to flail, her legs to kick and run, her mouth to scream.

Nothing.

"Tsk, tsk, tsk, my pet, you'll only hurt yourself if you struggle. Be a good girl and listen to me. If you fetch the blade and bring it to me now, I will spare your life and those of your friends and family when I seize control of Prague. I will even make you rich. Why, such an intelligent, resourceful young lady could do very well for herself under my rule. Consider it, my pet. Eybik ibn..."

Helena stopped struggling. Maybe Horymir *was* too powerful for a 13-year-old boy and a 14-year-old girl. Maybe it *was* useless to resist. Maybe restoring Prague to her former glory *wasn't* such a bad idea. If the sorcerer had the power to remake his body and raise an army he could control the way he was controlling her, what chance did they have? She had to protect her father...

"Yes, my pet. Yes, I will protect the ones you love. If you but fetch me the blade."

His voice dripped like rancid honey. Pushing away her thoughts, she gathered energy from her paralyzed limbs. She pooled all the breath in her body into her lungs. A sharp ache snaked through her temples; fear and lack of oxygen made her vision swim. She concentrated all her energy, her fear and dizziness, and her breath, amassing her entire will into a single, almost-solid thought. She held it all for one heartbeat, and then two.

She forced everything she held *out.*

"NEVER!"

Her cry echoed around the square. Tourists jumped and shopkeepers ran to the sidewalks and shoppers dropped their bags.

Helena sagged, draping her upper body over the two steps above where she sat, gulping in air.

After several moments of murmuring and pointed stares, the people in the square went back to their errands and jobs.

Slowly, Helena sat up. Her backpack lay open on the step above her. Horymir had vanished.

Hands shaking, she dug her phone from her front pocket sent a text:

'I'm sorry for texting so early, but I need your help.'

* * *

Helena pounded on the front door several times before remembering what Mr. Zeman said last night. She pulled her phone from her back pocket and sent a text:

'Sorry to bother you, Ms. Gordon. It's Helena. I'm at your front door.'

Moments later, Anna unlocked and opened the door. "I'm glad you texted, dear," she said, pulling a bathrobe over her pajamas. "I thought you must be one of those vagrants Mr. Zeman mentioned."

Arms wrapped around herself, Helena stepped inside. "I wasn't sure if my calls were going through. I'm so sorry to bother you so early. I hope I didn't wake you. Is Kat okay?"

"I've been up all night," Anna sighed. "Too wound up to sleep. I poked my head in her room about an hour ago. She and Nick are both out cold."

Helena winced. "That's good," she said. "I... I, um, was hoping to talk to Nick."

"Is something wrong, dear? You look pale."

"Just a chill," Helena replied. "I didn't sleep much either. I was worried about Kat. But if they're still asleep, I can come back later."

"You're fine, dear," Anna assured her. "I was actually getting ready to run some errands. I want to pick Kat up some medicine, and then I have a few things I need to take care of for the funeral. But you're welcome to stick around if Nick wants to hang out. And I'm sure Kat would appreciate the company too."

Helena froze in place. Fortunately, Anna was turned away looking for something in her purse. Helena had almost forgotten about the funeral with everything else going on. But beyond that, was Anna safe to leave the house? Would Horymir go after her just for being related to Damek and Nick? And how was she – a 14 year old girl – supposed to explain to an adult that they might be in danger if they leave the house because of an evil ghost?

"Hi, Mommy. Hi, Helena."

Kat stood on the staircase, clutching her Grogu squishmallow. Her long hair tangled around her head. Dark circles smudged the skin beneath her eyes and her lips were almost colorless.

"Sweetheart!" Anna hurried over to her daughter. She brushed Kat's hair back from her face. "Oh, honey, you look so tired. You should have stayed in bed."

"I'm cold," Kat said, voice faint, "and Nick keeps talking in his sleep."

"Oh no, I'm sorry, sweetheart. Let's bundle you up. Do you want to sleep in my bed? I think your uncle has a heated blanket here somewhere."

"Yes, Mommy," Kat said, swaying slightly.

"I can make her some cocoa," Helena offered, "I know where everything is."

"Does some cocoa sound nice?" Anna asked. Kat nodded and Mom picked her up. "Thank you, Helena. I'll wake Nick once I have her situated."

CHAPTER TWENTY-THREE - The Notebook

"Hey," Nick said, coming down the last flight of stairs. "I thought you had tour groups this morning. Is everything okay? I mean, besides everything obviously *not* being okay. Did something happen?"

"I called my boss at the last minute and canceled." Helena sat in Uncle Damek's chair, her hands fidgeting in her lap. She looked up at Nick, but a moment later her glance slid away, as if she was embarrassed.

The disquiet Nick had been unable to shake amped up to full-blown anxiety. "What happened? Are you okay?"

"Yes. I mean...no. I... I'm just really spooked."

"Yeah." Nick sat down heavily on the couch. "It took forever to fall asleep last night. I kept seeing his face. And then, when I did fall asleep..."

Helena covered her face with her hands. Her shoulders shook silently.

Nick was by her side in a flash, crouching next to the chair. He wasn't sure if he should put his arm around her or touch her leg or something. He patted her awkwardly on the back.

"I need to tell you something," she said. "Something awful."

"You can tell me anything, Helena."

She looked up, hands trembling a little. "Horymir showed up in the square while I was there."

Nick's back jolted straight. He stood up. "What? Are you okay? What happened?!"

"I'll..." Helena hesitated. "I'll explain everything, I promise, but I don't want to have to talk about it twice."

"Huh?"

"It's just, I wanted to get back here and inside the runes as quickly as I could. But I did something else, too." She hesitated. "Promise you won't be mad, but I might have..."

Three loud knocks rang out from the front door, cutting her off.

Nick crept out of the room and toward the front door. Helena emerged from the study behind him; for some reason, she didn't seem nearly as worried as him. Especially after apparently seeing Horymir again.

"Don't worry Nick, it's probably just..." She stopped herself, suddenly sizing up the door. "Except...I guess it's better to be safe than sorry."

Nick nodded. "Who's there?" he yelled, still not close enough to look through the peephole.

He jumped as a voice answered. It was even a voice he'd heard last night, too.

But not the one he'd been scared of.

"I admire your caution, Young Knight, but you have nothing to fear from me."

Nick stopped. "Mr. Zeman?"

He walked the rest of the way to the door, less anxious but still wary as he looked through the peephole. Indeed, the older attorney stood waiting patiently outside.

Nick opened the door a crack. "Um, hi, Mr. Zeman. Did you need something? My mom just left, and I'm not sure when she'll be back."

"Ah, I see that I've arrived before Helena could explain things. My apologies for the confusion."

"Before Helena could explain what?" Nick turned away from the door to look back at her.

"Nick, I was thinking about it all night. Damek had been investigating something before he died. His attorney just happens to get injured in a 'spelunking' accident right beforehand. You really think that's a coincidence?"

"So you're saying..." Gears turned in Nick's head, clicking into place one by one. "He was Damek's squire. He has to be! If every knight of the Brotherhood had one, then who else could it be?"

Mr. Zeman chuckled, drawing Nick's eyes back to the door. "Who else indeed?" He splayed his hands. "You two are very astute. Damek was right to put his faith in you."

With that, though, the attorney's face fell slightly. "He would be proud."

Nick looked down, not wanting the older man to see him tear up. He sniffed, then looked back up. "Um, well, we sure could use your help. But, um, I don't think Mom would like me letting an adult in while she's gone, even if it's you. I don't know how to explain all this to her either."

"Very conscientious of you, Young Knight. I presume, then, that I also arrived before Anna could make her call to Helena."

"Huh?" Nick said, just as Helena's phone started buzzing.

* * *

Mr. Zeman and Nick sat on the couch in the living room across from Helena, sipping some hot cocoa. Mom had called to let them know that Mr. Zeman was coming by to discuss some things with her and that she would be back soon but might not get there before he did. Before they sat down, Nick had checked on Kat. She was sleeping peacefully in Mom's bed.

"You didn't make yourself any cocoa?" Nick asked Helena.

She winced and shook her head. "No. My mouth is a little sore this morning. You know when you bite your tongue?"

"Ouch," Nick said. "I'm sorry. And I'm sorry to keep bugging you about it, but will you please tell me what happened with Horymir? I'm kind of freaking out."

"I, too, am quite anxious to hear what happened," Mr. Zeman said.

"Basically, I couldn't sleep so I went to Wenceslas Square to watch the sun come up. I thought I'd be okay. It was in public and there were plenty of people around. Plus, I thought I had the rune you carved for me in my back pocket," she said to Nick. "One minute I was sitting alone on the steps and the next there was a gust of wind and I turned around and he was there."

Nick's pulse pounded in his ears. He'd really hoped the runestone would work. He could only imagine how terrified Helena must have been.

She continued: "He...*locked*...my mouth so I couldn't talk, and then he made me march around in a little circle like a toy soldier and...he...he took the box. I'd completely forgotten it was in my backpack. I picked it up after Kat dropped it in the shop. I'm so sorry, Nick. I swear I didn't even remember I had it!"

Dread uncurled in Nick like leaves on a poisonous vine. It took him a moment to realize she was apologizing. "Are you kidding? You didn't do anything wrong, Helena. None of this is your fault."

"But you don't understand," Helena whispered. "He said he is going to remake his body. He commanded me to bring him the dagger, only he called it 'the blade.' He said that once he has his body back and gets the blade, he's going to build an undefeatable army to take over Prague."

"Did he say anything else, *davenka*?" Mr. Zeman asked, sitting on the very edge of the couch.

Helena nodded. "He asked if I knew about the legend of Rabbi Loew and the golem."

"Gollum?" Nick asked. "Like from Lord of the Rings?"

Mr. Zeman shook his head gravely. "Much worse, I'm afraid. Five hundred years ago, when the Jewish people living in the Prague ghetto were under attack, Rabbi Loew molded a giant golem out of straw and clay. He used words of power to bring the golem to life to help him defend his people. The golem had the strength of 20 men, did not feel pain, and could never die, as it had never been alive."

"That's not all, though," Helena said, eyes fixed on the table, hands clutched together in her lap. "He said that if I brought him the blade, he would spare me and my family. He said he would make me rich. What if he put a spell on me. What if I can't be trusted?"

"Well, did you?" Mr. Zeman asked, gazing deep into her eyes.

"Did I what?"

"Take   him   the   blade?"
"I... No. I didn't. But what if...?

"What did you do?" Mr. Zeman asked. "Instead of taking the blade to him?"

"I... I literally screamed at him louder than I've ever screamed before," Helena said, "and he vanished."

"You screamed at Horymir." Nick raised his eyebrows. "In the middle of Wenceslas Square. When you were under his control."

Helena paused, and hope flickered in her eyes. "Yes, I guess I did."

Mr. Zeman slapped his leg in approval. "This is why I am not worried."

Helena sat up a little straighter. "Really? You trust me?"

"Are you kidding?" Nick asked. "I trust you one hundred and fifty percent!" Then his shoulders drooped a little. "But what are we supposed to do? We've got the runes to keep us safe while we're in the house, but I'm the only one with the protection of The Brotherhood. I know I'm the heir or whatever, but there's no way I can do any of this by myself, not to mention I have zero idea how I'm supposed to find the clues to the weapon or whatever to stop Horymir."

"Do not discount the protection of The Brotherhood," Mr. Zeman said. "Without it, neither your uncle nor I would have made it out from beneath the mountain alive. I always enjoyed a modicum of protection when we were together."

"Beneath the mountain," Nick murmured to himself. "Spelunking." Images from his dreams of the door set in the mountainside flashed through Nick's mind. "Uncle Damek said he thought he could do what none of our ancestors had, that he could destroy Horymir. But he said he messed up and made things worse. What were you two doing beneath the mountain? How did he think he could destroy Horymir?"

Mr. Zeman opened his mouth to reply, but Helena beat him to it.

"By setting fire to his tomb," she said.

Eyes wide, Nick glanced from Helena to Mr. Zeman, who nodded a confirmation. "Did you have a dream, too?" he asked.

Helena shook her head. "No. Horymir basically told me. He said something about Damek and his squire turning his body to ash." She turned to Mr. Zeman. "And you said you were with him under the mountain. You mean Mount Blaník, right?"

"Very astute indeed." Mr. Zeman said.

"Mount Blanik?" Nick narrowed his eyes. "Where the knights of Blaník are buried?"

"According to legend," Helena said.

"According to fact," Mr. Zeman corrected. "The mountain's traditional name alone was enough to prompt the government to place a statue commemorating the knights at the mouth of a well-known entrance - on the wrong side of the mountain - along with a gift shop and a guided walk to attract tourists."

"Uncle Damek took me there," Nick said, "but he didn't say it was fake."

"He may not have known at the time," Mr. Zeman said. "And now, we are likely three of only four people in the world who *do* know the truth. Led by the diary, your uncle and I discovered the ancient entrance and the path to the burial chamber where the sorcerer's body had been entombed, guarded by runes and the Red Eagle, the sigil of the Knights of Blaník. I have not seen the place where the knights were interred upon their deaths, but Damek believed they were nearby, and that was enough for me. We thought to end the burden of Damek's lineage once and for all, but things did not go according to plan."

"It doesn't make sense!" Nick said. "I mean, I understand why Damek thought lighting Horymir's tomb on fire would destroy it, that makes sense, except then why wouldn't one of our ancestors have done it before?"

"That's what we need to figure out," Helena said. "Damek said he misinterpreted a passage or passages in the diary. He left a message saying we should find his notebook, that he'd translated the passage from an ancient language, though he didn't say which one."

"We looked for the notebook in his study," Nick told Mr. Zeman, "but it's like looking for a needle in a haystack. It could be anywhere."

"Something I can help with, at last." Mr. Zeman rose from the couch and limped quickly to the entry where he'd hung his windbreaker. He fished something out of his pocket and returned to the couch. "A municipal police officer called this morning to let me know they were releasing his personal effects. I was leaving the station when you called, *davenka*," he said to Helena. Reverently, he placed a smallish, nondescript notebook on the coffee table. "This was among them."

Nick recognized it at once. He didn't know if it was the exact same one Damek had carried when they'd last been together, but Damek had never gone anywhere without a similar notebook handy to record his observations in notes and sketches.

"What does it say?" Helena asked, on the edge of her seat.

"I came straight here," Zeman replied. "I have not opened it yet."

"You should, Nick," Helena said. "It belonged to your uncle, and you're the heir."

Silently, Nick picked up the small book and opened it. Instantly, his eyes swam with pages and pages of tight notes and intricate drawings in his uncle's strong, elegant penmanship. Flipping to the back, Nick thumbed through the pages until he found what he thought they were looking for: a poem five stanzas long, written in English. Each stanza consisted of two lines. The first stanza was underlined, and the second was highlighted in orange. It practically jumped off the page at him.

"This is it." He held out the book and made room on the couch for Helena. She sat down and leaned in close, as did Mr. Zeman while Nick read out loud.

Death piles stones twelve layers deep,
The Crimson Eagle sacred secrets keep.

Strike the light and fan the flame,
Without the body will the soul remain?

Time guards the key to hidden power,

A reflection of pride when the clock strikes the hour.

Beneath the place where heroes kneel,

The Knight and Squire will reforge steel.

Trust the Lion or all is lost

When Evil arrives at the Foot of the Cross.

"Oh, wow," Helena breathed, then tapped the highlighted stanza. "I saw this in the diary! I think I know what Damek got wrong."

Nick and Mr. Zeman looked at each other, raising their eyebrows. "Oh?" Mr. Zeman said, gesturing for Helena to continue.

"I couldn't translate much of the earlier stuff, but there were several places where the book stopped as I was thumbing through. You know, pages that had been read a lot, where it naturally fell open. And some of them had verses like this separated from the rest of the writing. Not all together like here, just two lines, which stood out to me. And one of them – this one – was underlined in pencil. I recognized the word 'soul'. But in the journal, that sentence wasn't structured like a question!"

"What do you mean?" Nick asked. "How can it *not* be a question?"

Helena took a deep breath. "Translating old languages like this can be tricky because the people who spoke them didn't always put their words in the same order we do today. So yeah, it might look like a question to us when it wouldn't to them. Imagine if the words were flipped around just a little so it read 'without the body, the soul *will* remain.' Also, we have to remember that this wasn't originally in English. I doubt it rhymed in whatever language it was written, that's probably just something Damek did because it seemed more natural. If you read 'the soul will remain' it's saying that even if you set Horymir's body on fire – strike the light and fan the flame – it won't get rid of him because his soul *will* remain. I could be wrong, but I don't think so."

"*I* think we're lucky you're so smart," Nick said, in awe. He knew she was right, the same way he'd known the verses were what they'd been looking for.

"The second stanza is what led Damek to believe we could end the threat by burning the sorcerer's body." Zeman's voice hitched with emotion. He began coughing so hard, Nick worried he'd run out of breath.

Helena pushed her glass of water into his hands, and he drank gratefully.

"Thank you, *Davenka*," Mr. Zeman said once his coughing fit had subsided. "My poor, brave friend," he lamented. "He was never one to take things lying down. Damek believed an acolyte seeking fame or power awakened the sorcerer, who then tried to infiltrate your uncle's dreams. Once he became convinced of the legend's reality, his goal was to end the threat and protect future generations – specifically your mother, your sister, and you – from its burden. I cannot imagine any scenario in which Damek would have sat back and waited for Horymir to attack."

"You're right," Nick agreed. "So he took the attack to Horymir. But Damek said he made the situation worse. How could lighting the tomb on fire set Horymir free if his soul was locked in the box?"

"We took the box with us," Mr. Zeman murmured. "Damek had it in his shirt pocket. I believe he meant to leave it there once the fire had been set, but the entire room exploded as soon as he struck the match."

"Oh no." Helena slumped back onto the couch.

In his mind, Nick watched the scene play out: the brief smell of sulfur as the match grated along the strike pad. A single orange flame flickering to life. The ancient trapped air in the tomb super-heating like a bomb. He groaned.

"The fire ate the air." Mr. Zeman's voice was quiet. "It howled as it chased us. We ran, but there was no oxygen to breathe and I stumbled, cracking a rib. Your uncle saved my life."

"Setting the corpse on fire must have released whatever magic was left in his body," Helena mused. "That's why your ancestors left the warning. They must have at least suspected that having the box and the body in close proximity would be bad, which is why they didn't bury the box in the tomb!"

"We released the wind." Mr. Zeman's voice was louder now, but also distant. "A single translation error defeated the great Dr. Maracek." He shook his head. "Damek spent hundreds, if not thousands, of hours of research to locate Horymir's burial place. In the end, he interpreted 'Death piles stones' as a reference to somewhere underground. That, combined with the legend of the King Wenceslas' knights entombing themselves beneath the mountain upon their deaths to protect Bohemia from a great evil...well, the pieces fell into place. "

"But what if...?" Helena sat up straight. Then paused.

"What if what?" Nick asked, not looking up from studying a charcoal sketch Damek had made of what looked like a map of some sort of catacombs.

"'Death piles stones twelve layers deep,'" Helena repeated, eyes widening. She turned to Mr. Zeman.

"What is it, *davenka?*" Mr. Zeman asked.

"Twelve layers deep! When I take tour groups to the Old Jewish Cemetery, I tell them that because Prague wouldn't give the Jewish people any more land, they had to bury their loved ones stacked up. In some places, they're twelve layers deep."

Nick watched as Mr. Zeman's mouth fell open. His lips moved, but Nick couldn't hear what he said. An image of the landscape from last night's dream rose in his mind: Damek picking the lock of a heavy iron gate, casting the beam of his flashlight around him to reveal slabs of crumbling stone markers.

"Nick?"

Helena's voice snapped him back to the present. He looked around at them, dazed, the howling laughter on the wind, the tortured crack of splintering wood, the sight of the heavy branch plummeting straight at him. But he had to tell them if it would help solve the riddle and stop Horymir.

"I had a dream last night," he said, fighting to keep his voice calm. He looked at Helena. "More than a dream. I saw Damek. He was somewhere that sounds exactly like what you're describing. I didn't recognize it at first – I just thought it was a bunch of weird stones. But it had to have been the Old Jewish Cemetery! He was searching for something, and the wind was following him. It made a huge tree branch fall..." He glanced at Helena and trailed off. "I think it was the night he died."

Silence swallowed the sitting room for several seconds.

"Young knight," he intoned, "why don't you describe your dream to us. From the beginning, if you don't mind."

CHAPTER TWENTY-FOUR - Midnight in the Cemetery

"...then the branch fell, and I woke up." Nick wiped away a tear as he recounted what he now knew to be his uncle's last moments; he hadn't even realized he'd been crying until now that he was done talking. His cheeks flushed when he realized, but only for a little bit. He didn't think he'd cried about any of this since maybe the first night he'd learned about Damek's death. Usually, crying in front of people – a girl and an adult, no less – would be the peak of embarrassment for him. Right now, it couldn't feel more right.

Besides, Helena's eyes were almost as wet as Nick's as she stared at Mr. Zeman. "Was Damek found in the Old Jewish Cemetery?"

Mr. Zeman bowed his head and made the sign of the cross. "I'd meant to relay this directly to your mother, but..." He paused for a moment as he dabbed a handkerchief to the corner of his own eye, "Yes. Your uncle was found in the Old Jewish Cemetery. You are a dreamer, young knight, just like Damek."

"Rabbi Loew is buried in that cemetery," Helena breathed, her eyes bright with intensity.

"That settles it." Nick locked eyes with Helena. "We *need* to go to the Old Jewish Cemetery. Like, right now."

"Whoa there," Mr. Zeman said. "You mustn't be hasty. Damek died in that cemetery. Clearly, Horymir will go to great lengths to prevent the knight from discovering the weapon that can destroy him."

"The night before he passed, I dreamt Damek passed the protection to me. I just didn't know what it meant at the time. But I've dreamt it since then, too. I think Damek did it because he believed Kat and I were in danger. He should never have left the house without it."

"I agree with you, young knight. But neither you nor I could have stopped him once he had his mind made up. And believe me when I say that although I didn't understand – or even agree with – your uncle's reasons and decisions, he was fully committed to them. To blame yourself would be disrespectful to his memory." Mr. Zeman was seized by another coughing fit.

Helena ran to the kitchen to refill the glass of water, returning quickly and handing it to him.

After drinking and composing himself, Mr. Zeman said, "My apologies. I suppose I still have some recovery ahead of me. Nicholas, it is admirable of you to pick up this task so readily, but none of us have the level of experience or knowledge your uncle possessed. I beg you, give me a little time to conduct more research, and then we can go together to the cemetery tomorrow. I can't imagine the police would be thrilled to find you sneaking around without permission, especially after your uncle's death. Besides, if Horymir is busy remaking his body, I'm confident you can wait one more day, at the very least."

"I don't think I can just sit here," Nick said, his knee bouncing with nervous energy. "I'll go crazy."

"You haven't had a moment's rest since you arrived," Mr. Zeman said. "I'm not asking you to nap, but you can look after Kat. Read the diary, perhaps, and explore your uncle's office. It is quite literally a treasure trove. You must be fully prepared if we are to overcome this evil.

"And I guess we need to guard the dagger, too," Nick said.

"Indeed, though I wouldn't fret over that too much," Mr. Zeman said. "As was demonstrated last night, the wards your uncle inscribed on the house seem to be holding Horymir at bay. As long as the dagger remains within the boundaries of his house..."

"The blade," Helena cut in. "Horymir called it a blade. He wants it badly. I think he needs it for his plan."

Mr. Zeman scratched his chin. "Odd that he is fixated on it. The dagger – or blade – has been passed down through centuries, though Damek never mentioned it, other than to say it was part of his inheritance. Still, the sorcerer wanting it is enough reason for us to keep from him. Hmmm. I wonder..."

After several seconds during which Mr. Zeman stared intently at his large hands, Nick finally interrupted his silence. "Wonder what?" he asked.

The old squire shook himself, returning to the present. "Oh, nothing, young knight. A sudden, wild hunch. An idea, at least, of where to start my research."

"I guess that's better than nothing," Nick said. "And tomorrow we'll go to the cemetery together. What time does it open?"

"Nine o'clock," Helena said.

"It's settled, then." Mr. Zeman rose from the couch. "Trust in each other, and keep each other safe. That goes especially for you Nick: trust your squire and guard your sister with your life. The fate of Prague may depend on it."

"Your mom is back," Helena said, nodding out the window as Anna walked up the alley carrying several reusable grocery bags. Helena stood up and went to the door just as her phone buzzed. "Perfect timing, too, because

I have to go," she said, after reading her text. "My dad's come home for an early lunch and wants to speak with me.

"Is everything okay?" Nick asked.

Helena nodded. "He probably just left something behind and came back for it. And I left before he was up, so he might just want to say hi." She turned back to them. "Mr. Zeman, please text me if you have any news, and I'll come over right away to let Nick know. And Nick, if you need anything, I'll just be next door."

"Same goes for you," Nick said. "I'll be here all day. And Helena, I'm really sorry about what happened this morning."

"None of this is your fault," Helena said, her hand on the doorknob. "We've just got to figure this out."

* * *

Helena's father, Jiri, was waiting for her when she came through the kitchen door. "Good morning, young lady," he said from his seat at the small dining table. He'd set out two cups and a plate of scones. "You were gone before I left this morning. Mind joining me for a quick tea?"

"Papa!"

Jiri opened his arms wide and beckoned his daughter in for a hug. "I hope I haven't interrupted any plans you've had with Damek's niece and nephew."

Helena gave him a bear hug, then sat down in the chair next to him. "Not at all," she said "I was just chatting with Nicholas and Mr. Zeman, actually. We don't have any plans for today. Katarina – Damek's great niece – has gotten ill, so I think they'll all be staying in. Besides, I have some summer reading assignments I've been trying to catch up on."

"You look a little pale yourself, Lena," Jiri said, "and you feel cold. I hope you haven't caught the little girl's illness."

Helena shook her head. "The doctor said she isn't contagious. I just woke up early and couldn't get back to sleep, so I went to Wenceslas square to watch the sun rise. I guess I am a little sleepy." She shivered, and rubbed her arms. "And a little cold. It's been so windy lately."

"Yes, it has." He filled her cup with hot tea and pushed it toward her. "Well, I hope you'll have a chance to slow down today," Jiri said. "You've certainly been busy showing the Gordons around."

"I really like them, Papa, but I'm sad for them, too." She sipped her tea. "It's their first time visiting the city in so long, and they're here for such a sad reason. But Nick knows so much about Prague already. I'm actually learning things from him!"

"Are you, now?" Jiri asked. "And quite a handsome boy, judging from what I saw just now through the window." He winked at her playfully, and Helena rolled her eyes. "Now," he said, his tone becoming serious, "you know I trust you to look out for yourself, but please be extra careful this week. Prague is usually such a safe city, but there have been some odd things happening lately."

Helena tensed. "What kinds of odd things? Anything serious?"

"You mentioned the wind," Jiri said, setting an unfinished scone back on his plate. "Well, people have been calling in to report that they're being 'attacked' by it. There was some sort of...weather event...yesterday at an antiques shop in Old Town yesterday, and apparently the wind was strong enough that it sent an umbrella flying straight into a plate glass window. But it isn't just the wind. Several tourists rang the embassy this morning to report seeing a transparent figure harassing an adolescent in Wenceslas Square this morning. You didn't happen to see anything, did you?"

Beneath the table, Helena's hands gripped the edge of her seat. "I... It all sounds so strange, Papa."

"Normally, I would agree with you," Jiri said, voice grim. "But I've seen footage of several people seemingly being pushed onto tracks at the metro, only no one pushed them." He paused for a moment, dabbing the side of his mouth with a tea towel. After setting it down, he reached for Helena's hand. "I'm not trying to frighten you, Lena, just to ask that you be vigilant when you're out. A man was found dead in an alley last night. His clothes and all his personal effects had been taken."

"Oh no."

"You're cold as winter, Helena!" Jiri exclaimed. He rose from the table and retrieved a blanket from the living room couch, which he tucked around Helena's shoulders. "I'm sorry for upsetting you, but I'm glad you understand how serious this is. Prague is one of the safest cities in Europe. I considered asking you to stay in and cancel your tours until things settled down, but I don't want to be alarmist. You have your mother's keen perception, and I trust you to make good judgments. Just please be safe."

Helena nodded. "I will, Papa." She hoped he didn't hear the anxiety in her voice.

He squeezed her hand. "That's my girl. Now, I'd best be getting back to the office. The Prime Minister has called a session of parliament, and I'll want to be prepared." He placed the back of his hand against Helena's forehead. "You don't have a fever. Are you sure you haven't caught something?"

"I'm fine, Papa," she said, sitting up straight. "Just thinking of that poor man."

He smiled and stood up, seemingly satisfied with her answer. As he left the room, Helena tugged the blanket around her as tight as she could.

But no matter how hard she pulled, she couldn't get warm.

* * *

Nick couldn't sleep.

The day had dragged on forever. He'd tried exploring in Damek's study but couldn't seem to focus on anything. Then he'd read practically the entire *Legends of Old Bohemia* to Kat while she rested in Mom's bed. Several times, he stopped reading and shut the book, sure she'd fallen asleep. Yet every time the cover closed, her eyes would pop open and she'd stare up at him begging him to keep reading.

How could he refuse? She lay so still, so limp and pale and cold; Nick was afraid she'd wither away and disappear. Every second his brain spun like a hamster on a wheel, searching for something he could do – anything – to make Kat well.

When the book was done, Mom took a turn sitting with Kat. Brimming with nervous energy, he'd gone up to the attic and fiddled around with the marionettes and scoured through Damek's notebook while keeping a close eye on the roof in case Helena came out.

She didn't.

Twice, he'd almost gone to knock on her door. But she'd said she'd come over if she heard anything from Mr. Zeman, so he just had to trust that everything was okay.

If something bad had happened, you'd know, he told himself. But it didn't *feel* good. It felt like he'd set loose an ancient evil sorcerer on Prague and was just sitting around doing nothing to stop him from remaking his body and raising an unbeatable army.

From three stories below, Nick heard the grandfather clock strike 11:00 P.M. He adjusted his position in bed again and groaned. No matter how he laid or how many pillows he put under it, his hip, knee, and ankle of his bad leg wouldn't stop yelling at him. He threw back his covers and sat up. Surely Mom had packed some ibuprofen. Hopefully, she wasn't asleep yet.

Tap-tap-tap-tap-tap!

Spinning on his heel, Nick crouched down, out of the moonlight, eyes scanning the window like a hawk. The runes didn't light up, and he didn't hear any wind. Had he imagined it?

"Are you going to let me in, or what?"

Helena!

Nick scrambled up on the bed and unlatched the window. "You almost gave me a heart attack!"

"Shhhh," Helena hushed him as she climbed in through the window and dropped to the bed. "Keep your voice down. As much as your mom likes me, I doubt she'd be thrilled with you letting a girl in through your window at night."

Nick blushed. He actually wasn't sure if Mom would be more upset or surprised, but he didn't want to risk finding out. "Thank God you're here, I've been going crazy! Did Mr. Zeman text?"

"No, I haven't heard from him."

"I keep telling myself that no news is good news."

"Not today," Helena grimaced. "I'm guessing you haven't been online or watching TV or anything?"

"The only TV is in Uncle Damek's room where Mom is sleeping. Why? What's going on?"

"My dad said weird things are happening all over Prague."

Her half-guilty, half-concerned frown made Nick's restlessness take on an anxious edge. "Tell me," he said.

"Most of it was about us, actually. The umbrella breaking the window, the mess at the antiques shop, and my little run-in with Horymir in the Square this morning..."

"Did you tell your dad about what's going on?" A strange hopefulness surged in Nick. "The government is way more powerful than I am. We should have told them straight away, they can handle this!"

Helena shook her head. "I didn't tell him. I feel terrible keeping secrets from him. But Nick, you're wrong. The government probably won't do anything about what they'd assume is just a ghost story. Damek would have gone to them if he thought they could do something. But I think we're running out of time. Other things are happening too. Really bad things. People are getting hurt. People are dying. I don't think we can wait for Mr. Zeman to finish his research. I think we need to go to the cemetery now."

"I figured," Nick said. He didn't even ask specifics about what her dad had told her. What good would it do? "You got some flashlights in there?" he asked, nodding at the rucksack slung across her back.

"Absolutely I do, but...wait, so you agree?"

Nick grinned. "I know I worry a lot, but you're right. Damek asked us to deal with this, and now that's all we can do. I know Mr. Zeman just wants to keep us safe, but we can't just do nothing while Horymir is out there hurting people. Not when it's our responsibility to stop him."

Now it was Helena's turn to blush and look away. "Thank you for trusting me, Nick," she said. "But you said 'us,' and we both know Damek trusted *you* specifically to handle this."

He shrugged. "Every knight needs their squire."

A cold breeze blew in through the window. Helena shivered and zipped up her thick sweatshirt.

"Hey, are you okay?" Nick asked.

"I mean, not really. I'm kind of freaking out."

"No, I mean..." Nick didn't want to say she looked bad, but she absolutely did. The shadows under her eyes and in the hollows under her cheekbones made her face more angular than usual. "Are you hungry? We can eat something before we go?"

"I haven't had much of an appetite," Helena shrugged. "Plus, we need to hurry. We're running out of time."

Nick turned and stared out at the dark night sky so Helena wouldn't see the alarm on his face. She was sick, the same way Kat was sick. "Maybe you should stay and get some sleep," he said. "I can go to the cemetery by myself."

"Ha!" Helena covered her mouth with both hands to quiet her laughter, but it poured out her eyes and her body shook until she was gasping for breath.

"It's not that funny," Nick grumped. "I was being serious."

Helena wiped her eyes and laid back on the bed, catching her breath. "Thank you," she sighed. "I needed that."

"So glad I could help." Nick rolled his eyes, but was happy to see the color had returned to Helena's face.

"You ready for this?" Helena asked.

"Absolutely not." Nick shook his head. "You?"

"Nope," she said, determination glowing in her eyes. "Let's go."

* * *

Fifteen minutes later, Helena led Nick through the ticket-booth leading to the Jewish Cemetery. A key from her keyring opened a locked door labeled 'Pouze Zaměstnanci: Employees Only.' After a short corridor, another door opened into the night air.

Nick and Helena quietly stepped out into the cemetery, the beams of their flashlights dancing over the crumbling gravestones. The markers tilted at odd angles, casting grotesque, elongated shadows. Nick shuddered as he surveyed the graves all stacked on top of each other, just as they had looked in his dream. The air seemed thick with tragedy and suffering. Nick shivered and imagined weeping families burying their loved ones on top of the graves of other loved ones.

"How are we supposed to find one tombstone in thousands?"

"There's only one Rabbi Loew, and luckily, *everybody* knows where his grave is."

"Not *everyone*," Nick said.

"Right," Helena amended. "Luckily *I* know where his mausoleum is. You're very fortunate to have me as your squire. Not that you really had any choice."

He knew she was trying to lighten the mood by teasing. He just wished it actually helped. "There's no one else I'd rather have as my squire. I'm so glad you're here."

Helena ducked her head, and Nick could have sworn her cheeks turned red.

"Come on, she said. "It's this way."

They worked their way deeper into the graveyard, squeezing past the narrowly packed tombstones as respectfully as they could. Nick only just avoided scraping both his knees and one of his elbows as Helena came to a stop in front of him.

"We're here." She shined her light on the gravesite in front of them.

"Wow," Nick muttered. Even without Helena guiding him, he would have known this spot was important. The memorial was shaped like a church, only miniature, with a tall entrance and rear, and a lower section connecting the front and back. He trained his light on the front of the mausoleum, taking in moss stains covering the time-gouged symbols carved on the grave. "This doesn't look like Czech." Nick pointed at the etched figures.

"It isn't," Helena confirmed. "It's Hebrew."

"Is your Hebrew as good as your English and ancient Bohemian?"

"Ummmmm...no," Helena admitted. "I only started studying it recently. But that's why we brought your camera."

"This is stupid." Nick couldn't keep the frustration from his voice. "We're running out of time! Couldn't we have found pictures of Rabbi Loew's mausoleum on the internet or at the library? How will taking pictures help?"

"There must be something here, or Damek wouldn't have come here that night. He's seen this marker a thousand times. I don't have any other ideas, Nick. If you do, I'm happy to listen to them. This is where all the clues lead: your dream, Horymir's obsession with Rabbi Loew, the first stanza in the poem. We have to try."

"You're right," Nick said. "I'm sorry."

"Good, because I know someone who speaks Hebrew. And I'm pretty sure he'll help. Don't worry, I can vouch for him."

"I don't care who it is. If you trust him, so do I."

The snap of a twig nearby stole the breath from Nick's lungs. He froze, not even daring to blink. For a moment, everything went quiet.

Then he heard it: shuffling footsteps, moving closer. From the corner of his eye, he saw Helena motioning for him to follow. She ducked behind a large tombstone and clicked off her flashlight. Nick copied her exactly, plunging everything into darkness just as the vague outline of a large man appeared a stone's throw away. He lumbered along the narrow path between the grave markers in their direction.

Nick's heartbeat hammered in his ears. *Is it Horymir? Has he already reformed his body?*

Helena peeked around the grave marker, then whispered. "It's the night security guard. I'll distract him. You take as many pictures as you can. Quick!"

Before he could protest, Helena leaped to her feet and took off noisily down the path.

The security guard yelped in surprise, springing into action. "Stůj!!" he yelled, running right past Nick in hot pursuit of Helena down the narrow dirt path between the grave markers.

Nick waited until the guard was out of sight before inching out from behind the tombstone. *I hope she runs faster than I do,* he thought. For a moment, he paused, listening for the sound of a struggle, but could only hear the gentle rustling of the leaves on the trees. *Trust your squire!* he told himself.

Shadows grew thick around him as he made his way back to Rabbi Loew's mausoleum. Fumbling at the strap, he lifted the camera from around his neck. Making sure the flash was on, he started taking quick bursts of pictures from left to right, top to bottom, like he was reading a book.

Every time the flash went off, Nick squeezed his eyes shut, trying to avoid the blinding bright light. *What if there's more than one guard? What if Mom wakes up and sees that her keys are missing and then checks my room and sees that I'm missing? She'll call the police for sure!*

NICHOLAS!

Startled, Nick looked up instinctively to where he could have sworn he'd heard Damek's voice calling his name. Of course, no one was there.

Except... What was that moving up in the tree?

CRACK!

Nick covered his face with his hands as he fell onto the ground, waiting for the impact he knew would be coming any second.

Click!

What was that?

It took several heartbeats for Nick to realize that there was no tree branch plummeting down toward him. It had been a trick of his imagination, replaying the moment he'd seen in his dream. The image Uncle Damek had seen right before his death.

He felt sick. But he couldn't think about that right now. Picking himself up, searched the grass around him for his camera. *That must have been the clicking sound I heard.* Once he had it pointed the right way, he began taking more photos from random angles, moving as quietly as he could around the entire marker. The underbrush and headstones in front of him lit up, illuminated repeatedly by the camera's flash.

Beepbeepbeep!

The memory stick was full. Crap.

Crouching low, Nick blinked slowly, waiting for the afterimages to disappear.

A shadow darted from one gravestone to another, coming back down the path Helena had taken only minutes before, but coming toward him. Something *sparkling?*

Was this another trick of his imagination? He blinked again to clear his vision.

No. It was real. Helena's dangling silver star earrings reflected the pale moonlight, sparkling.

"Helena!" he whispered.

"Nick?"

He stood up and switched on his flashlight.

"Oh thank God," she exhaled sharply, joining him on the path. "You nearly gave me a heart attack! Come on, let's get out of here. I gave the guard the slip over by the gate near the back."

"Gave him the slip? What are you, a ninja?"

"Hardly!" She took a ragged breath. "I got all freaked out by myself out there in the dark. I kept seeing shadows everywhere. I thought you were Horymir for a second." She paused, still breathing heavily. "Weren't you scared?"

"Terrified. But I got as many photos as my camera could hold. Now what?"

"Now we go home and try to get some sleep," Helena said. "I'll be outside your house at seven o'clock. Set an alarm, okay?"

"Can you at least tell me where we're going? And shouldn't we text Mr. Zeman first?"

"We're not going anywhere dangerous. And I'm not texting Mr. Zeman at one in the morning. If everything goes to plan, we'll be home before he's finished his breakfast and we can tell him then."

"Great," Nick said as he followed her out of the cemetery. "But can you least tell what the plan is?"

"Oh, right." Helena cleared her throat. "Tomorrow, young knight, we'll be visiting the Old New Synagogue."

CHAPTER TWENTY-FIVE - The Old New Synagogue

Nick floated in endless mist while the thunderous pounding of fists against a wooden door filled his ears.

This is a dream, he told himself. The same dream I had the night Damek died.

As if on cue, the mist separated, revealing Damek as Nick had seen him before, desperately pressing his back against a barely-closed door, trying with all his might to keep whatever was on the other side from getting out.

Horymir.

Why do I have to see this again? *he thought, barely able to look at his uncle, at the fear and sorrow so plain on his face.* I already know Horymir escapes. I already know he manipulated Kat. But she has the pendant now. It must be Horymir trying to mess with my head. There must be a way to wake myself up, or at least go somewhere else...

"Štít projde. Nicholas, rytíř i řádu, čas nést toto břemeno je nyní na tobě."

Damek spoke the words loud and clear this time – not muffled like before. But that wasn't the only difference. Nick could see the words, too. They formed in corruscating golden light, floating around him. Suddenly, the letters shimmered and shifted, morphing from Czech to English.

'The shield will pass. Nicholas, knight of the Brotherhood, the time to bear this burden is now yours.'

A deep tremor of emotion ran through Nick, combined with a strange kind of confidence that seemed to flex around him like invisible, shatter-proof glass.

The splintering of wood yanked his attention away from the glowing words to where Damek pushed back against the door, just in time to watch his uncle's body launch through the air as the door exploded, sending debris flying in every direction.

No! *Nick shouted,* **NO!**

But there was nothing he could do. This dream had already come true. He'd been right about Damek passing the protection of the Brotherhood before his death.

Nick's heart weighed too much for his body, but he knew he couldn't undo the past. As he watched, evil poured out from its prison and surged forward. Frantically, Nick turned, searching the mist for Kat, but couldn't find her. Instead, Horymir's formless presence shot straight at him.

Every instinct told him to run, but just as the shapeless malevolence rose to swallow him whole, the words hovering around Nick sparked brilliant white, as if all the energy in the entire world had been funneled through the radiant script. The light blinded him, plunging the dream into violent afterimage shades of violet and indigo.

A rage-fueled scream pulsed around him, piercing his eardrums. Just as he thought they would burst, it vanished entirely.

As the light faded, he found himself standing in a new place: a ruined cobblestone street on the outskirts of some ancient town.

He wasn't just in a new place. He was in an entirely new body. Not Damek's, like in the dream he'd had the previous night.

In this dream, he wore a tunic of chainmail from neck to knee and shoulder to elbow, topped with a heavy metal breastplate. Thick, leather gauntlets protected his hands and forearms, and steel-toed boots rose to the middle of his thighs.

"Hold true, Ansel."

Nick turned as a heavy hand grasped his left shoulder from behind. It belonged to an old, grizzled man dressed the same as he – Ansel, he guessed – wore, and sporting a scar that crossed his right eye.

"Have faith in our protection, young knight. The sorcerer cannot harm us physically."

Nick's hand fell to his chest. Resting there was a pendant: a twin to the one Nick had given Kat down to the exact detail, only it felt fresh in his hands, thrumming with newly bestowed power. Still, Nick hesitated. Nick's lips moved of their own accord, and a man's voice escaped. "You saw what he did, Bodhi. He bewitched Boleslav, the King's own brother. What hope do we have?"

Bodhi grimaced. "You are young, Ansel, barely raised from a squire, so you have not witnessed Boleslav's greed. It did not take much to bewitch him. Rest sure, the protection of the brotherhood safeguards our bodies, and the lion protects our dreams. But more importantly, as Knights of Blaník, it is our duty to safeguard the kingdom. We must stop the sorcerer before he can inflict more harm."

Nick watched through the eyes of the young Knight Ansel as he fell into step with half a dozen other knights behind Bodhi, who approached the stone dwelling of the local herbalist and healer. The wooden door seemed wedged into its crumbling stone archway, like it had been forced into position after the fact.

Without hesitation, Bodhi raised his foot and kicked the door. It crashed to the ground with a single, solid thud.

Light from the midday sun spilled into the small hut, revealing gnarled roots and pungent herbs hanging in bunches from the low ceiling. Countless strange curios crowded the shelves in the miniscule dwelling. At its center a figure hunched low over a tall, cluttered worktable, chanting as he mixed something with a mortar and pestle. The curtains had all been pulled tight.

The knights stood shoulder to shoulder in the small room. They drew their swords. The figure paid them no heed.

"Sorcerer!" Bodhi's voice commanded attention.

"Good sir Knight." The sorcerer set down his mortar and turned from his work, bowing low and sweeping his hands toward the shop's dirt floor. In one of his hands he clutched a small, unadorned box. "I am yours. Take me where you will, I will not resist."

By way of answer, the knights stepped forward as one, raising their swords to heart level and aiming them at the sorcerer.

"I see." Horymir sneered. "Do what you will then."

Clearly, the sorcerer knew they were coming and had prepared some enchantment to defend himself with. But it didn't matter. Confidence surged through Ansel's body as he held the sword in his hand. The weight felt good – right – almost as if it were an extension of his body and mind. He was proud to have been the one chosen to wield it. He would cleanse the kingdom of this evil sorcerer once and for all!

Shock filled Nick's mind as he – as Ansel – lunged, swinging the sword at Horymir's neck.

"You've done it!" Bodhi exclaimed. "The evil is finally..."

The sword shattered in Nick's hand. A burst of light filled the room, and...

Nick startled fully awake at the first buzz from his watch alarm and sat up straight in the attic bed. It was 6:30 A.M., just under four hours since he'd climbed in bed after getting back from the cemetery.

Oddly enough, he wasn't tired. Maybe it was just the adrenaline from the dream spilling over into real life. Details flooded his senses, not like the other dreams that had been hazy and confusing.

"You're a dreamer, Nick," he said out loud. "This is important." He knew he had to remember as much as he could. *Write it down.*

Grabbing the notebook he'd borrowed from Mom yesterday and a thick workman's pencil from the workbench, he started scribbling.

1. Pounding on the door
2. Damek holding the door
3. Damek passes the protection to me
4. Door breaks, Damek flying through the air
5. Evil pours out and flies straight at me

He paused, pencil in the air. A lot of that was a repeat of his previous dream, except this time he knew he was in a dream and knew what was going to happen. Up until the evil targeted him. Last time, it had gone for Kat.

Okay, obviously Horymir can't attack Kat anymore, so he's coming for me. Nothing new there. And I'm getting better at dreaming. That's good, if I can use it to help us figure out the clues. The dream from the night before led us to the Old Jewish Cemetery and Rabbi Loew's mausoleum, but we still don't know if we've found anything.

The same frustration he'd felt in the cemetery reared up in him again. What good was it to be a dreamer if he couldn't figure out what his dreams meant?

Focus, he told himself. *Remember: we have to try.*

Pressing his pencil to the page again, Nick went back to the dream.

6.   I'm a knight named...

Crap! Why can't I remember his name? Adam? No, something more unusual. Axel?

Panic gripped Nick as he grasped at the images from his dream that had been so vivid only moments before. Now, when he reached for them, they slipped through his fingers, fading faster and faster the harder he tried to hold on.

Something about being a knight and kicking in a door...Horymir's door!...and an old vegetable smell, like mold, but that couldn't be important. Unless it was. His fingers and palms thrummed with his pulse, as though he had just released an incredibly tight grip on something he couldn't seem to remember.

Groaning, he dropped the pencil and fell back on his pillow.

I suck at dreaming.

A second alarm went off on his watch. It was 6:45 A.M. He'd slept in his clothes, so he rushed to brush the cotton from his mouth and put on a double layer of deodorant, then hurried down the stairs, notebook and pencil in hand.

Tearing off a sheet of paper, Nick scribbled a quick note in case he wasn't back before Mom realized he was gone. He had no way of even guessing what his day would entail, but he didn't want to stress Mom out more than she already was.

* * *

"And here, we can see a stunning example of 19th century sculpture work," the tour guide swept a single hand to his right, indicating the large statue of a man on a horse that dominated the square, flanked by four smaller statues of standing saints on each of its corners.

Members of the tour group 'oohed' and 'aahed' appreciatively.

"Sculpted by Josef Václav Myslbek, this particular statue depicts none other than Wenceslas the First," the guide continued. "If that sounds familiar, it's because the whole square is named after him!" He waited until the chatter amongst his group died down, then held up a finger. "If you think that's impressive, just wait until you see *this!*"

He turned to face the statue behind him, pointing to the nearest standing figure. "If you look closely, you can see the earliest known example of..."

The crowd's intrigued murmurs turned into cries of shock. One older gentleman stumbled backwards, steadying himself on his wife's arm at the last minute.

Silence descended on the group, their mouths working soundlessly to find words for what they'd just seen.

"Did it...?" the older gentleman tried.

"I... I...it m-m-must have just..." the tour guide stuttered.

"Mommy, I want to go home," a little boy whimpered to his mother.

"Honey, there's nothing to worry about," his mother tried to assure him, though she didn't sound so sure herself.

"I...um...well," the tour guide said shakily. "Prague truly is a city of wonders!" Then, under his breath, "What in the world was that?" He cleared his throat and, somewhat hastily, moved to the next spot on his route. "Now," he said, beckoning his skittish followers away from the statue *that had just turned its head and winked at him,* "if you'll follow me this way...and remember, keep your eyes peeled for magic...we'll be entering the room where..."

The sound of the tour's chatter faded into the distance. No one was there to once again gasp in shock as the statue's lips twitched into a sinister smile, as if the corners of its stone mouth had been pulled up by hooks.

Or maybe by puppet strings.

* * *

"Whoa," Nick stared in wonder at the steeply pitched roof and gothic gables of the Old New Synagogue. The angles and peaks made it look like a frozen flame shining over the surrounding buildings. "I've never seen a building like this before. How old is this place?"

"It's been standing in this spot for more than 750 years, and is one of the oldest operating synagogues in the world." Despite her chills and achiness, Helena couldn't help but slip into her professional tour guide persona when describing famous landmarks. "Legend says that angels brought the stones from the temple in Jerusalem on the condition that they would be returned to the Holy Land when the Messiah comes."

"Angels?" Nick raised his eyebrows.

"What's the matter? You don't believe angels flew around the world carrying giant stones?" Helena elbowed him in the ribs.

Nick elbowed her back gently. "I'd rather believe in angels than undead sorcerers raising an undefeatable army. Kinda makes you wonder what else is real that we thought was myth."

"It changes everything," Helena said quietly, studying the exterior for a moment longer before motioning to a side door covered with elaborate iron work. "But it doesn't change the fact that we have a job to do. This way."

Nick followed her across the street, noticing that the hair on the shaved side of her head had grown out a little. When they reached the door, she knocked.

The door opened slowly to reveal a wizened man wearing what looked like a black coat-robe combo. White streaked the man's gray beard, and a smile creased his face at the sight of Helena.

"Helena, so nice to see you. No tour group today?" the man asked, peeking behind her.

"Not today, Rabbi. I came because I need your help."

"Are you well, child? You look like you might be under the weather. Some tea, perhaps?"

"Thank you, Rabbi, but I'm fine. What I need is urgent."

"Well, come in, come in, and introduce me to your friend." He ushered them over the threshold.

Nick followed Helena and the rabbi inside and up nine steps to the interior. He gaped up at the huge brass chandeliers filled with candles hanging from the soaring, ribbed ceiling. Narrow gothic windows casting fascinating shadows on the stone arches flanked the sides of the open vestibule.

"Rabbi, this is my friend Nicholas Gordon. He's from Chicago."

"Ah, Nicholas." The Rabbi inclined his head. "I am very happy to meet you."

"Nick, this is Rabbi Sabatka. Your uncle introduced us so the Rabbi could tutor me in Hebrew and Aramaic. He's one of the wisest men I know."

The Rabbi chuckled. "Helena, you must not confuse antiquity with intellect. But, I would be honored to help you in any way I am able." His smile disappeared as he turned to Nick. "You must be Professor Maracek's nephew. I was very sorry to hear about your uncle. He was well known and loved by the Jewish community of Prague. I have known your family for many years. Your grandfather passed before you were born, but I can tell you, he was the most worthy of men. I remain devoted to him and his memory."

Nick bowed his head. "Thank you." A pang of sadness rang through him. This time, though, it was...less piercing, somehow? More muted maybe? The grief was still there, but Nick was able to let it roll over him rather than linger and sting. It was strange. He wasn't sure if he should feel happy or not, to have such a monumental tragedy loosen its grip on him. *Maybe it's okay that I'm not surprised by it anymore.*

He pulled the camera from around his neck. "I took pictures at the cemetery last night." He turned it on and brought up the photos of Rabbi Loew's mausoleum before handing it to Rabbi Sabatka. "I think my uncle was looking for clues at this marker as part of research he was conducting about an ancient legend, but I'm not sure what clue he was looking for. I'm hoping you might be able to tell us."

The rabbi took the camera and scrolled through the images. "I've seen these engravings many times before. May I ask why you are so interested in Rabbi Loew's marker that you would visit the Jewish Cemetery after closing time? Why not visit during the day? The carvings would have been easier to see."

Nick and Helena exchanged nervous glances.

"You've got to tell him, Nick." Helena said quietly. "I trust him as much as I trusted Damek and as much as I trust Mr. Zeman. We need all the help we can get."

"My uncle sent me a book, *The Legends of Old Bohemia*, before he died." Nick hesitated. Telling Mr. Zeman had been one thing. The old squire had been dropping hints since the ride back from the airport. But the rabbi was a stranger.. *Trust your squire,* he reminded himself. *Trust yourself.*

Looking up at Rabbi Sabatka, Nick continued. "There was a note inside the book that said Damek believed an evil presence had awakened and that Prague was in danger. We've seen the evil with our own eyes. We believe the writing on the grave may be able to show us how to stop it."

The Rabbi considered Nick for a moment, contemplating him through his keen, narrowed eyes. "You've seen this evil with your own eyes?"

"Yes, sir. First as a wind, and then as a spirit. It tried to get into Damek's house, and it put a spell on Helena yesterday." Beside him, Helena nodded.

"So, the seal has been broken," the rabbi said, his voice grave. "The box has been opened. No wonder you look ill, Helena." Then to Nick he said, "You still have the box, the diary and the dagger, yes?"

"You know," Helena gasped.

"You knew my great-grandfather." Understanding dawned on Nick's face. "Were you...*his* squire?"

"My service was not nearly as exciting or noteworthy as yours, Helena," the rabbi said. "If I'm correct in assuming that is the position you hold?"

Helena nodded.

"The sorcerer didn't stir while the artifacts were under your great-grandfather's care. I heard from your uncle that he'd begun searching for the weapon. But when I learned of his passing, I prayed that it had truly just been a tragic accident. I am sorry this task has fallen to you. I know that was your uncle's greatest fear."

"He and Mr. Zeman tried to end the threat once and for all by burning Horymir's corpse, but instead of destroying him, it set him free. Damek realized he'd made a mistake and went to the cemetery to try and fix it, but Horymir was already strong enough to use the wind and..." The words died in his throat.

Rabbi Sabatka nodded solemnly. "Do you know what pointed Damek to Rabbi Loew's marker?"

Nick pulled the notebook out of his pocket and opened to the page with the stanzas Damek had translated. He handed it to the rabbi.

"'Death piles stones twelve layers deep/Sacred secrets the crimson eagle keeps,'" the rabbi read slowly.

"Helena figured out that the first part is about the Jewish cemetery," Nick said, "and the crimson eagle is a symbol of the Knights of Blaník, right?"

"We think Horymir has gone back to the tomb where he was buried to remake his body," Helena said. "He took the box from me, and commanded me to take him the dagger. He said once he has it, he's going to raise an undefeatable army, only he called it 'the blade', not the dagger."

"Is the dagger still under your protection, Nicholas?" Rabbi Sabatka pressed.

"It is."

"Thank goodness," Rabbi Sabatka said. "Most among Jewish mystical scholars considered tales of the Knights of Blaník and their descendants to be nothing more than fantasy. But according to your great grandfather, Horymir anticipated he would be executed for turning Prince Boleslaus against his brother Wenceslaus. He prepared a box..."

The floor of the synagogue seemed to tremble under Nick's feet, and a bout of dizziness struck him as Rabbi Sabatka spoke.

"...in which he placed a lock of his hair and an alchemist's stone," the rabbi continued. "After Boleslaus murdered his brother, the king's guard captured Horymir..."

"And when they executed him, his soul went into the box!" Nick exclaimed as his dream came rushing back. "I was there! I saw it! At least...I saw some of it. Not everything is clear."

Helena gasped.

"You are a dreamer," Rabbi Sabatka murmured, considering Nick. "Did you see what they did next?"

"No," Nick sighed in frustration. "That's when I woke up."

"Your ancestors took every precaution to ensure Horymir would never be freed. The box contained a word of power that would rebind Horymir's soul, should it ever escape. And only the key originally used to lock the box could open it again. But it was lost many generations ago. Do you know who discovered it and where?"

"My little sister. Horymir got into her dreams and now she's really sick; her body temperature keeps falling. And there's a man. He was at the airport when we arrived and it turns out he owns an antiques shop. We think he's an acolyte."

"Your uncle must have been looking for the 'sacred secret' kept by the order of the Crimson Eagle." Rabbi Sabatka's tone was low and reverent.

"I still don't understand how the knights and Rabbi Loew are connected, though," Nick said, handing the camera back to Rabbi Sabatka.

"Legends of the Knights of Blaník are well known to the people of Bohemia," Rabbi Sabatka said as he studied the photos more closely. "Some say they periodically rise from their tomb beneath Mount Blaník on misty nights to scout the city for evil doers and those who would cause Prague harm. But something that is not widely known is that the Rabbi Loew was admitted into the Order of Blaník as an honorary knight."

Goosebumps covered Nick's entire body. "No way," he whispered.

"See this round emblem on the front of the grave? Do you know what this figure is?" Rabbi Sabatka turned the screen so that Nick and Helena could see, too, and zoomed in on the upper part of the ancient marker. He indicated the strange beast that almost looked like a griffin standing on its hind legs, one clawed paw raised in the air in front of it.

"That's a lion," Helena replied.

"It is, indeed," Rabbi Sabatka nodded. "In fact, Loew is derived from the German word 'löwe,' meaning lion. Rabbi Juddah Loew referred to himself as the 'Young Lion.'"

Nick zoomed in on the lion on the screen. "Wait! Does it have two tails?"

"Excellent eye, young man," the Rabbi said. "Is that of some significance to you?"

"I thought the two-tailed lion was the symbol for Bruncvik. The lion became Bruncvik's faithful companion after he helped it defeat a nine-headed monster. It was even with him when he found his magic sword."

"Yes," Helena said in tour-guide mode. "Legend says that when things are at their worst for Prague, King Wenceslas will return and defeat Prague's enemies with Bruncvik's sword."

"It's all connected." Nick's voice was barely audible. Louder he said, "Too bad all we have is a dagger, not a mystical sword. Does anyone know where the actual sword is?" Nick asked. "Isn't it just in the Charles Bridge like the legends say?"

"People have been searching for Bruncvik's sword for much longer than I have been alive. You are correct that rumors speak of King Charles hiding it in the Charles Bridge," Rabbi Sabatka said, distracted. Nick looked up to see the old holy man peering at the camera screen, which he was holding very close to his face. "Young man, I haven't seen this carving before. Which marker did you take this photograph of?"

Nick stepped closer to the Rabbi. "I only took photos of Rabbi Loew's marker. Except, wait. The camera went off once when I dropped it. It must have been on the underside of the gravemarker or something so you'd have to lie down to see it."

Helena pointed to the upper right corner of the screen. "Are those part of the Aramaic alphabet?"

"That is indeed an ancient Aramaic letter," Sabatka said, "but it doesn't mean anything. It's just the letter 'N', which obviously isn't a word."

"What if it's part of a word?" Helena stepped back, eyes wide, glancing from the rabbi to Nick and back again. "You said there's a word of power that can stop Horymir if he ever got out of the box, right? And we're searching for clues that lead to a weapon to defeat him. Damek's letter said that the descendants of the knights have had to relocate the weapon throughout the centuries, probably each time Horymir could turn someone into an acolyte through their dreams! What if the clues your ancestors left are letters that spell the word of power? What if this is the first letter to the word of power?"

"Excellent work," Rabbi Sabatka praised. "I think Damek placed his trust in you well."

"Thank you so much, Rabbi. I think we can...whoa!" Nick stopped abruptly when Helena yanked him forcefully toward the door.

"Thank you, sir!" Helena echoed. Then, to Nick, "Come on! We're running out of time!"

CHAPTER TWENTY-SIX - Vanity's Mirror

"Where is everyone today," Nick asked, as they left the Jewish Quarter and entered a quiet park. The normally bustling streets were eerily empty, and the few people who were out rushed their steps as if desperate to get back home. Even the birds had gone silent, and there were no tourists taking pictures in front of the statue of Moses that the park was famous for.

"I see it too," Helena said, glancing left and right. "Everyone seems hyper-alert, like they're waiting for something bad to happen. If they're smart, they'll go home and stay there."

"They have no idea," Nick said. "Do you really think that'll save anyone from Horymir?" he asked, hopeful.

"No. I think *we* have to save everyone from Horymir. At least he's leaving us alone right now. Let's figure out where to look next."

They sat down on a bench and Nick opened Damek's notebook to the verses.

Death piles stones twelve layers deep,

The Crimson Eagle sacred secrets keep.

Strike the light and fan the flame,

Without the body will the soul remain?

Time guards the key to hidden power,

A reflection of pride when the clock strikes the hour.

Beneath the place where heroes kneel,

The Knight and Squire will reforge steel.

Trust the Lion or all is lost

When Evil arrives at the Foot of the Cross.

"Right. So, we've figured out the first and second stanzas the hard way," Helena said.

"Hopefully."

"No, not hopefully. *Actually.* Everything points to it – even your dreams, right?" Without waiting for him to agree, Helena continued: "So, 'hidden power' is obviously talking about the word of power we're looking for. 'Time guards the key to hidden power/A reflection of pride when the clock strikes the hour.'"

"Is there a reflecting pool in Prague? Maybe one that you can only see at a certain hour?"

"A pool you can only see at a certain hour?" Helena scrunched her nose at him. "What does that even mean?"

"You know, like in *Raiders of the Lost Ark* when Indy sticks the staff in the ground and the sun shines through the jewel and shows the secret entrance to the Well of Souls?" Nick's eyes glowed. It's how he'd always pictured his uncle's adventures. "That would be *amazing*."

"Excellent film," Helena said, "but there are no public reflecting pools that I know of in Prague."

"Maybe a really big mirror? In a fancy shopping area?"

In the distance, chimes rang out from the Orloj Astronomica.

"Crap, what time is it?" Nick asked, momentarily forgetting he was wearing a watch. "Seven fifty-eight," he said, answering his own question. "Hopefully Mom won't notice I'm gone for another hour."

"That's it!" Helena punched Nick in the nose, then hopped up from the bench and headed for Pariska street.

"What's it?" Nick asked, limping after her.

"The four evils!" Helena called over her shoulder.

Nick caught up, panting. "What are you talking about?"

"The four evils: Vanity, Greed, Death, and Lust! On the Astronomical Clock!"

"'When the clock strikes the hour,'" Nick whispered..

"Exactly! 'Time guards the key to hidden power/A reflection of pride when the clock strikes the hour.' Vanity is pride! He's even holding a mirror!" Helena grabbed his hand. "Come on!"

Nick's hip complained loudly as he jogged along beside Helena. Her energy was definitely fading, and while he worried, he was also grateful for the slower pace.

The procession of the twelve apostles had already ended by the time they reached the town square. Nick stared up at the two wooden sculptures on the left hand side of the astronomical dial: brown-cloaked Greed with his stick and bag of gold, and Vanity in his green robes and red cloak gazing into his golden-framed mirror.

"Come on!" Helena tugged him along the checkered walkway in front of the tower.

"Where?" Nick asked, confused. "We're as close as we can get without climbing straight up the tower!"

"The statues you see on the clock aren't the originals," Helena explained without stopping. "The real ones are kept inside the tower to protect them from the elements and vandalism."

"Wait, then how are we supposed to get to them? I doubt two random kids are allowed to just walk inside." Nick said.

"Do you trust me?" Helena asked over her shoulder

"Always."

"Then come on!"

Nick followed as Helena elbowed past an elderly couple. With a final shove and mumbled apologies in English and Czech, they emerged from the crowd right in front of a hulking security guard wearing a frown. His biceps bulged as he folded his arms across his chest.

"Hi, Vaclav!" Helena greeted, smiling cheerfully.

"Don't 'hi' me, young lady." Vaclav's accent was thick, but his English was clear. "You promised to bring me koláče last week." He held out his empty hands. "Every day, I wait. No koláče. Some old-lady tour guide come instead. All the tourists so bored they sleeping on their feet following her around."

Helena's smile faltered. "I know. I'm sorry. I... Something came up. But I'll make it up to you, I promise."

Nick watched the exchange. Helena and the burly guard were obviously friends, and Helena seemed genuinely sad to have disappointed him. *Because of me,* he reminded himself. Helena had dropped everything since they'd met to help *him.* "It was my fault, Mr. Vaclav, sir," he said. "My uncle died and she's been staying with my family."

Vaclav's frown softened. He glanced from Nick to Helena, a question in his eyes.

"This is Nicholas," Helena said quietly. "Damek Maracek's great-nephew."

The security guard cleared his throat and uncrossed his arms. "I heard about that. I am very sorry. And sorry for you, broučku. Damek Maracek was a great man. "

"Would it be all right for me to show Nicholas the original statues?" Helena asked.

Vaclav scratched his head. "Hmm." He pursed his lips, considering Nick and Helena. "You know that section of the building has been closed for repairs, broučku..."

Nick's mind scrambled, trying to think of something he could say that would convince the guard. *An evil wizard is raising an army to overthrow Prague and the only thing that can stop him is a secret letter hidden somewhere in the Vanity statue. At least we think?*

"*...but,* this is special circumstance," Vaclav continued, "to cheer you up, Nicholas." He spoke quietly, glancing around furtively from beneath his bushy black eyebrows. Without looking at her, he handed Helena a small key ring he'd fished out of his pants' pocket. "Big silver key," he whispered, "you know the way. Please be careful, and don't let Gizela see you. She wring my neck."

Nick followed Helena in through the main hallway entrance to the left of the massive dials. He craned his neck to look up at the ceiling, taking in the brightly painted vaults depicting Wenceslas and the two-tailed lion, Brucvik's sword, and a knight protecting a castle. He'd been here before with his parents, but his memories were all of the clock outside. If things were different, if Kat and Helena weren't sick and getting sicker, if he weren't afraid of dreaming every time he closed his eyes, if Horymir weren't threatening Prague and everyone in it, he could spend days here exploring and learning.

"There are lots of stairs, and they're steep," Helena whispered as they navigated through tour groups and visitors waiting for their turn to see the Old Council Hall and the Assembly Hall. "Are you able to..." she hesitated, glancing at him sideways, "...we've been walking a lot. How's your hip?"

Nick's hip groaned with every step he took. "Never better," he answered through only mildly gritted teeth.

Helena opened the ornate door at the back of the chapel and slipped inside like she'd been sneaking around the Old Town Hall all her life.

Nick followed her into a shadowy stairwell that seemed to go up and up forever. *Just keep your eyes on the step in front of you,* he told himself. *One step at a time.*

They climbed the steep wooden staircase until eventually reaching the door leading to the room where the clock calendar and statues of the twelve apostles were kept. Elaborate clockworks filled almost the entire space, with the complicated wheels and gears rhythmically clicking and clacking away to keep everything in motion.

Everything moved except for the statues. Those hung motionless near the center of the room, temporarily lifeless as they awaited the next chiming of the hour.

"It's almost like they're puppets waiting for the next marionette show," Nick mused. "I wonder if..."

"You heard Vaclav, we have to be quick!" Helena strode toward the mechanism. "Come on, young knight, we've got some Ancient Aramaic to find!"

Helena was right. Nick steeled himself and stepped towards the statue of Vanity and went straight for the mirror.

A flat, wooden surface stared back at him. He didn't know what he expected. Why would it have been made out of real glass?

And what would he see staring back at him if it was? Probably a tired, grieving 13-year-old boy with purple shadows smudging his eyes and pale skin hiding underneath a tan. He probably looked like someone who'd been living underground and just emerged into the sun for the first time in years.

But he at least hoped he didn't look terrified. His terror had downgraded to anxiety and an enormous amount of pressure. It didn't feel great, but was better than being scared all the time. Or maybe it would be more accurate to say fear still followed him like a shadow, but he was doing his best not to let it make decisions for him.

That's when he saw it. At the bottom of the mirror, what initially looked like small scratches in the glass surface caught Nick's attention. "Helena!" He shouted. Helena sprinted over. "Please tell me these are Aramaic letters."

"It's another one! This one is hard to pronounce on its own, but it should sound like 'shruh.'" She turned to Nick, smiling widely. "I still don't know what it means, but we were right! The poem is telling us where to find the rest of the word of power!"

A flicker of movement in his peripheral vision caught his eye. Without hesitation, Nick dove to the floor, pulling Helena with him.

"What the...?"

A heavy, carved blade lodged into the wooden floorboards exactly where she'd been standing a split second before, somehow slicing through the material as if it were made from real steel. Death leered down at her, partially detached from the chains and bolts that had secured it to the clock's mechanisms. It yanked its scythe from the wood as Nick and Helena scrambled back to their feet. Its joints jolted at odd angles like a deranged puppet as it freed itself one snap at a time until it was standing completely on its own, scythe raised high for its next strike.

247

CHAPTER TWENTY-SEVEN - Battle at the Clock

Nick stared in horror as the suddenly-animated statue of Death advanced on Helena. She scrabbled back, staring at Nick with terror in her eyes

"Nick," Helena shouted, "DUCK!"

Without thinking, Nick flung himself to the floor, rolling to the right. Vanity's mirror swung up into the air, missing his chin by inches.

As if pulled by invisible strings, Vanity lurched its way forward, crouching eerily next to Death. They stood like tag-team wrestlers posing for an invisible audience, basking in imaginary cheering. Death's gaunt, uncloathed, skeletal figure brimmed with violent energy. Vanity, dressed in foppish courtier clothes from medieval times, suddenly didn't look so funny to Nick.

"Run?" Helena suggested, quickly springing to her feet.

"Run!" Nick concurred. They leapt for the door behind them...

...only to find it wouldn't budge.

They both turned, pressing their backs to the door and facing their assailants. In tandem, the statues hunched their wooden forms and dashed forward with inhuman growls, Death brandishing his scythe and Vanity his mirror.

Nick and Helena dove in opposite directions, narrowly dodging the onslaught. They barely had time to get back to their feet as Vanity and Death readied their next attacks, Death aiming at Nick and Vanity moving toward Helena.

"I guess Horymir is back to not ignoring us again," Helena panted, dodging a slashing swipe from Vanity's mirror. "Now what?"

"I have no idea!" Nick panted, jumping back and away from an upswing from Death's scythe.

Jerk. The statues lowered their weapons again. *Jerk.* They swung forward as if synchronized, driving Nick and Helena further back.

Nervously, Nick glanced at the other three pairs of wooden statues while narrowly sidestepping another attack. At least they weren't suddenly coming to life. Not that two reanimated statues weren't bad enough.

Nick wiped away the sweat building up on his forehead and stepped back on his short leg, preparing for another dodge, when the back of his shoe struck the wall. With no weapons and nothing to fend off blows, it was only a matter of time before one or both of them got badly injured.

This is it, Nick thought as he stumbled awkwardly to the side, raising his arms helplessly to guard his head. *This is how Death gets me.*

But Death couldn't adjust fast enough. Its arms followed through with its strike, scythe clanging against the wall where Nick had been standing even as its head followed Nick's new trajectory.

Nick jumped backwards. Death brought its scythe around in a backhanded swipe, its elbow striking the wall and its weapon bouncing off harmlessly.

Gears whirred in Nick's mind like clockwork of its own. Obviously, Horymir controlled the statues just as Kat had described him masterfully controlling his puppets on in her dream. He must be able to see him and Helena, but what if that was it? What if he couldn't see the room they were in?

"Helena!"

"Kind of busy, Nick!" she yelled back as she rolled away from Vanity, its mirror clanging off of the floor so hard, Nick half expected it to shatter.

Despite all the near-misses and too-close swings of Death's scythe, the confidence that came with the protection from the Brotherhood surged through his bloodstream.

Will it work for Helena, too? Mr. Zeman said *he* had enjoyed the protection when he was with Damek. *Focus, Nick!* he told himself. He still had to be careful. Comic books and movies were full of people who lost battles because they'd been too confident. *Now is not the time to be distracted. Figure it out when giant puppets* **aren't** *trying to kill you!*

Death's scythe cleaved the air inches from Nick's head for the dozenth time in the last few minutes. They had to end this.

"I have a plan," Nick shouted. "We need to get them close together!"

Without a word, Helena immediately changed direction, dodging, weaving, and leading Vanity step by step closer to where Nick maneuvered around Death in the middle of the room.

From the corner of his eye, he gauged Helena's movements, positioning himself directly in her path. In the span of only a few ragged breaths, her back brushed against his.

"Duck on three!" Nick yelled. "One, two... Three!"

Helena ducked in perfect timing with him, the moment before the statues let their weapons fly...

...right into each other.

An awful clanging rang out through the room. Death's scythe sent Vanity's head sailing off of its neck, and Vanity's mirror completely caved in the left side of Death's face. The two statues twitched for a moment, then collapsed.

Nick and Helena both stood doubled over, huffing and puffing to regain their breath.

"That...was too...close," Nick said, standing up straight and wiping sweat away.

"Seriously," Helena agreed. "But Nick, that was incredible! How did you do that?"

Nick blushed a little. "I realized Death could see me, but not much else."

"How?"

"He kept running into the wall."

Helena grinned briefly, but then groaned. "Horymir is getting stronger. I'd bet he'll be able to animate anything he wants and see just fine before very long. Do you think this means he's done remaking his body?"

"If it does, we may not find all the letters in time. We don't even know how many more letters there are!"

"There's gotta be at least one more."

Heavy footsteps sounded outside the door.

"Oh, no!" Helena's hand flew to her mouth. "Vaclav! And look what we've done! These statues are priceless!" Tears welled in her eyes.

Nick surveyed the damage, a knot of regret forming in his gut. But he shook his head. "We didn't do this Helena. Horymir did."

The door flew open. Vaclav entered. His eyes went wide and his jaw went slack. He grabbed his bald head with both hands. "What did you two do!?"

* * *

Mr. Zeman slammed the book shut with a heavy *thud*. He had it! The last piece of the puzzle.

He fished his phone from his trousers' pocket. After all, he'd promised to alert Helena with any news. He typed rapidly, surely making a few mistakes he couldn't be bothered to correct. He had to tell her what he'd found. This new information may very well change how they looked for the clues, if not allow them to...

Whoosh.

Too late, Kyril turned toward the sweeping sound rushing down the empty walkway toward him as he crossed the brick-paved street. He barely had time to scream before he was lifted off the ground, tossed around like a tumbleweed, and slammed onto the cobblestone.

He laid there, head pounding, hand clutching his phone, trying to pull air into his lungs when the wind picked him up again. He hovered weightless above the ground for just long enough to shield his head with his arms before he was hurled back down. Again and again the wind assaulted him until finally, the world went black.

Nearby, someone screamed. The rustling wind swirled up in a vortex before fading down the street toward the Church of St. Giles, seemingly satisfied with its violent work.

Kyril's arm twitched as he regained consciousness. Blinding pain shot through his neck when he tried to turn his head.

From a great distance, he heard the blare of sirens approaching.

CHAPTER TWENTY-EIGHT - The Final Piece

"Listen, we didn't mean to..." Nick pleaded, but Vaclav completely ignored him.

"I *knew* I shouldn't have let you two up here," the security guard muttered, ushering them toward the exit like a very cross mother hen. "I don't know what you do to make such loud noise. You try to wake the dead! You are lucky nothing breaks. It sound like many things broken!"

"I swear it wasn't our fault, it was...! Wait, what?" Nick glanced over his shoulder as they reached the door, expecting to see the wreckage of the two priceless statues. But Vanity and Death hung lifeless in their original places. Relief surged through him, quickly followed by fear. He stopped and turned around. What if they jumped back down and attacked them again?

"No stopping!" Vaclav grabbed Nick by his collar and steered him back around, pushing him gently through the doorway. "I could lose job for this, Helena," he growled, shutting the door. He held out his hand, in which Helena placed the set of keys he'd given her. After locking the door, he hurried them down the steep staircase and out into the main hall. He didn't stop until he had dragged them to a side entrance, pushed them through with straight arms, and slammed the door shut.

"Come on." Nick pulled Helena through the thin crowd of tourists milling about outside on the checkered black and white public square. Neither of them spoke until they stopped beneath a lamppost out of the way, but still in the open. "Here, sit down."

She let Nick help her sit down, then leaned back against the lamppost and closed her eyes. "I just need to catch my breath."

Nick glanced around furtively, afraid someone might sneak up on them. He peered anxiously into the faces of anyone that wandered too close. "Do you think he'll really get fired?" he asked, his voice low.

"I...don't think so?" Helena said. "I really hope not. But that might be the least of his problems. Did you see the statues? It looked like nothing had happened! What if Horymir decides to animate them again and attack the tourists?"

"It makes more sense that he's trying to slow us down," Nick said. "Hopefully they're safe for now. For a second I thought I'd imagined it."

"You didn't." Helena held out her arm. A long gash ran up her arm from her elbow to her shoulder.

"Oh my gosh, are you okay?"

"It's not deep." Helena dropped her rucksack on the ground and crouched down, to rifle through it. She pulled out antibacterial wipes and several bandages. "A little help?"

Nick crouched down beside her, cleaned the gash with some wipes, and then began dressing the wound. "He's getting stronger, isn't he?"

"He is," Helena said through gritted teeth. "But you are, too. You were dodging like a ninja in there. Your leg didn't slow you down at all. How bad does it hurt?"

Nick blinked. He tensed the muscles in his right leg, sensing for any joint pain. Sure enough, the aching waited for him right where it'd been when he'd climbed up the stairs to the chapel. "It hurts," he finally said, "but it's manageable."

Helena's cell phone buzzed.

"It's gotta be Mr. Zeman." She shoved the first aid supplies back in her bag. "I never texted him about the cemetery, or Rabbi Sabatka! But maybe he has news. Maybe he's figured something out!" She stood up, pulled her phone out of her back pocket, and answered the call. "Hey Mr. Zeman, we've found the first two... Oh! Hello, Mrs. Gordon."

"Ask her how Kat's doing," Nick whispered.

Helena nodded at him. "Yes, he's with me." She put her finger in her other ear. "Sorry, what was that...?" Suddenly, her posture went ramrod-straight. "Oh my god!" she gasped. "Is he okay?"

* * *

The steady *beep beep* of a heart monitor greeted Nick and Helena as they entered Mr. Zeman's hospital room. They'd gotten there as fast as they could, hurrying past the ornate statues in the courtyard and barely stopping to ask for the right room at the desk inside. They panted as they looked down on Mr. Zeman's wounded body. The big man was ashen, either unconscious or sleeping. A white bandage wrapped his head, standing out in stark contrast to an ugly purple-black bruise spreading across the entire left half of his face.

Mom and Kat stood at the foot of his bed with a doctor in scrubs.

Nick heard the doctor say, "...he's in stable condition, but he'll need to stay overnight for observation. He's developed pneumonia as well. His lungs were badly damaged due to smoke inhalation from the fire three weeks ago. He should really have been on bed rest for at least another week."

"What happened?" Nick asked after the doctor left.

Mom shook her head. "It doesn't make any sense! I tried calling you earlier when I left to bring Kat to her follow-up visit with Dr. Smithe. We were leaving when they brought Kyril in on a stretcher."

"What did Dr. Smithe say about Kat?" Nick asked. Kat leaned up against Mom, bundled in several layers of clothes. She gripped Mom's arm with one mittened hand, and clutched her Grogu in the other. She hadn't said a word since they'd arrived, seemingly in her own little world.

"She said Kat's body temperature has stabilized, but isn't going up. She said that it's a positive sign that she had the energy to come in today, but that it will likely take time for her to recover..." she choked off a sob and wiped her eyes with a tissue. When she continued, her voice was steady and cheerful, but her eyes were still haunted. "They think Kat caught a bug on the plane and that because of her recent loss, her body is having a tough time fighting off illness. Trauma affects everyone differently, so she hopes she'll make a full recovery with some rest and time. She also mentioned that she has a friend who can help her process her grief, didn't she, Kat?" Mom stroked Kat's hair.

Kat looked up at Mom and nodded.

"But there's nothing they can give her, to warm her up?" Nick asked, and immediately wished he hadn't when Mom's eyes clouded.

"They took a blood sample and they're running some tests," she answered, voice quiet.

Kat turned and gazed at Nick, eyes hollow. A lump formed in his throat. "Does anybody know what happened to Mr. Zeman?"

"The police told the doctors that witnesses saw him have a seizure outside the Klementinum."

Nick and Helena exchanged glances. Mr. Zeman had been doing research on how to defeat Horymir. It was too much of a coincidence. Nick clenched his fists, his insides churning like spoiled milk. Just when he'd finally allowed himself to consider the possibility that they might actually be able to stop Horymir, this happened.

"The doctor said he's in stable condition," Mom, wiping her eyes again. "I'm sorry for being emotional. It's just been a lot recently."

"He shouldn't have gone out," Nick muttered, angry at himself. "He wasn't protected. I should have said something!"

"You can't blame yourself," Helena said, but her voice wasn't convincing.

Kat let go of Mom's hand and reached under her collar. She pulled the lion pendant out from under her collar and slipped it over her head then walked over to Mr. Zeman and placed it silently on his chest.

"No, Kat." Nick picked up the lion. "Uncle Damek gave it to *you*. He wanted to protect *you*. You need to wear it.."

"Nick?" Mom's voice spiked with alarm. "What is going on? What are you talking about?"

"The dagger..."

Everyone spun to stare at Mr. Zeman, but whatever he was going to say was lost in a fit of coughing that racked his body and ended in a muffled groan.

Nick and Helena rushed to join Kat by his side.

"Mr. Zeman?" Nick leaned close.

Mr. Zeman's eyes opened, zeroing in on Nick. "...just a piece..." More coughing seized him, then, "...mustn't let him have it." The old squire struggled as if he was trying to sit up. "Must keep it...safe."

The monitor by his bedside sounded a warning and a nurse rushed into the room, pushing Mr. Zeman down flat on his back.

Still the old squire struggled, reaching for Nick. "You must take care...he will be waiting...at the foot of the cross."

"Where is the foot of the cross?" Nick asked, leaning closer even as Mom tried to drag him back.

Mr. Zeman wheezed, gasping for breath. "...A clue, hiding in plain sight...all this time..." More coughing. "...Where the real...adventure begins."

The heart monitor's beeping grew erratic.

Nick let himself be pulled away as two more nurses came in, one with a long needle. It took two nurses to hold Mr. Zeman down while the other administered the sedative. The beeping returned to normal and Mr. Zeman's body went still, his head listing to one side.

"Nick? What is going on?"

He heard fear and confusion in Mom's voice. He couldn't pretend nothing was happening anymore. "Mom..." he began.

The hospital went completely dark.

Mom yelped in surprise. Nick turned in a slow circle checking every corner of the room, and the hallway. "Come on, come on!" he murmured, urging the generator to kick in.

"He's coming," Kat said.

Helena gasped.

Nick whipped around. In the darkness, he could barely see the outline of his little sister's face. She stared at the wall behind Mr. Zeman's head, mouth hanging open, eyes blank, mouth open wide with terror.

Nick slipped the pendant in his hand over Kat's head. Immediately, she startled as if waking from a bad dream.

"Sweetheart?" Mom sank to her knees in front of Kat. "Honey, what happened? Are you alright? Who's coming?"

"She'll be okay, Mom," Nick said. "I'll explain everything, I promise. Just give me a second, okay?"

Mom stared first at Nick and then at Kat. Anger, worry, and relief each flashed across her face. She nodded.

Nick crouched down until he was eye level with Kat. His pulse quickened as he realized her gaze was no longer hollow. "What did you see?" he asked.

"I saw him, Nicky. Only, not see-through like when he was on the porch."

Dim emergency lights flickered on, though nowhere near strong enough to dispel the chill in Nick's bones.

"You have to stop him, Nicky," Kat said, voice hard like rock. "I can watch Mr. Zeman and Mommy. You have to stop Horymir."

"Please tell me what's going on!" Mom was on the verge of tears. Her hands pressed against her chest like she was trying to keep her heart from leaping out.

"Kat is right, Nick." Helena stood at the head of Mr. Zeman's hospital bed. Her hand looked impossibly small on top of the old squire's bandaged hand. She swayed slightly. "We've got to get out of here. We've got to find the weapon and stop him before he gets any more powerful. Everyone is doomed if we stay. Besides, Horymir used Kat to try to stop us. He hurt Mr. Zeman so he couldn't help us. Maybe he won't bother them anymore."

"Are you sure you're strong enough to go?" he asked.

"Are you calling me weak?" With effort, she stood up tall and gave a lopsided grin. "I'll feel a lot better when we've found the weapon."

Nick turned to Mom and swallowed hard, "I'm really sorry." To Kat, he said, "Stay with them, okay? You're fierce, just like the two-tailed lion. You can keep them safe."

"I will," Kat said solemnly.

"Horymir wants to stop me and he wants the dagger," he said to both Mom and Kat. "I'm pretty sure he'll focus on me if I leave."

Kat nodded and Mom made a whimpering sound.

"Mom, I know you're scared, but we need you, okay? You're a Maracek, and that means the blood of knights runs through you, too. Tell her what's going on, okay, Kat? And remember: you have the lion. Horymir can't make you do anything, right?"

"Right!" She stomped her foot, bared her teeth, and growled.

"Yes!" He kissed Kat on the forehead, relieved her skin felt almost warm. He kissed Mom on the cheek. "I love you both," he said.

Then he grabbed Helena's hand. Together, they ran out of the room and toward the main entrance.

Between Mom's shouts and his own growing sense of doom, Nick barely noticed the door slam shut behind them on its own accord as they ran out onto the streets of Prague.

CHAPTER TWENTY-NINE - The Foot of the Cross

Thick fog draped itself over all of Prague like a shroud. Mist clung to buildings and street lamps. Gloom rolled slowly down alleyways, curling and slithering like vaporous snakes. The main streets were eerily empty, save for one or two people hurrying somewhere.

Nick hoped they had somewhere safe to go.

He stopped briefly, glancing over his shoulder and straining his ears for sirens or desperate cries or any disturbance that would signal Horymir's arrival. But all he heard was silence. Too much silence.

"I think I know what Mr. Zeman meant about a clue hiding in plain sight," Nick said. "I think it's in the study. I used to beg Uncle Damek to take me with him on one of his digs, only when I was little I called them treasure hunts. He knew what I meant, but still, every time I asked, he'd take me to his study. He said all real adventure begins with learning."

"That sounds just like him." Helena smiled but then her face quickly changed to a frown. "It's not very helpful right now, though. There are at least a million books in that office, and we've already searched it. I didn't see any clues hiding in plain sight. Did you?"

"No. But that has to be what he meant, I'm sure of it. How close are we to the house?""

"*This* close!" Helena led him around one final turn, and Damek's front door loomed out of the fog at them.

* * *

"What do you mean, none of the exits will open?" Mom asked the bewildered-looking nurse who had stopped outside Mr. Zeman's room. "How is that even possible?"

Kat watched from beside Mr. Zeman's hospital bed as Mom interrogated the anxious-looking nurse. The emergency lights had taken over ten minutes ago, and this was the first person who had stopped to talk to them.

"I don't know, ma'am," the nurse responded, his eyes darting up and down the hallway as she spoke. "That's just what they told me."

"But my son is out there!" Mom failed to keep her voice level. "There has to be a way out! Someone should break down the doors!"

"Paní – Ma'am, we have patients in critical condition. They need our attention. Excuse me." He hurried off in the direction he'd been heading before Mom had stopped him down the dimly lit hall.

Mom retreated back inside Mr. Zeman's room and paced back and forth along the tiny patch of linoleum between his bed and the bathroom while punching numbers into her phone and muttering to herself.

Kat knew that Nick was right: Horymir really wanted the dagger, not her. He was only trying to scare her.

The steady *beep beep* of the monitor had gone silent when all the lights went out, but Mr. Zeman's coughing had subsided after the nurses gave him the shot, and his breathing was steady. Kat didn't like the ugly purple bruise on Mr. Zeman's head, though. That must have hurt.

Sighing, she slipped her small hand inside his big one. "Don't worry Mr. Zeman," she whispered. "I'll protect you."

"What was that, sweetie?" Mom rushed from the doorway and knelt down in front of Kat.

"I was just telling Mr. Zeman that he doesn't need to worry because I'll look after him." With her small fingers, she tried to smooth away the furrows on Mom's forehead. "You don't need to worry either, Mommy."

Mom took Kat's hand and kissed it. "Oh, Kitty-Kat, your hand is almost warm! How are you feeling, Sweetheart?"

"I'm tired, Mommy," Kat said. "But I'm okay. I'm sorry I didn't tell you about Horymir before. He told me not to, but he can't boss me around anymore."

"Oh, honey!" Mom pulled Kat into a hug. "I don't know what's going on, but I know that whatever it is, it isn't your fault. I'm sorry for not paying more attention. Since your uncle's accident, I haven't been sleeping much." Her eyebrows furrowed and she shook her head. "Such strange dreams whenever I close my eyes," she murmured to herself.

"You've been having scary dreams, too, haven't you, Mommy?" Kat asked.

"No, not scary, really," Mom said, still speaking to herself. "I don't remember them very well, just that they wake me up and leave me with the feeling that something bad is coming. And there's a voice. A strange voice, but it speaks a language I don't understand."

"That's Horymir, Mommy. He woke up and I... I let him out of his box."

"Horymir?" Mom came back to the present and looked at Kat, confused. "Your imaginary friend?"

"He's nobody's friend. He's bad and he tricked me and made me sick. He hurt Uncle Damek and Mr. Zeman. He wants to hurt everyone, that's why Nick and Helena have to stop him."

First disbelief, and then alarm spread across Mom's face. She hesitated before asking, "Kat, what does this...Horymir...look like?"

"All crooked," Kat said, "like this." She hunched her body the same way she had when describing her nightmare to Nick.

"Does he have...yellow teeth?"

"*Pointy* yellow teeth," Kat nodded. "You're a dreamer, too, Mommy."

A muffled sob escaped Mom's lips. But then she looked at Kat standing there bravely. Mom smoothed her expression and nodded. After a moment, she stood up and pressed the red button on the wall next to Mr. Zeman's bed repeatedly.

Nothing happened.

"That's it," Mom muttered. "First the wi-fi goes down and now the nurses aren't responding." She grabbed Kat's hand and tried to pull her out into the hallway.

Kat resisted. "Mommy, no! Nick said to stay here and protect Mr. Zeman. He doesn't have a necklace! Nick and Helena are going to get the dagger. They're going to stop Horymir!"

"I don't care who has a necklace, Katarina! I pray for Mr. Zeman, but I am *not* going to let my son and the neighbor girl run around Prague during a blackout with a *dagger* trying to destroy some creepy old ghost with fangs who terrorizes people's dreams!"

A gust of wind rushed through the hallway, screaming like a lost soul. As it passed, it slammed the door to Mr. Zeman's room shut tight.

* * *

Nick pounded down the last flight of Damek's stairs with the dagger clutched in his hand. His bad foot seemed to land slightly harder than his good one on every step, sending a jolt of pain up his leg. Clenching his teeth, he joined Helena in the study, where she dug through a pile of papers, maps and books on Damek's desk, looking for anything that might offer a clue.

"Any luck yet?" Nick asked.

Helena shook her head, mouth tight with frustration. "Like I said, it could be anywhere in here. It'll take days to go through everything!"

"Except Mr. Zeman said it was hiding in plain sight. It has to be something obvious."

"You're right!" Helena stopped digging and pulled Damek's notebook out of her backpack. "Okay, what do we have left? Let's see. There are still two stanzas..."

Beneath the place where heroes kneel,

The Knight and Squire will reforge steel.

Trust the Lion or all is lost

When Evil arrives at the Foot of the Cross.

"That's two more places." Helena couldn't hide the exhaustion in her voice. "The place where heroes kneel, and the foot of the cross." She sat down heavily on Damek's desk chair and lowered her head to her hands. "Do you know how many heroes and crosses there are in Prague?"

"Hey." Nick crouched down in front of the chair and spun it slightly until Helena faced him. "I know it seems impossible, and I know you're sick and cold and so tired. But you keep figuring things out, and you know so much more about Prague and her history than I do. Damek wanted you to be my squire for so many reasons."

Helena lifted her head, brushing back her long hair from the unshaved half of her head. "Maybe," she said, "but I don't know anything about reforging steel."

"Yeah, that part's insane. I'm ignoring anything about smelting and forging for the time being."

"One step at a time," Helena nodded. "Thanks," she said.

"For what?" Nick asked. "For needing you?"

"For believing in me."

Nick blushed and had to look away, moving his eyes anywhere else so he wasn't just staring back at her. They came to rest on the large painting that hung on the wall behind his uncle's desk.

"Nick?" Helena snapped her fingers in front of his nose. "Are you okay?"

"Hidden in plain sight," he murmured.

Helena followed his line of sight to the painting of the lone knight below the cross at Charles Bridge, and gasped. She leaned forward to read the small plaque inset in the ornate frame. "I swear I've seen this painting a dozen times, and I never bothered to read the title," she murmured.

"The Foot of the Cross," Nick whispered.

"Nick, that's it! You really *are* a genius!"

Nick's whole body glowed with hope as he zipped the dagger into his backpack. He still didn't know what Horymir wanted with it, and maybe it would be safer here in the house. But whatever happened when they found the final clue, Nick figured they'd need all the help they could get. Leaving the dagger behind just felt *wrong* somehow.

"Come on," he said. "We still have time."

CHAPTER THIRTY – The Hospital

The hospital had descended into total, eerie silence. The only sound Kat could hear was Mom grunting as she shoved all of her weight against the door to the hallway again and again.

It wouldn't budge an inch.

"Shhh," Kat hissed loudly. "Listen."

Mom stopped pushing and strained her ears. Very faintly at first but growing louder every second, she heard the click-clacking of something moving down the hallway. Something coming closer.

Click-clack...click-clack...click-clack.

"I... I thought you said Horymir couldn't hurt us?" Mom stuttered.

"He can't get in my dreams anymore," Kat said. "And he can't make me say and do things I don't want to do while I'm wearing the pendant. And he couldn't come in the house because we didn't invite him."

"Damek's house?" Mom's voice rose in pitch. "He tried to get into Damek's house? When?"

"When you went to dinner with Mr. Zeman."

The single pair of clittering-clattering footsteps in the hallway had been joined by several others.

"Ah, Katarina. My young acolyte. We meet in the waking world once more."

Mom gasped at the sound of the voice coming from the hallway, but Kat only glared at the window set in the metal door.

A stone face peered in from the other side, its round, sightless eyes staring right into Kat's skull.

"Is that...?" Mom's question hung in the air for a moment before she answered it herself. "No, Anna. This is insane. Pull yourself together!"

"It's one of the statues from outside the hospital," Kat confirmed. "Horymir is a magician. He can make things move like Uncle Damek made puppets move."

"Ahh, this must be your mother, Anna, all grown up." The statue's lips weren't moving, but the sound was definitely coming from its head.

The statue turned its face toward Mom. "As you may know, Anna, my access to your daughter's mind was cut regrettably short. She has been remarkably helpful until very recently. You should be proud to be raising such an obedient young lady."

"Shut up, you stupid butthead!" Kat half-shouted through gritted teeth.

Mom's eyes widened, but she didn't say a word. She hurriedly turned the lock on the doorknob and stepped back.

"Oh, ho, ho! Such a fierce little lion!" The statue threw its head back, cackling laughter emanating from its permanently-open mouth. "I would love to stay and play, but I am afraid all my resources will shortly be needed elsewhere."

The statue's face disappeared from the window and the hallway fell silent.

BOOM!

Mom pulled Kat tight against her.

BOOM!

A bulge appeared in the metal door.

BOOM!

And another.

"Kat?" Mom walked backward, pulling Kat with her until they both stood huddled up against the far wall of Mr. Zeman's room.

The door crashed open. Two stoney figures discarded a third, smaller statue they'd used as a battering ram on the ground. Its head promptly crumbled to pieces.

Mom's horrified scream punctuated the military march of the two remaining statues as they marched into the room and unceremoniously pulled Kat from her arms, dragging her out into the corridor where another half-dozen statues waited at attention.

"NO!" Mom plunged into the hall after them, grabbing at their arms and legs, but every hold she found was easily shaken off.

"Be still, wench!" Horymir's voice echoed in the silent hall. "I have underestimated your brats before. I will not do so again. This one will remain in my possession until the knight kneels before me. If I am feeling generous.

Immediately, a stiff wind blew open the double doors in front of the marching statues. The wind raced toward Mom, whipping her hair around her head, sending her tumbling to the ground, pushing her further and further back until she crossed the threshold into Mr. Zeman's room.

The door swung closed. Mom lay in a heap on the linoleum floor, panting for breath, tears streaming down her bruised cheeks.

"Anna..."

Mr. Zeman's voice was so weak that at first, Anna thought she'd imagined it. But then she heard it again.

"Anna. It is time to call for help."

Painfully, she pulled herself to her feet and limped to Mr. Zeman's bed. "I'm so sorry," she said, clutching his hand. "The phone lines are down. Wifi, too, and the button isn't working. I didn't want to leave you or Kat..." She broke off in a sob.

Mr. Zeman squeezed her hand gently. "Not the phone..." he rasped. "Your mother's ring. You must...twist the ring and call them. You must wake them."

Anna shook her head. "That was just a game." Vividly, she remembered her mother placing the ring on her too-small finger. It had been in a hospital room not unlike this one, when she was eleven. Her parents had been in a car accident. Her father had been killed instantly, but she'd gotten to say good-by to her mother.

"This ring will keep you safe, Anna," her mother told her. "And when you are sad, it will remind you of me. Wear it always, and know that I am always with you, even if you can't see or hear me. And if you are ever in danger and have nowhere to turn, twist the ring three times. Our family is strong, Anna. Your ancestors are watching over you."

For several months after the funeral, Anna had been unable to bear the sight of the ring. Why would she ever believe it could keep her safe when it had failed so miserably to protect her parents? But after time passed, Anna looked for as many ways as possible to feel close to her mother.

"It was...not a game."

Mr. Zeman's voice was barely audible.. Anna leaned in close to hear his words.

"Remember what your uncle told you...when you were old enough...to go out...on your own?"

How could she forget? Every time she'd gone out with her schoolmates, and later, when she'd begun to date, Damek made sure she was wearing her mother's ring whenever she left the house. She'd had to have it resized over the years. At times, she believed her uncle was more concerned with the fit of the ring and making sure she wore it than he was about scheduling her yearly dental visits. When mobile phones had first become available, she begged to get one, but Uncle Damek had insisted she didn't need one until she had finished high school.

"If you ever need help, divenka," he'd say, somewhat teasingly, "you can use your mother's ring to call our ancestors. That ring can wake the dead!"

Now, looking down at the gold band, these memories came rushing back. Despite the dark hospital interior and the terrifying circumstances, she imagined a comfort and strength encircling her, like the memory of her mother's embrace.

"He told me it was Queen Neomenia's ring," she murmured, fondly. "I haven't thought of that in years."

"Bruncvík gave Neomenia the ring to protect her in his absence."

Once, as a young adult, she'd bristled at the tale of the supposedly heroic knight leaving his young wife for seven years while he roamed the land with his two-tailed lion seeking out adventure. The ring hadn't been left for protection, she was certain. It had been left as a sign of ownership.

"You have a gift for seeing beyond the legends men tell to the truth of the matter," Damek had nodded when she'd told him what she thought. "But this ring's story has never been about the man who gave it away. Rather, it is about the women who wear it."

Sirens wailed outside the hospital, punctuated by screams and blaring alarms. Anna knew that things didn't always turn out all right. So many things in her life had not turned out all right. Right now, things were definitely not okay.

It had been a long time since she'd felt she'd had much control over much of anything, but she had control over one thing at least. She could stay here in the hospital and insist that there was no such thing as ancient, power-hungry sorcerers, or she could twist her ring three times and then go and find her children. And she could rip to shreds anyone who got in her way.

CHAPTER THIRTY-ONE - Kneel, Knight

Faint beams of moonlight penetrated the thick fog that continuously hung over everything, bathing Nick and Helena in a deep, pale glow as they ran through Old Town toward the east end of the Charles Bridge.

A chill ran through Nick as he realized it was only 7:30 P.M. – way too early for it to be this dark. The statues flanking each side appeared and disappeared as the beams from their flashlights zigged and zagged across the mist in time with their footsteps.

"Here it is." Helena came to an abrupt stop in front of the third grouping on the north side of the river. She bent down with her hands on her knees, catching her breath.

Nick played the beam of his flashlight along three figures that made up the Crucifix and Calvary, crisscrossing Helena's beam as they searched for any ancient-looking letters. Two statues, one of Mary and one of John the Baptist, flanked three plaques detailing the display in English, Czech, and Hebrew. Up above, the figure of Jesus hung below giant, golden letters forming an arc above his head. "I hope they aren't up there." He indicated the highest point with the flashlight. "The cross must be at least 20 feet tall. Are any of those big gold letters in Aramaic?"

"I wish," Helena sighed. "That would be so helpful. But no, they're in Hebrew. This statue is quite controversial, actually. The legend is that during

World War II, the Nazi's turned one of the letters backward, which changed the entire meaning." She shivered, wrapping her arms around herself. "It reminds me of when Rabbi Loew used a single letter to bring the golem to life. Horymir mentioned it in Wenceslas Square. He said something like 'if a single letter has that much power, imagine what a whole word could do.'"

Nick stared down at the worn spot on the bridge directly in front of the statue's base; the stone had become smooth and glossy there from centuries of faithful women and men kneeling to pray.

The distant cries and shouts from both ends of the bridge seemed to be getting nearer. It sounded like every car alarm in Prague was going off at once. As Nick stared at the shining spot, the image of Kat's face frozen in scream after terrified scream crowded his mind. Horymir had done that. Horymir had made his little sister afraid to go to sleep. He'd made her sneak around and lie and shout at him. He made her so cold that nothing could get her warm. And now it was happening to Helena, too.

Think, Nick, THINK. He ran over the final two stanzas in his mind as he stared down at the glossy stone: *Beneath the place where heroes kneel/The knight and squire... Wait, that's it!*

He dropped to his knees.

"Nick, what are you doing?" Helena asked, joining him in front of the statue. "Are you hurt?"

"'...the place where heroes kneel...'"

"Oh my gosh, that's it!" Helena trained her flashlight on the bridge. "Scoot back a little – you're covering half of it!"

"Hold the light steady...right there!" Nick pointed. In the glow of light, what had looked like random scratches resolved into the final letters of the word of power.

"It says... *'ah,'*" Helena murmured.

"So an 'N,' 'shruh,' and 'ah'...?"

"Most Aramaic letters are just consonants," Helena's arm began to tremble again. "You have to just guess the vowel sounds if you don't know them already. So maybe something like *Nashroah*?"

"Or *Neshrea*?" Nick guessed.

A low rumbling sprung up from all around them, and the ground shifted. Slowly at first, then all at once, the stone beneath Nick's feet sank and then slid outwards from the symbol he'd just found. He scrambled back from the widening hole that opened right in front of him.

"Whoa."

Helena muttered something in Czech that Nick didn't catch as the two of them stared open mouthed at the chasm that had just opened in the middle of the bridge.

"We did it, Nick!" Helena threw her arms around him. "We found the clues and it worked!"

"This is what the knights wanted us to find," he breathed, peering into the dark pit. Finally turned to Helena. "Did it mean anything? The word?"

"I don't know much Aramaic," Helena said slowly, "but in Hebrew, *Neshir* is the word for eagle. I wonder if it has something to do with the Red Eagle..."

As the sound of the rumbling and grinding stone died down, a new sound took its place, silencing Helena: faint footsteps approaching them from the same direction they'd arrived. Footsteps, and...*chanting*.

"He's here," Helena whispered.

Instinctively, she and Nick flattened themselves against the surface of the bridge, laying as still as possible, their eyes locked on the source of the echoing sound drawing closer. Soon, the outline of dark figures emerged from the shrouded mist, close to the bridge.

"He's going to see us," Helena whispered, voice shaking.

"No. He's not." Nick grabbed his backpack and tossed it into the gaping hole that had opened beneath them.

Helena nodded, steeling herself. "Lower me down."

"No way." Nick shook his head. "I'm going first.

The strange chanting drew nearer.

Nick handed his flashlight to Helena and slid his feet into the hole, shimmying over the edge on his belly. His breath hitched as his bad hip caught on a rough rock shard.

Helena took his hands and lowered him, straining, as far as she could. "Can you touch?" she whispered.

Nick shook his head. "Hand me my flashlight!"

"Are you nuts? You'll fall!"

"I'll probably fall anyway." He let go of one of her hands. "I'd like to see how far before I land."

Muttering to herself, Helena grabbed one of the flashlights and handed it down to him. Nick shone it around the chamber. "Nick, it's huge! Are you sure you can..."

Before Helena could finish, and before he could psych himself out, Nick let go and fell.

"Nick!" Helena's eyes were wide with fear. "Are you okay?"

He nodded up at her. "Come on," he whispered.

Helena dropped her flashlight into Nick's outstretched hands, then twisted her body around and backed into the hole, lowering herself down feet first. She started to slip, her elbows giving way, but Nick's hands were already at her knees.

"I've got you," he said again.

She let herself fall.

Within seconds, Horymir's footsteps sounded overhead. Nick and Helena clicked off their flashlights, huddling together as far back from the opening above them as they could, together, staring up without breathing.

The chanting continued on past the statue, walking towards the west end of the bridge.

"What do you think he's doing?" Helena asked, releasing Nick.

"I don't know," Nick breathed, switching his flashlight on, "but check this place out!"

"It smells so...old and dark and wet down here," Helena covered her nose and mouth as she switched hers on, too, shining it around the interior of a claustrophobic chamber of crumbling stone and packed dirt.

Nick crouched to keep his head from brushing the clumps of roots and debris hanging from the ceiling.

"It looks like some kind of shrine or something," Helena whispered. "Look, those stacked stones must have been an altar."

Together, their flashlight beams skittered over the surface of the hole above the ancient altar like metallic bugs.

A deafening grinding of stone against stone above made them both jump. Nick dropped his flashlight.

"That can't be good." Helena's voice was barely audible above the noise.

A *BOOM* like a cannonball hit the bridge. The underground chamber quaked, knocking them both off their feet. Dust and gravel showered down onto their heads.

"That sounded like artillery!" Nick whispered.

"That doesn't sound like guns." Helena ducked as the next *BOOM!* dislodged more dirt and debris.

BOOM!

"You're right," Nick muttered, "it sounds like tanks." A few fist-sized rocks crumbled from the wall near the opening they'd made, revealing a thin glint of metal beneath the bedrock.

"Nick, look!" Helena pointed her flashlight. "What's that?"

BOOM!

More rocks and mortar fell, exposing the edge of something steel lodged high up in the wall of the chamber; the nicked, dirt-covered, hiltless blade sparkled in the light.

"Wait!" Nick scrambled to his backpack.

"What?" Helena demanded.

"Look! That's the blade of a hand-and-a-half sword without a hilt!"

"So?"

He unzipped the backpack and pulled out the dagger, holding it up."

"Wait. No way. You don't mean...?"

"It's not a dagger. See how the metal matches? It's a hilt and the rest of that sword."

"It's the weapon! I think I can reach it!"

BOOM!

Helena clenched her fists. Grime covered her pale face and clung to her hair. She inhaled deeply, then launched herself into action, leaping onto the altar stone and springing up to grab the blade.

But just as her fingertips reached out for it, a loud, metallic CLANG filled the chamber and Helena's body flew back from the blade in a shower of sparks.

"Helena!" Nick raced to where she lay crumpled on the ground.

"I'm okay," she said, cradling her right hand, "but there's definitely some kind of magic protecting it. No wonder Horymir hasn't attacked us directly yet. I'm guessing you're the only one who can touch it, young knight."

He shook his head. "But I can't jump like you just did," he said, reaching down and pulling her to her feet. "There's no way I'll be able to reach it unless you have a ladder in your backpack."

"You can either try or not, but if you don't, we're probably going to die. So maybe just try?"

"You should be a motivational speaker."

"It's not easy being right all the time," she moaned. "And I know I keep saying this, but I'd really rather not die."

Nick backed up to the other end of the chamber. The hilt of what he now knew was a sword felt right in his hand. He measured the distance between him and the blade in his head. Then he approached, fast-walking at first, then speeding up into a jog, then a run, then a sprint. Right before he reached the wall, he jumped.

For a brief moment, as he soared up and forward, he wasn't in some secret chamber hidden under a bridge in Prague. He was back home in the forest by his house, sailing over the creek. There were no other people, no bullies, not Tony, not Jeremy, not even the rope. Just him, flying through the air.

He was going to make it. When he was a split second away from smashing face-first into the wall in front of him, he shouted: "Neshrea!"

In a flash, a dance of white stripes overwhelmed Nick's vision.

Surrounded by a wall of blinding light, his hand wrapped around the hilt of the dagger, Nick's body floated, suspended in the air. Time stood still, and the world went silent except for the singing of metal meeting metal as the broken pieces merged.

Nick's feet hit the ground, jolting each bone in his body. He barely noticed it. The reforged sword gleamed in his hand.

"The sword of the Golden City!"

Blinking away the swirling after-image, Nick's vision finally cleared. Helena stood a few feet away, shielding her face with her arms and squinting her eyes, mouth open in awe.

"The what?"

"Nick, that's Bruncvik's sword! The sword of the Golden City. That's why Horymir wanted the dagger so bad: he knew it was the hilt of the sword! He already has the power to animate an army, but if he has Bruncvik's sword, no one can stop him. All he'd have to do is yell 'Blade. Heads off!' and his enemies will all fall at his feet!"

Bruncvik's sword...?

Confidence surged through Ansel's body as he held the sword in his hand. The weight felt good – right – almost as if it were an extension of his body and mind. He was proud to have been the one chosen to wield it. With it, he would cleanse the kingdom of this evil sorcerer once and for all!

His dream came back to him. He understood now. The answer had been with him the whole time.

BOOM!

The banging sound from above snapped them both out of their reverie. By the sound of things, Horymir had reached the west end of the bridge and was now making his way back. With several some*things* that sounded HEAVY.

"C'mon! Let's go kick Horymir's butt!" Lacing her fingers together, Helena made a stirrup with her hands and held them out for Nick.

Without hesitating, Nick stepped onto her cupped hands and kicked up. With her boost, he made it out of the sinkhole to the surface of the bridge. Once he had his footing, he reached down to pull her up.

Standing on the bridge once more, Nick palmed the hilt of the dagger-turned-legendary-sword. The weight of the blade rested heavy in his hand. The length was definitely fitted for an adult. Still, holding it felt *right* somehow.

He turned the sword this way and that, mesmerized by the balance and the razor-sharp, double-edged blade. It was real. Brucvik's magic sword was real. Not only was it real, he…Nick Damek Gordon…was holding it in his hand.

BOOM!

Helena pulled him down into a crouch beside her. They both turned in the direction of the Earth-shaking rumble.

Horymir strode slowly across the bridge toward them from the west, chanting something Nick couldn't hear. His fingers and hands wove patterns in the air, and his eyes glowed with unholy light.

He wasn't alone.

Polished, angular, impossibly heavy figures crowded the bridge behind him, following in his wake. Every set of statues on the north and south sides of the bridge groaned to life as the sorcerer walked by.

Screeching metal and cracking of marble echoed through the night as carved and cast images of saints, heroes, and knights broke free from their pedestals. Stretching their limbs, they flexed before stepping down and landing with a crushing *BOOM!* onto the bridge. One by one, they fell in line behind Horymir, mutely following their master on huge, stiff, marble legs. The features of their stony faces stared blankly ahead, unseeing.

"I think I know where Horymir is going to get his army from," Helena moaned.

CHAPTER THIRTY-TWO - Heads Off!

Several of the animated statues broke free from the main group at some silent command from Horymir. They stepped off the sides of the bridge, splashing down into the Vltava River and briefly submerging before walking straight up onto the riverbanks and advancing into Lesser Town at the west end of the bridge, and Old Town on the east end.

Nick's head swiveled from side to side, eyes growing wider as he watched the statues begin destroying the city. In front of him, the sorcerer advanced step-by-step to where he and Helena stood beneath the Crucifix and Calvary statue. His grip tightened on the sword.

"By the time he's here," Helena breathed, "he'll have almost 30 statue-golems just from the bridge, and that's not counting the groups with multiple figures. Plus, who knows how many other statues from Lesser Town he reanimated on his way here? Nick, we have to do something! There are statues literally *everywhere* in Prague!"

The sorcerer and his golems were only yards away. Now feet. Nick sucked in his breath. He'd never seen Horymir in the flesh before, but he was somehow taller than he expected. Or maybe it was that his back wasn't nearly as crooked as Nick had pictured.

Without thinking, Nick moved his sword arm behind his back.

At that exact moment, Horymir turned his head and locked eyes with Nick. "Thank you for retrieving my sword, young knight," he said. "Hold it for me just a little longer while I awaken the rest of my soldiers."

The sorcerer's voice whispered quietly in Nick's ears, and the chaos around him seemed to fall away. Though he fought with all his might to keep it still, his hand holding Bruncvik's sword inched out from behind him..

"Look out!" Helena grabbed Nick's free hand, pulling him out of the way as the two statues above them split apart from Calvary Hill and jumped down onto the bridge.

Whatever spell Horymir had put on him was broken as Nick and Helena sheltered on the west side of the broken pedestal.

Police arrived on the scene, parking their cruisers on either end of the bridge. The shrill wail of sirens echoed, muffled in the dense fog; flashing lights strobed red and blue, casting strange shadows in the mist.

The officers milled around, bewildered and unorganized. Nick doubted anything in their training had prepared them for this.

One officer approached Horymir and his golem from the barricade the police had set up between the bridge Old Town. But before she could reach him, the statue of St. Ivo stepped in front of her. It was flanked by two orphan statues – a baby and a young boy.

The orphan statues flung themselves at the police officer. The stone baby – as tall as the officer's waist – scampered up to the woman's torso, pinning her arms to her sides. She screamed, and then screamed again as the little-boy statue crashed into her legs. She sprawled backward over the stone safety wall. Her scream went suddenly silent as she hit the water with a splash.

The statue of a beggar, its thin body carved with hunger, advanced on a squad car parked just behind the barricade. Two officers exited the car and sprinted off just before the statue's fingerless fists caved in the car's roof.

"Do something, Nick!" Helena gasped. "Wield the sword! Over there!"

Wield the sword? The words couldn't connect with the command center of his brain. He stared at the blade clutched in his hand like he'd never seen it before.

From somewhere nearby, Horymir cackled.

"Focus, Young Knight," he heard Damek's voice speaking calmly in his mind. *"You know the words to say: 'Blade! Heads off!'"*

Relieved, Nick raised the sword above his head, turning to see where Helena was pointing only to find...

...she was gone.

Nick spun, eyes scanning the bridge. Where could she be? "Helena!" he yelled. "Helen..." His voice cut off as he smacked face-first into a marble wall.

No.

Not a wall.

A leg.

An enormous, stone leg protruding from King Wenceslas' armored statue.

Head spinning, Nick gazed up at the statue towering above him. Wenceslas' hands were no longer clasped together in prayer. One held an enormous lance. The other rested empty at its side.

Aas if it had just thrown something as hard as it could.

Oh no.

Nick stumbled back and looked up just in time to see Helena as she landed in a heap more than halfway down the bridge near the statue of St. Jude. She didn't even twitch on impact.

The only thought in Nick's head was that she'd be crushed underfoot if he didn't move her out of the way. *Now.*

He took off running, ignoring the protests from his hip. He'd taken only a few steps, though, before a faint breeze brushing across his cheekbone. Instinctively, Nick raised the gleaming sword defensively above his head. The next second, stone Wenceslas' 15-foot lance collided with Bruncvik's sword...

...and shattered.

Nick's sword arm vibrated so hard from the impact, he was shocked his bones hadn't fractured.

The statue stumbled back but quickly regained its footing. Moving remarkably fast for stone, the sculpted Wenceslas repositioned its shield from bicep to forearm and swiped at Nick, but Nick somersaulted out of reach.

Nick raised Bruncvik's sword and shouted: "Blade! Head off!"

An audible *CRACK* rippled from the statue's neck. Its whole body *shivered* with a shrill, resonant ringing. Wenceslas' statue clasped at the source of the crack with both hands as if hoping to hold it in place, but it was too late. The head toppled to the ground and landed at Nick's feet with a *THUD.*

Hope surged inside him as King Wenceslas' statue teetered and swayed, falling to one knee.

The victory was short-lived. A fresh statue clambered over King Wenceslas, wildly swinging at Nick with a large club.

Dodging the blows, Nick sprinted west as fast as his twisted leg allowed. He was almost there. Only a few more yards to go.

A terrified scream rang out from behind him at the east end of the bridge. Dread latched onto Nick's heart. He stopped in his tracks. He knew that scream.

Kat.

"Nicholas Damek Gordon."

Nick turned.

Horymir stood backlit by flames that licked at buildings, burned cars, and torched trees. At least 100 statues from all corners of Old Town stood on either side of him. Their ranks now included shop mannequins, eyeless CPR dummies from the hospital, and even rougher-looking figures that look like they'd been formed from bricks and mud.

He's making more golems, Nick thought in horror. *I'll never be able to take them down fast enough, not even with the sword.*

Four statues – Nick recognized them from the courtyard outside the hospital – clutched Kat between them. She kicked and screamed like a wildcat. Behind him, booming steps warned him more statues were approaching. He jumped out of the way just before being plowed down by a statue stomping past him with Helena's lifeless form slung over its shoulder.

"I told you to hold the blade for me, not use it against my soldiers." Horymir's words snaked across the bridge to Nick's ears, infusing the fog-filled night air. "Now I have your precious Katarina, among other things you value. Perhaps you'll agree to a trade?"

"You may have caught her, but you can't hurt her!" Nick yelled. "She's protected by..."

"By this?" Horymir cut him off, raising his right hand.

Nick's stomach clenched as he recognized the lion pendant dangling from the sorcerer's hand, gently swaying back and forth.

"I no longer need to toy with her mind now that I control her body." Horymir cast the pendant on the ground at his feet. "What kind of brother leaves his baby sister with no protection other than some ancient bauble?"

A wave of guilt washed over Nick. Horymir was right. He should never have left Kat and Mom alone. His sword-arm ache and his hip burned.

"Now, now, young knight. You must not blame yourself. You are far too young to be burdened with parenting your sister *and* saving the world." The sorcerer's voice brimmed with mock-sympathy. "It is time to end this. Give me the sword, and I will release your loved ones."

An overwhelming sense of helplessness joined the guilt weighing Nick down. What choice did he really have? He couldn't let Horymir hurt Kat, but he was just one boy against an undead madman's army.

"There, there," Horymir continued. "You have done admirably, Nicholas. You made it much farther than that foolish uncle of yours. St. Anne, bring me my sword."

At the mention of Damek, the helplessness and guilt vaporized, replaced by steel-cold anger. Nick growled deep in his throat.

A dozen yards away, the statue of St. Anne sprang into action. Its voluminous stone robes seemed to billow around it as it snatched the large stone ball from a parapet and stalked toward Nick. He raised the sword above his head and shouted, "Blade! Head..."

Before he could finish the command, St. Anne threw the stone ball straight at him. He dove to the side – a fraction of a second too late. The ball struck a glancing blow to his right shoulder. His arm spasmed, each nerve on fire. The sword clattered to the bridge.

St. Anne's feet pounded across the bridge toward him.

Clutching his arm to his side, Nick dove on top of the sword. He may be just a boy and he may be outnumbered a hundred to one, but he wasn't going to make this any easier for Horymir. All at once, it became clear to him that even if he handed over Bruncvik's sword, Horymir was never going to let anyone go.

As St. Anne barreled closer, Nick fumbled beneath his body with his left arm. When the statue was five steps in front of him, he grasped the sword's grip, held it up, and shouted: "Blade! Head off!"

With a concussive *CRACK!* St. Anne's head split from its body, rolling forward until it bumped against Nick's shoulder. Its marble body hit the bridge hard, thrashing about.

"Bruncvik, attend this rabble," Horymir commanded without a hint of concern.

The heavy footfalls of six approaching feet warned Nick that the statue of the legendary knight and his two-tailed lion were only a few dozen yards away.

"It's not your sword!" Nick yelled. Stiffly, he rose to his feet, heavy with exhaustion. His right arm hung slack and useless by his side. He gripped the heavy sword in his left hand and raised it awkwardly. "This is the real Bruncvik's sword. It belongs to the people of Prague!"

"That sword severed my soul from my mortal body," Horymir said, "not to mention my head."

At once, every animated statue on the bridge snapped to attention, standing completely still, even the two without heads.

"You have fulfilled your part in my plan by reforging the sword...something only an heir could do," the sorcerer continued, "and for that you have my thanks. However, now that your purpose has been served, you are no longer needed." The puppeteer strode toward the middle of the bridge where Nick stood, followed closely by the statues carrying Kat and Helena.

They stopped about 20 feet away from Nick, clearly obeying some silent signal from the Horymir, who continued forward.

Nick blinked. Horymir was...*different*...somehow. Less sinister. In fact, as he drew closer, Nick gasped. The cruel lips that had pulled tight over the sorcerer's pointed, yellow teeth in Nick's dreams were gone. This man's lips were dry and thin, but they were gentle and caring, too. And his eyes that had glowed wickedly before now shone with concern.

Concern for me, Nick realized. He found his muscles beginning to relax, and shook himself back to attention. *It has to be a trick.*

"I am sorry, son," the man said as he approached. "I am sorry for what they have done to you. I grieve for your loss and for your pain. This burden should never have fallen to one so young, so vulnerable. Not just the responsibility of recovering the sword, but the well-being of your sister and mother, and your friends, too. You are tired, Nicholas. Let me help you carry your burden."

The tears that had dried up just days after Damek passed suddenly welled up in Nick's eyes again. He'd thought he would never cry again. But this man - this kind man whose voice almost reminded him of his uncle's - was going to help him. Finally, Nick would be able to rest and grieve properly.

"Come now, son," the compassionate voice soothed. "Hand me the sword and I will take you to your mother. She's waiting just there with your sister. They are very worried about you."

Nick's eyes followed the man's finger to the east end of the bridge. Sure enough, Kat and Mom stood together, hands clasped, waving and smiling at him.

He lowered his left arm gratefully, letting the tip of the sword rest against the surface of the bridge. "Thank you," he said. "I *am* tired. I've been having such strange dreams..."

"That's it," the nice old man said. "Just close your eyes and I will take care of everything."

Nick's eyelids sagged.

"There, there," the old man crooned, his voice like a lullaby. "Don't struggle. That's it, let your mind and body relax."

As his eyes closed, Nick was aware that the nice, grandfatherly man had almost reached him, was stretching his arm toward the sword. In a moment more, none of this would matter. Once he gave the sword to the man, he could lay down and sleep soundly. All his worries would disappear...

...in his dream, Nick stood on a beach. A massive tsunami roared out at sea, climbing into the sky, blocking out the light of the noon sun as it hurtled toward the shore.

Instinctively, he dropped to his knees and then to his side, curling into a protective ball.

This is a dream, a calm voice whispered in his head. There is no giant wave. Open your eyes, Nick, and see.

He knew this voice. He trusted this voice. He opened his eyes.

The wave had disappeared. Now an enormous lion stood before him, pawing at the sand with dangerous-looking claws.

"Kat?"

The lion tossed its shaggy mane, bared its teeth, and roared.

"Kat, the nice old man says I shouldn't have to do this. I'm too young to hold the sword, too young to protect everyone. I'm so tired, Kat, and the sword is so heavy."

The lion reared up on its hind legs. Words flashed through Nick's mind: "That is Horymir, Nick. He's not a nice old man. He LIES, remember? You can't trust someone just because they tell you what you want to hear. You are strong enough to do hard things. Wake up, Nick. You need. To Wake. UP!"

The rearing lion's split-tail writhed behind it like a double-headed serpent. With a final roar, it lunged forward, shoving against Nick's chest with its powerful forepaws...

...Nick's back hit the bridge hard. The sword of the Golden City clattered loudly on the ground beside his feet. He raised his head to see Horymir leering down at him, eyes glowing greedily as he grabbed for the sword.

Desperate, Nick kicked the sword away from Horymir with his bad leg, grunting in pain.

"Not quite whole, are you, young knight?" Horymir rose casually. "I could straighten your hip for you. You obviously have strong potential as a dreamer if you were able to break free from my spell. If you give me the blade willingly instead of making me take it by force, I will heal your deformity and grant you a place of great honor in my regime."

Still on his back, Nick dug in with his elbows and heels, painfully inching his way toward the sword. "Do you really think," he asked through gritted teeth, "that I care more about having a disability than I do about helping an insane murderer?"

"You stupid, cripple boy," Horymir snarled. "Bruncvik. My blade!"

Bruncvik's titanic stone foot smashed down a hair's-breadth away from Nick's outstretched hand, right on top of the sword of the Golden City.

"Adalbert!" Horymir called. "Luthgard! Methodius! Take the boy and bind him along with his little sister and their friend. I have a city to conquer. I will waste no more time bartering with a child."

Bruncvik's gigantic hand scooped up the blade. Terrified screams, alarms, and wailing sirens assaulted Nick's ears. Lying on his back in the middle of the bridge, Nick had no way to shut out the screech of twisting metal and the crunch of toppling buildings. No way to help.

Two pairs of stone hands reached down and grasped his body, hauling him up and away from the sword. "I'm sorry, Damek," he whispered.

But in the distance, a rhythmic pulsing joined the pandemonium of the city, thrumming like the thundering of a thousand horses' hoofbeats and the muffled thump of a drum.

CHAPTER THIRTY-THREE - The Red Eagle

"Statues!" Horymir's voice boomed, his head snapping to some point in the distance. "Drop everything and fall in line!"

At once, the stone soldiers released Nick, letting him free fall a few yards to the bridge.

His breath whooshed from his lungs and stars spun in his vision. His tailbone and lower back throbbed like live wires. Part of him prayed for the relief of unconsciousness. But hope sparked through him, too.

Horymir's voice had wavered with fear.

As he sat up, the rush of blood in his ears momentarily blocked out the sounds of chaos. His gut heaved as he staggered to his feet. In front of him, the reanimated army stood in straight lines, shoulder to shoulder and at least five rows deep.

What happened? Why did they let me go? Is it already over?

Rubbing the bump forming on the back of his head, Nick turned around, searching for any clue about what had happened.

A bright gleam from further down the bridge caught his eye.

The sword of the Golden City.

No moonlight or lamplight traced the surface of the blade. Nearly covered in rubble, the sword shone from within, calling to Nick. He scrabbled back toward the spot the statues had picked him up.

But how? I saw Bruncvik's statue pick it up!

Horymir's command came back to him: "Drop everything and fall in line!"

But what had made the sorcerer give such a strange command? And why had he sounded scared?

Reaching down, he grasped the hilt of the sword.

A bugle's call pierced the night.

"THE QUEEN'S HEIR HAS SUMMONED US. STAND DOWN, SORCERER."

Confusion flooded Nick's mind. Who was the Queen's heir? And who was speaking? Who had been summoned?

Nothing in any myth Nick had studied had he ever heard anything about a queen's heir. Had there? Of course, there were queens, but...

Helena would know what's going on, he thought. *Focus Nick. There's no time for this now. I need to get to Kat and Helena. Maybe I get away with them while Horymir is distracted by the queen's heir.*

Quietly, he limped as quickly as he could to the rear of the statues standing in formation. Once he reached the back row, he knelt down and crawled between the rows of statues' immobile legs, careful to keep the blade from hitting the ground and making noise.

Sweat dripped down his face, streaking through the dust and grime that covered him. His knees ached and his hip burned, but he clenched his teeth. One stomp from a statue could end his life in a second. But he couldn't stop. He had to get to Kat and Helena

He reached the front line and peeked around the stone robes of Frances Borgia's statue.

Horymir stood less than ten feet away.

Nick's pulse spiked.

"You are too late!" Angry spittle sprayed from Horymir's mouth, but the gleam in his eyes held fear, too. The sorcerer glared into the dark, past where the police barricades had been to where the bugle call and the commanding voice had come from. His hand opened and closed reflexively around nothing.

The sword.

Menacing shapes shifted in the night beyond the end of the bridge. Nick heard the impatient stomp of a horse's hoof accompanied by a whiny, and all at once, he knew:

The Knights of Blaník had awoken.

As if on cue, a single, noble figure on horseback emerged from the swirling mist, bathed in an eerie, unnatural light. Upon his helm rested a simple golden circlet. A blood red eagle emblazoned his breastplate.

Nick nearly dropped Bruncvik's sword. *King Wenceslas!* Not the statue. The actual King.

The enormous warhorse's armor glowed, reflecting the burning city's flames, and a twin flame flickered furiously in its eyes as it advanced.

A dozen feet away from Horymir, King Wenceslas reined in his steed. The animal tossed its head and pawed the ground.

"MAGICIAN, STAND DOWN."

For a moment, Nick couldn't understand what the king was saying. His accent sounded like Horymir's, but the words were garbled.

"Your majesty." Horymir bowed low, his arm sweeping the ground in mock respect. "You are looking much better than when last I saw you."

Ignoring Horymir's jeer, King Wensceslas turned his head, gazing directly into Nick's eyes. "STEP FORWARD, YOUNG KNIGHT," he commanded. "BRING ME THE SWORD OF THE GOLDEN CITY."

Heart pounding in his chest, he rose from his crouch and stepped out from behind the statue of Francis Borgia. *Everything will be okay now. The King will defeat Horymir, and Kat and Helena will...*

"Nick!"

Nick froze at Kat's panicked cry. He whipped around.

The statues carrying Helena's unconscious form dropped her body unceremoniously in a heap on the bridge just behind Horymir. Those carrying Kat had set her on her feet. One held each arm, and another had its hands wrapped around her neck. The fourth held a long, jagged shard of stone to her neck. She stared at Nick, eyes wide with terror.

Red spots of anger floated across Nick's vision. He wanted to tear Horymir to shreds. He wanted to bash the statues to pieces.

He had to save Kat. He had to help Helena. But how? Hoyrmir's soldiers outnumbered him a hundred to one.

"Ah, my little acolyte." Horymir casually approached the spot his statues restrained Kat. He placed both hands on Kat's small head. "How easy it was to gain your trust and exploit your innocence. Has no one ever taught you not to speak to strangers?"

A snarl rose in Nick's throat as Horymir stroked the side of Kat's cheek. She stared up at the sorcerer, eyes as blank as one of his statues.

Horymir held out his hand, into which the statue placed the stone shard. Then he yanked Kat's head back by her hair and pressed it to her throat

"Now, young knight, relinquish my sword, or young Katarina dies."

It didn't matter that he held the Sword of the Golden City, or that the legendary King Wenceslas waited mere yards away. If either of them tried anything, Kat would take her last breath.

Movement on the bridge a few feet from Horymir's feet caught the corner of Nick's eye. A pale face he knew by heart appeared above Helena's forgotten body.

Mom.

She raised a finger to her lips to signal quiet. The glow of an ancient ring flickered in her eyes.

Hope ignited in Nick's chest. He had to keep Horymir's attention so he wouldn't notice Mom. "You're nothing but a disgusting coward!" he shouted as Mom carefully rolled Helena onto her back and brushed back her hair from her face

Horymir narrowed his eyes in irritation, pressing the scalpel hard enough against Kat's neck to draw a trickle of blood.

Nick's mouth went dry, but he had to keep going. "No one with real power would use a little girl to do their bidding," he shouted. "I reforged the sword, and I can break it again, too."

"You wouldn't dare sacrifice your sister," Horymir sneered. "Hand the sword to my soldier unless you want to see more of Katarina's blood."

The statue that had given the stone shard to Horymir approached Nick with its hand outstretched. Nick took two steps back.

"DO AS HE SAYS, YOUNG KNIGHT."

Surprised, Nick whipped his eyes to meet the gaze of King Wenceslas atop his warhorse.

"I AM SORRY, NICHOLAS. THE WORLD CAN BE AN UGLY PLACE. YOU HAVE SERVED PRAGUE WELL AND FAITHFULLY. NO ONE CAN FACE SUCH EVIL ALONE. NOW, YOU MUST RELY ON THE STRENGTH OF YOUR FAMILY AND FRIENDS."

Horymir threw back his head and laughed. "The strength of the Maracek family has failed."

In his peripheral vision, Nick watched Mom and Helena slowly creep between the motionless statues' legs until they were an arm's length away from the sorcerer. They took up positions, each on one side.

"Do you promise to let her go?" Nick asked, the tremble in his voice part faith, part fear.

"You have my word." Greed and hunger glittered in the sorcerer's eyes. "Once I have the sword, she will be of no use to me any longer."

"I will listen to the king." Nick limped forward several steps to where the statue stood, hand open and waiting. He stretched out his swordarm, but instead of placing the blade in the statue's hand, he leaned forward and whispered: "Blade. Head off!"

The statue began to vibrate.

"Now!" Nick shouted.

In the moment the statue's head *popped* off its neck, Helena buckled Horymir's left knee with a vicious elbow-strike, and Mom tackled him the rest of the way to the ground.

Kat's eyes sprang open as the sorcerer crumpled like a bag of bones.

"Run, Kat!" Mom shouted as she struggled to hold Horymir down. Kat bolted straight for Nick's arms.

"KNIGHTS OF BLANÍK, ATTACK!" King Wenceslas' voice carried across the bridge.

In response, the single bugle note rang loud and clear.

Immediately, hundreds of horses' hooves pounded from the far side of the bridge as generations of Knights rode forward, devouring the distance between them and the stone-still army of statues.

"End them all!" Horymir screeched. "Destroy th..."

The sorcerer's cry ended in a muffled scream as Mom stuffed the wad of tissues she always carried in her bag into his mouth. But she was too late.

The golem sprang into action. Pandemonium engulfed the Charles Bridge.

Nick caught Kat in his arms. Hands clutched tightly, they zigzagged, dodging giant feet and weapons. A split second before being pulverized by an enormous stone fist, Nick pulled Kat beneath the mound of earth where the word of power had split the bridge apart. She clung to him limply.

Shots from mist-wreathed bows rained down everywhere, thunking solidly into the ground before disappearing in a puff of smoke. But when the arrows hit a golem, bowling-ball chunks of stone, metal, or brick exploded into gaping holes. Some knights rode through the streets with lances lowered, speering golem to buildings or knocking them from walls.

With the blade beneath him, Nick curled his body protectively around Kat, swiping gritty rock dust from his eyes. He knew he needed to get the sword to King Wenceslas, but he wasn't willing to take Kat out into the madness.

"There!" Nick heard Mom's voice from close-by. "Under the outcropping. By the sinkhole!"

Before he could react, he and Kat were swooped up onto the back of a galloping horse behind an armor-clad knight.

"Kat! Hold on, tight!"

The commotion must have revived her, because her little arms locked firmly around his waist.

A blur on his right pulled his attention. He blinked in surprise to see Helena gripping the back of a mounted knight whose horse galloped apace with his. He turned to his left to see Mom riding behind another. The horses didn't miss a stride as they sped to the north end of the bridge, and then veered sharply to the right.

Nick squeezed his eyes shut, sure the stallion was going straight over the safety wall and into the water below. Instead, the steed's muscles bunched as its legs gained the air. He opened his eyes again, shocked to realize they'd risen above the fog.

"Look!" Kat's small voice breathed in his ear. He looked to where she pointed, down at the bridge,

Below them, King Wenceslas strode through the melee toward Horymir just as the puppeteer rose to his feet.

Without any indication of distress about the battle raging around him, King Wenceslas continued forward. He ducked beneath a blow from the statue of Cosmas, aimed directly at his head. He dodged a vicious swipe of the two-tailed lion statue's massive claws. The king leapt up, hovering in the air above a statue that was trying to unseat knights from their mounts with a long, stone flagpole, despite missing half of one leg. Suspended in the air, King Wenceslas kicked out with both feet against the statue's chest, sending it flailing backwards into the statue of a polished-bronze dog.

King Wenceslas landed nimbly on the bridge 15 yards away from where Horymir stood. The sorcerer's black robes were in tatters, his hair a matted mess as he muttered to himself, glaring at the King while he waved his hands around in front of him.

"He's casting a spell!" Kat cried.

"Knight!" Nick yelled as loud as he could. "Ride closer to the King!"

Immediately, the knight reigned his warhorse around, wheeling him toward the bridge and the King. The stallions carrying Mom and Helena turned as well, churning the air beneath their hooves as they galloped groundward.

"Hold on, Kat!" Nick shouted.

Before he could blink, they'd closed the distance. Now they were mere yards away, charging ahead, only a handful of meters above the bridge.

King Wenceslas continued toward Horymir one measured step after the other, closing the gap, less than 10 feet away.

As his stallion rode directly overhead, King Wenceslas looked up, straight into Nick's eyes. He nodded.

Nick dropped the sword.

In a heartbeat, the three horses had raced past the bridge. Once again, they mounted the sky. Beyond the horizon's curve, Nick glimpsed the morning sun, impatient to rise. In the city, emergency lights flashed and fires burned, polluting the beautiful city with soot and ash. But Nick also saw the rest of the Brotherhood battling Horymir's golem wherever they stood.

BLINK.

Below the horses hooves, the sword landed in King Wenceslas' outstretched hand, and the world *flexed* around him.

BLINK.

King Wenceslas covered the last five feet as if nothing existed except him and the evil sorcerer plaguing Prague.

Horymir's spine hunched in fear. Nick saw the enchantment of the younger, stronger man fall away. Once again, the King raised his eyes, saluting with the sword of the Golden City against the red eagle on his breastplate.

Everything went still. The King's words echoed throughout Prague.

"BLADE! HEADS OFF!"

EPILOGUE

Nick's legs trembled as he gazed out over the congregation. He didn't recognize most of the people who had gathered to pay tribute to his uncle. The chapel pews were completely filled, and men and women stood at the back and in the aisles, all looking up at him with compassion. Some dabbed at their eyes with tissues or handkerchiefs.

So many people loved Uncle Damek, he thought, knowing he'd never be able to count them all even if he tried.

He glanced at the notes he'd painstakingly written in his notebook.

After everything he'd survived since his uncle's death, the most difficult challenge he'd faced had been writing this speech. *How do you sum up a lifetime in three to five minutes?* he'd asked himself over and over again while staring at the page. The obvious answer, he'd realized, is: you can't.

The words swam below him on the paper as he blinked back tears. He closed the notebook and found Kat's face in the crowd. Her small face was still somewhat paler than usual, but her eyes were bright as she smiled up at him.

"My uncle did things in his life that most of us only ever read about in books or see in movies." His voice wavered, but he kept going. "When I was younger, I asked him once if he'd ever met Indiana Jones on one of his archaeological adventures."

A wave of chuckles ran through the congregation. Nick smiled to see Damek's friends turn to each other, leaning close and nodding at their own memories.

"A few weeks ago," Nick continued, "my uncle left the safety of his home and went out into the dark night alone. Not because he wasn't afraid. He was. But because his love was stronger than his fear. His love for this city. His love for me. His love for you."

Whispering rose again in the congregation. Nick saw Vaclav – the security officer from the Orloj – clasp the hand of a man seated next to him. His lips pressed into a grim line and his eyes shone with unshed tears. He nodded at Nick, pressing his free hand to his chest in salute.

"My uncle wasn't perfect. No one is. But he did what was right, even in the face of overwhelming odds. In his final hours, his goal was to protect Prague and her people - to protect me. In the last letter he sent to me, he wrote that he had failed."

Nick's voice broke, and he paused until the lump in his throat shrank enough for him to continue. He didn't bother wiping away the tears wetting his cheeks. "But even then, he didn't give up. He didn't let failure stop him. He kept trying, doing everything in his power to achieve his goal."

Nick's eyes fell on Kat again, her expression sent a small jolt of electricity singing through him.

He recognized that look!

It was the same look he'd worn when he peered through the nursery window in the hospital the first day they met.

The expression he'd had when he watched Mom galloping across the bridge only the week before on the back of a warhorse, Queen Neomenia's ring glowing on her finger.

The same look he'd always worn when gazing up at Damek while sitting on his knee, listening to one of his stories, or when watching him make a marionette dance.

It was a look of absolute love and admiration.

In that moment, Nick realized that Kat loved him as much as he loved her.

As his eyes scanned the row from Jiri Olbrycht sitting at the end next to Helena, to Kat, to Mom, to Mr. Zeman in his cast and sling, he saw the same emotion reflected back at him in each of their eyes.

"I know that when you look at me, you might just see a skinny 13-year-old kid from Illinois, who walks a little funny and could probably use a haircut. But that's not what Uncle Damek saw. To him I was a young knight, strong enough to face an evil sorcerer. Brave enough to stand up to the worst bully of all time. Damek believed in me when I didn't believe in myself. From him, I learned that with the right friends, a little determination, and the wisdom of legends, the only way I can fail is if I give up for good."

There were so many other things Nick could have said. But all of them strung together still wouldn't be enough.

He gripped the sides of the podium and gazed at the enlarged photo of Damek on an easel a few feet away. It was the same photo that sat on his bedside table at home in Chicago: Damek holding Myslík's silver fish. "I love you, Damek. I'll find you in my dreams."

The next few seconds blurred a little as he limped quickly down from the stand and hurried to the pew. Helena's father stood to let him past, and Helena scooted to the side, leaving a spot for Nick between her and Kat.

Mom reached over and squeezed his hand. "I love you," she whispered.

He nodded, head bent, face flush with the awkwardness of so many shining eyes watching him. But in the next breath, Helena's father ascended the short flight of stairs and took his place behind the podium. Nick sighed with relief.

"I have had the privilege of living next door to Damek Maracek for the past 15 years," Jiri began. "He was truly the best of men. Recently, I had the honor of becoming better acquainted with his young nephew – whom you've all just heard – along with his little sister, Kat, a lion of a young lady if ever there was one."

Nick raised his head and returned Jiri's warm smile. A rush of pride swelled in his chest. On his right, Kat threaded her arm through his and leaned her head against his shoulder.

"I am here today not only as a friend and neighbor," Jiri continued, "but also in my official government capacity on behalf of our Prime Minister, who has asked me to convey her condolences to Damek's family, friends, and community. With his death, our great city of Prague, and indeed the entire Czech Republic, has lost one of its brightest minds and most valorous hearts.

It is with great honor that I share with you that last week, the Prime Minister and I met with Damek's family to posthumously confer upon him the honorary rank of Knight Commander in the Order of the Red Eagle for his bravery and service to our beloved country. Thank you, Damek Nicholas Maracek, for your life of service."

A gasp, followed by a murmur of approval ran through the assembly. Helena took his hand in hers, lacing her fingers through his. Her fingers were warm. She leaned in to rest her head on his shoulder.

From where he sat to the right of Mom, Mr. Zeman caught Nick's attention, tapping his own chest with his finger and nodding solemnly. Nick returned the nod, touching his hand to the heraldic pin on his lapel: an eagle set with ruby eyes embossed against a field of gold and red.

What Mr. Olbrycht didn't mention - out of respect for their wishes - was that in the private ceremony, the Prime Minister had dubbed Nick as Knight Champion in the Order of the Red Eagle, making him the only living Knight of Blaník.

It had been proposed that Mr. Zeman and Helena be dubbed Knight Bachelors, and Mom and Kat Squires of the same order. Both Helena and Mr. Zeman refused the honor but requested, and were granted, the lower rank of Squire, while Kat happily accepted the assignation of Page.

Mom refused any rank altogether. She said that nothing could surpass the gift of her children' s safety. That, and Queen Neomenia's ring. Still, Nick saw her name had already been inked with scrolling letters in the Book of Heraldry on the Prime Minister's desk, and he sincerely doubted it would be crossed out.

What Mom *did* accept was lifetime travel expenses assured for the family, both to and from Prague. Nick, Kat, and Helena were each awarded scholarships to Charles University, should they wish to attend in the future, and Kat and Nick received dual citizenship.

Nick received a replica of the Sword of the Golden City, which now hung in Damek's office. The original — which had been retrieved from the bridge after the Knights of Blaník and King Wenceslas had disappeared into mist - was inducted into the Prague National Museum, surrounded by more security than Nick even thought possible.

Kat had been disappointed to learn that Horymir's detached head and 'reformed' body had vanished as well. But the small wooden box, containing a lock of his hair and his enchanted stone, had been recovered. The hair and the stone had been promptly incinerated.

Nick, Helena, and Kat - equipped with state of the art gear, and accompanied by a team of professional spelunkers - had buried the box in the cave beneath Mount Blaník, surrounded by the legendary Knights, sworn protectors of King Wenceslas the First and of the Realm.

Only Kat and Helena were with Nick when he opened the secret compartment in Damek's attic and reverently placed the ancient diary back where it belonged.

As he sat in the pew, surrounded by the people who loved him, listening to Jiri speak about the impact of Damek's life, Nick turned over a question in his mind: *Am I different today than before Uncle Damek passed?* As far as the world outside this chapel knew, he'd just happened to be traveling in Prague with his mom and sister over summer vacation at the same time the city received a terrorist threat.

The citizens of Prague had learned from the news and an official announcement that the Prime Minister had received a letter demanding she give up control of the government. When the terrorists' demands weren't met, they carried out a coordinated attack on the Charles Bridge and the hospitals in Old Town and Lesser Town. The unnamed terrorists were ultimately defeated in a joint effort between the brave first responders, the military, and the police. The news reported that renowned scholar, Damek Maracek, uncovered the plot and helped the government apprehend the terrorists, tragically losing his life in the process.

He was a national hero. That last part, at least, was true.

And as for Nick? A lot had happened, but how much had really changed? Well, besides the fact that he was holding hands with a really cool girl, who was already thick into planning their foreign exchange student trips.

And besides being dubbed a literal knight. He'd felt funny about that, being an American and all, but the Prime Minister assured him that The Order of the Red Eagle didn't *officially* exist. The Czech Republic had discontinued the practice of dubbing knights long before, so the title was just a formality.

What will I tell people when I get back to Chicago? he wondered. *What will I say to Jeremy? What will I say to anyone?*

Probably that his uncle had passed away and he'd gone to Prague to attend his funeral. That he was still grieving – that he probably wouldn't ever stop grieving.

It surprised him a little that he wasn't eager to tell anyone about how he and his little sister and his new friend had solved an ancient riddle and helped a legendary king defeat an evil, undead sorcerer. Not that anyone would believe him, anyway. But in examining his feelings, Nick found that he was one hundred percent fine with that. Maybe he wouldn't tell a single person.

And maybe – if anything *had* changed in him – it was that he didn't care what The Pack thought or said about him anymore. That he'd learned a lot about himself in the past few weeks. That he could truthfully say he had absolutely nothing to prove to anyone.

As the ceremony concluded and the crowd of people filed out through the church doors, Nick looked out over the Prague skyline. The sun – with a ways to go still before reaching its apex – cast everything in a warm, softening glow. It was beautiful. It was irreplaceable.

It was safe.

Nick knew Damek wouldn't have it any other way.

About the Authors

Jane is the award-winning author of novels and short fiction, best known for Riven and Secret Keeper, the first two books in the soon-to-be-complete My Myth Trilogy. She writes memorable, character-driven fiction that blends fantasy, humor, and psychological horror with real-world contemporary issues to create layered stories that engage and transport.

When she isn't working on her own manuscripts, Jane teaches private creative and academic writing classes. She specializes in coaching young and neurodivergent authors to connect with their imaginations and confidently develop their voices.

Jane insists that frolicking is an absolutely vital part of the writing process. If you can't find her, it's because she's lost herself somewhere in a primeval forest, meadow, or waterfall, listening to the stories trees and flowers and rushing rivers tell.

Ruston is a storyteller. While earning his university degree in film, he sharpened his skills taking as many screenwriting classes as he could. He has made his living for over 20 years with a camera and editing software working on diverse projects ranging from documentary films and television series to travel and yoga videos.

For Sword of the Golden City he made the switch from film maker to novelist, partnering with Jane Alvey Harris to adapt his screenplay into book form. Ruston has been researching and creating this story for over a decade and is ridiculously excited to share it with readers everywhere.

When you have finished reading Sword of the Golden City, you will likely need a good stretch and might want to join one of Ruston's yoga or meditation classes. When not at the computer or on the yoga mad, you will usually find him in the basement designing and sewing the new collection for his upcoming fashion shows.